Readers love J.S. Cook

Come to Dust

"If you like a good, solid, murder-mystery plot set in an historical background with a touch of M/M romance thrown in and with a sprinkling of spooky supernatural on top, then this book has the lot!"

—Sinfully Sexy Book Reviews

"…throughout I was glued to the pages."

—MM Good Book Reviews

A Little Night Murder

"It is well written and the characters are well drawn. It is also a book that will keep you on the edge of your chair as you keep turning pages as quickly as you can."

—Reviews by Amos Lassen

But Not for Me

"*But Not For Me* is a very fun, lighthearted book with a great plot with plenty of twists!"

—Top 2 Bottom Reviews

By J.S. COOK

But Not For Me
Come to Dust
A Little Night Murder
The Lovely Beast
Sixteen Songs About Regret
Valley of the Dead

Writing as JOANNE SOPER-COOK
Eye of Heaven

Published by DREAMSPINNER PRESS
http://www.dreamspinnerpress.com

THE LOVELY BEAST

J.S. COOK

Dreamspinner Press

Published by
DREAMSPINNER PRESS

5032 Capital Circle SW, Suite 2, PMB# 279, Tallahassee, FL 32305-7886 USA
http://www.dreamspinnerpress.com/

This is a work of fiction. Names, characters, places, and incidents either are the product of author imagination or are used fictitiously, and any resemblance to actual persons, living or dead, business establishments, events, or locales is entirely coincidental.

The Lovely Beast
© 2014 J.S. Cook.

Cover Art
© 2014 L.C. Chase.
www.lcchase.com
Cover content is for illustrative purposes only and any person depicted on the cover is a model.

ISBN: 978-1-62798-843-8
Digital ISBN: 978-1-62798-844-5
Library of Congress Control Number: 2014940022.
First Edition July 2014

Printed in the United States of America

This paper meets the requirements of
ANSI/NISO Z39.48-1992 (Permanence of Paper).

To Paul, who makes everything possible.

PROLOGUE

THE DREAM begins the way it always does: I am standing by myself in a great hall. The ceilings stretch away into infinity, and the dimensions are so large that they are entirely meaningless. I can hear faint strains of music from an orchestra not readily visible and the subtler noise of people whispering together. When I follow these sounds to their origin, I find myself standing before a set of double doors, each hewn of a dark and sturdy wood and carved with curious symbols and strange devices. The doors part for me, as if by magic, and I am suddenly in the midst of a gathering of some hundreds of people, all dressed in fine costumes and dancing slowly—gracefully—around something I cannot see. There is no one there whom I know, whom I would recognize in any other milieu, but I am content and comfortable. I am satisfied to stay as long as I am wanted. I realize I have somehow traveled to the past, but I am not concerned. I feel absolutely safe.

A glass is pressed into my hand, brimming with a warm liquid in whose depths I can see myself reflected back in miniature. The orchestra is playing Faure's "Clair de Lune," a composition so new it has hardly been heard anywhere outside of Paris. No one is singing, and yet the words come to me, unbidden:

Your soul is a chosen landscape

Where charming masqueraders and bergamasquers go

Playing the lute and dancing and almost

Sad beneath their fantastic disguises.

The crowd parts, and I see the object in the center of the room: a coffin made of glass and etched with a beautiful and delicate gold tracery that blooms in the chilly silence like a frost flower. Yet the figure in the coffin lives and breathes, and there is a palpable heartbeat—patient, persistent, eternal—throbbing underneath the music and the chatter. The woman in the coffin turns her head to look at me and smiles a beneficent smile. Her hands are thrust into the air, her palms flat against the inner surface of her glass sarcophagus. I realize with a thrill of horror that what I had mistaken for a smile is actually a rictus of terror. She is trying to escape. I raise the goblet to my lips and drink. The carmine liquid warms me, heating my blood with an insistent, arcane fire.

DIARY—JACOB VAN WILLIGEN

January, 1897

This cold is deadening. Even with the warmth of my compartment's woolen lap rug, my hands and feet have been reduced to lumps of lifeless matter. I resolve to draft a letter to the esteemed Mr. Brunel, stating exactly what I think about the paucity of warmth in his atmospheric railway. One wonders—since the network of pneumatic tubes extends practically everywhere in Europe nowadays—why some little expense could not be put toward the engineering of more heat in the passenger compartments. I am thoroughly chilled to the marrow of my very bones.

I am no great stranger to the cold, having spent some years of my childhood and young manhood in the northern regions of the earth. During my final semester at university, some fellows and I planned to engineer a sojourn to the great steppes of Mongolia, where we intended to spread goodwill and Christian charity to the heathen tribes. But the second Data War put paid to our attempts, and we did not think it wise to venture so near to China or any of its neighbors. The Korean countries were also in a state of extreme dissolution, having entered the war on the side of the Axis powers—an inevitable reaction to the death of Governor Hao, who had perished with all his entourage when the vice-regal transport exploded in the pneuma tube between Pyongyang and Seoul. There were other discussions, other plans to bring Christ's light to the remaining heathen nations of the world, but nothing ever came to fruition. By the time I might have indulged in such an expedition, my formal education had ended. A few months later, the war started, and, like other able-bodied men of my age and social station, I volunteered. I was sent almost immediately to Belgrade, where I served the remainder of the war as an administrative clerk attached to a squadron of Allied dirigibles. These weren't even war dirigibles, but common cargo ships employed in ferrying supplies and materiel to the front. I was disappointed, to say the least.

After hostilities ended with the signing of the First Accord in Ulaanbaatar, I journeyed back to my homeland and spent a few weeks in Maastricht, where I was born and where my widowed father still lived, attended in his daily needs by my younger sister Annika. I wandered by the banks of the Maas, considering my future and where I would locate myself in the world. At university I had studied theology and the law, but I could not imagine combining these two in any practical way, and the thought that I might have no true vocation tormented me at every turn. I was young, strong, practical, and clever, and eager to turn my hand to whatever work presented itself to me. To supplement my meager student's allowance, I had worked as a farm laborer, a shop assistant, and a bookbinder. I had tutored endless streams of baffled younger classmen who lacked the ability to effectively parse the more laborious theological texts. I had hoped a week or two spent among the worthy remembrances of childhood bliss might propel me in some appropriate direction. I never suspected my search would lead me to the Society of Psychical and Esoteric Research, or that my commission would take me to the wilds of a place steeped in myth and legend. Before the war, this region of Europe was closed to all but the most hardy adventurers. After the cessation of hostilities, the pneuma network was extended to include Eastern Europe, comprising a series of transit tubes especially built for the harsh climate in this area.

The views I have had of this countryside thus far have been breathtaking. I cannot recall when I ever saw a landscape more magical and more forbidding, with great mountains on all sides seeming to frown down upon us with not a little aggravation, like giants newly awakened from the sleep of centuries. I imagine this place must be glorious indeed in summer. I would have much rather waited until the advent of the warmer months, but Brother Inish was implacable: I must go *now*, immediately, as soon as possible, and here was my ticket. I had barely time to pack a valise and gather the necessary papers when I found myself whisked off to St. Pancras and stuffed aboard the first continental express bound for one of the wildest and most isolated parts of Europe.

I, of course, understood the nature of my mission. We are always briefed in advance; the Society prefers to avoid mistakes whenever possible. My prefatory interview with Brother Inish effectively dispelled any ideas I might have had about this journey: this was not a holiday, nor could I expect to spend much time in contemplation and study. As proponents of both the scientific and the sacred, we battled the forces of darkness, using such tools as were readily at hand and any means necessary. This would be as rigorous a test of my training as any I had yet undergone.

I remembered it well. I had been sitting in the library, transcribing my notes from an earlier journey to a small village just outside Madrid. A local priest there had contacted Brother Inish, afraid of an ominous presence that had taken up residence in the bell tower of the church. Many of his congregation, terrified of the creature, preferred to risk their immortal souls rather than attend the Mass. Baptisms, marriages, and burials had all but ceased, and those few who were brave enough to make their Confession later suffered the torments of the damned. The priest had tried everything he knew to banish the specter but had no success. In writing to Brother Inish, he requested not only the Society's support and help, but the Vatican's permission to enact the Rites if necessary. Thankfully, there had been no need to involve the Holy See: we managed to defeat the demon ourselves.

Later, when we had returned, I felt a hand on my shoulder and looked up to see Brother Inish's smiling, lined face. "Jacob, I must speak with you. It is very important. Take your books and your papers and come with me." Like any properly instructed member of the Society, I obeyed immediately and without question, following Brother Inish's plain brown robe through the silent, narrow hallways and up a short flight of stairs near the back of the building. "Come into my office." He ushered us both inside and shut the door, then beckoned me forward. "That chair, next to the shelf. We can speak freely in here." He sat down behind the desk and waited for me to compose myself. "Jacob, you are an asset to the Society. You know I do not say that lightly." He waved a hand as if brushing away flies. "But the time for compliments is not now. I must ask you to undertake a great journey."

I clenched the arms of the chair until my wrists ached. "You have only to command me, Brother."

"Do not be so hasty." He held my gaze, then shook his head. "This is dangerous. It is very dangerous. I may be sending you into the mouth of Hell itself, and with no easy way to recall you, should you happen upon some unusual peril." His eyes were a particular shade of blue—quite pale, with large, lustrous pupils that lent him an air of great compassion. His face was much lined, and his hands as well, yet none of us knew how old Brother Inish was. He was almost as old as the Society itself, which some whispered dated back to the great king Solomon, although I couldn't see how. A just man, it's true, may live a long time, but no one, not even one as virtuous as Brother Inish, lives forever.

He told me about a certain European gentleman, recently transplanted from America, whose young wife was stolen away in the prime of her youth and died a most ignominious—and possibly unnatural—death by drowning in a great river. This same nobleman, possessed of great ancestral wealth and possibly driven a little mad by the premature death of his beloved, was conducting the most heinous sort of experimental procedures, using travelers and strangers as well as the unwitting sons and daughters of the local people as his subjects, in the hope of restoring his dead wife to life again. The villagers held him in high regard because, like a noted ancestor before him, he enacted certain hereditary duties upon which the superstitious villagers depended.

"It's monstrous, certainly." I didn't see what it had to do with us. "He cannot possibly succeed. The resurrection of the dead is the sole province of our Lord and Savior. This is blasphemy."

"It is blasphemy, true. Moreover, we suspect he may be consorting with certain spirits of darkness." Inish regarded me carefully. "You recall, of course, the punishment required for such... activities." He folded his hands in his lap and waited, as patient as the Sphinx, for my reply. A stray shaft of sunlight illuminated one side of his gentle face and lit up the silver in his hair. A multitude of tiny dust motes twirled in this same column of light, spinning slowly down to settle on the polished surface of his desk, his books, and the rich wool carpets underneath our feet.

I did. "Quite apart from excommunication, and if there is sufficient evidence, then he can be brought before the ecclesiastical court." I still didn't see what that had to do with the Society. We were hardly what one would call policemen. "Surely his blasphemy can be mediated by some other means," I said. "A message can be dispatched over the pneuma networks. I'm willing to draft and send the pod with your permission, if that's what you wish."

He shook his head, got up, and strolled slowly over to the opposite wall, where he stood for some time examining the spines of the books. A tiny clockwork sweeper, no larger than the palm of a man's hand, clung valiantly to the window drapes, cleaning them of dust. I watched as it reached the terminus of a fold, turned itself about quite nimbly, and hovered in place like a bumblebee. "This man has gathered the best minds of his generation to create a device which will, under the right conditions, animate his dead wife, a probable suicide."

"Clearly he's mad," I said. "The woman's soul is damned. Already she burns in the fires of Hell."

"No, he isn't mad." Inish traced the gold lettering on the spine of David Hume's *On Superstition and Enthusiasm.* "It's been speculated, however—" He left the bookshelf and moved to where I stood. "—that he isn't human."

The tiny hairs on the nape of my neck prickled and, had I chosen to adopt the traditional monastic tonsure, I'm sure they would have been standing straight up. "Not human? So he's a demon, then. Some incubus or devil of the pit."

"The nature of his being has never been established. There is much speculation, however. He is of a curious physical character that seems never to age, or at least not in the usual way. He claims to be a direct descendent of an ancestor for whom he was named, but there are those who suspect he is that ancestor." Brother Inish shrugged. "His hereditary duties, services he enacts in the presence of the village, somehow guarantee or vouchsafe the harvest—at least this is what we've heard. We aren't entirely sure what he does or how it is accomplished, but he has written—" He picked up a slip of parchment from his desk and waved it at me. "—that he wishes to be released from the ritual his family has enacted for all these many years."

"He wants an exorcism?"

"He wasn't entirely clear about that. Even with the pneuma networks, it's difficult to get much news from those parts. We're talking thousands of miles of heavily forested and very remote mountain landscape, a region without benefit of modern conveniences such as we take for granted." He moved to put the parchment on his desk and lingered near it, gazing out the window. The set of his shoulders was as resolute as ever, but something weighed on him—a weariness that pressed him down.

"So you're saying that it isn't Khovd or Wellington."

"Or Maastricht. The Council of Elders thinks he may be—" He turned to me, his expression grave. "—a Watcher."

The declaration struck me as an odd thing for the Council to say, considering. "A Watcher? Brother Inish, with all due respect, he would have to be—"

"Hundreds of years old, yes." He shrugged. "You can see why we've chosen to send you."

I recoiled from his insinuation. "My nightmares may be merely phantasms, the lies of the Deceiver. You said yourself there is no proof of anything beyond the usual." My breath came short in my chest, and my throat was tight. "I have been thoroughly examined by the Council of Elders, and you know that both Brother Malachy and Brother Salomon concur. My visions are of unknown and neutral origin." I was on my feet. "If you like, I'll submit to further examination. Procure whomever you wish. I will offer myself for such tests as you feel are necessary—"

"Ease yourself, my dear Jacob." He laid a hand on my shoulder, and calm flowed into me like cool water. "Let peace be upon you. Your visions—the origin of them, their meaning—are not at issue here. What I am trying to say is that this man, if indeed he is as we suspect, a Watcher, is best handled by a veteran with your kind of experience in the field. Do you agree?"

I didn't truly believe this was what he meant, but I did not say so. "I am ever at your service." I sat down. "He cannot be a Watcher," I said after a minute or two. "The Watchers were to be bound in the valleys of the earth until Judgment Day, you know that."

"I believe," Brother Inish said dryly, "that the remote reaches of Eastern Europe would qualify. From what we know of sacred scripture and the apocryphal writings of Enoch, the Grigori, or Watchers as we know them, were dispersed throughout the world. He is not the only one of his kind. There have been others, but our investigations could find no trace of them. It is a monstrous undertaking. I need you to go to him, study the situation, and destroy the machine so that this abomination can never be." His smile held none of its usual warmth. "He believes you are coming to aid him in casting off the shackles of his inherited curse." He drew a folded sheet of paper from his robes. "He wrote to me, himself, and asked that I send aid. Ironic, I know, but…." He lifted his shoulders and let them drop. "What God has brought to fruition…"

"If he is as old as you suspect," I said, "wouldn't he already know the purpose of my visit? Surely a man with such a span of years is wiser than most others?"

And so it was that I found myself en route to the heavily forested, remote mountains of a country many believe exists only in the imagination, and which I will not reveal here, for the sake of confidentiality. I carried a sealed letter from Brother Inish, indicating the tacit approval of both the Society and the Vatican. I also carried with me the traditional tools of the holy warrior: a stake of blessed, blooming dogwood, the tree upon which our Lord was crucified; an iron dagger formed from the burning heart of an ancient meteorite; an amulet of Saint Michael to protect against evil; and a vial of holy water, which I wear on a silver chain against my heart. I hoped it would be sufficient. There are those in the Society, of course, who scoff at what they call my "monster killing kit," and yet they are safe in London while I am here, hurtling toward what may be the greatest hour of my destiny.

I AM waiting at a hotel here for a coach, which I am told will call for me presently. The proprietress—a very proper elderly woman wearing a surfeit of crucifixes and other holy objects—has just handed me a letter. The writing is in an oddly antique hand. "My friend," it says, "I am sending a conveyance to meet with you. I anticipate making your acquaintance." The letter is unsigned and there are no other instructions, nothing that would hint at my correspondent's identity. Of course it will be all right: this is a homely sort of place and these are good people, despite their backward ways and their curious superstitions.

Yet some warning is ticking away at the back of my brain, admonishing me to remember and be careful, and I wonder if everything in this place is as it seems. There are the mountains, covered in a cloak of snow, and the naked trees—their bare limbs unfurled heavenward—and the narrow strip of road leading to a cold and narrow pass, a treacherous journey in even the best of weather. The wind has died away, save for an occasional whisper of breeze that lifts handfuls of the powdery snow and twirls it round and round. Darkness, they say, comes early in these parts at this time of year. It will be dark when I board the diligence that will take me up the mountain. It will certainly be dark when I arrive, alone and friendless in a foreign land.

Just now the proprietress has come back. The diligence is waiting. The inn's other guests have been apprised of the note, and they regard me with something approaching fear. This does not encourage me. The proprietress is insistent: I must take a crucifix and wear it about my neck, for God alone knows what will happen to me if I do not. The Society frowns upon the outward show of spiritual tokens, likening the use of such to mere superstition, but I will take it, if only to appease the old woman. When the diligence arrives, we board it, travelers all, but the old woman stands watching the progress of the vehicle until we are around the last bend in the road. Her concern for the state of my soul does nothing to assuage my worries.

I HAVE never in all my days experienced a ride like that, and I suspect I never will again. I have made a mental note to write the whole thing out in more detail once I am properly settled, if only to convince myself it was not a dream. The diligence that called at the hotel was a more or less regular affair—an automated coach such as one sees nearly every day on any London street. Except this one was equipped with toothed, metal belts to drive it forward, a necessary adaptation in this environment, where the weather is, I am told, most violent and capricious. There were seven of us, including myself, and the driver, situated at the front of the vehicle, was seated on a sort of cantilevered bench, which allowed him a sweeping view of the surrounding countryside. The engine was, I fear, not in the best of repair, for it commenced to belch great clouds of foul-smelling smoke as soon as we had started forward and seemed to be in imminent danger of falling to pieces.

We ascended the narrow road precipitously, going higher and higher into the mountains until we came to a level place where we stopped, but only long enough for the driver to toss my luggage off the coach. I have never seen a man as frightened as he was then: he stopped to set me down, and his fervor in racing the engine gave me pause. Then the machine was gone, and I was alone in the midst of a deserted mountain pass in the freezing cold.

The wind, which had earlier died out, now sprang up with a viciousness that seemed almost personal, and I cursed my poor judgment in leaving my warmest gloves behind in London. The particle warmer I had brought (at the insistence of my friend Hayes, who assured me it would get very cold indeed where I was going) was packed deep inside my valise. In order to reach it, I would have to disgorge the entire contents of my luggage upon the ground. I huddled into my coat and stamped my feet to keep the blood going, wondering at the same time if perhaps this was some kind of ill-timed joke. It might be that this gentleman intended to keep me waiting until the last moment, enjoying my discomfort and secretly laughing at me.

Luckily, I hadn't long to wait. Presently I spied a pair of lights in the distance, which eventually materialized into an old-style coach with the studded iron wheels common to this part of the world and a primitive, woodburning engine. The driver pulled up beside me and indicated by signs that I should pass my bags to him, which I did. It being dark, I could not see his face, which was shadowed by the heavy traveling cloak he wore. He nodded to me and I climbed inside, and directly we set off at an impressive rate of speed. We seemed to be negotiating a series of switchbacks—places where the road had been laid more or less flat and in a progression of upward steps—in order to climb the mountain. Were it not for the cold, I would have liked to get out and walk a little, but the freezing temperatures and the driver's forbidding manner put an end to any such thoughts. I contented myself with observing such topographical features as could be made out, but I regret to say the darkness hid practically everything, and I passed much of the journey with my gaze directed inward.

At length the carriage pulled up in front of a massive stone structure—a medieval manor house set at the highest reaches of this mountainous country. In appearance and scale, it bore no resemblance whatsoever to the venerable old halls that we have in England. It was at once larger and more imposing and seemed to crouch upon the landscape like some fearful monster or golem. I could discern casements above me, the window glass glimmering in the scant light thrown by flaming torches that had been affixed to the outer walls. The door was wooden, bound about with iron straps, and fully three times as tall as a man. If my host was on the same scale as his door, he was surely a giant.

The driver flung the carriage door open and threw my bags onto the ground. By this I assumed I was to disembark. He then whipped the vehicle round and disappeared into the darkness. I was left to my own devices before the great dwelling. I could discern no other soul nearby, and the thickness of the walls and the great wooden door before me would surely hinder any attempt I might make to hail the house's inhabitants. I stood shivering and wondering what to do when a faint point of brightness pierced the dark beyond the door and shone between the gaps in the wood. The unmistakable sound of approaching footsteps sounded from inside, and at once the door was flung open.

My host held a candle directly before him, and thus I could make out very little of his features, but his voice, when he spoke, was rich and welcoming. "Come in, quickly, and warm yourself. I must apologize for my driver. He is the descendent of some wild mountain tribe and often forgets himself." His accent was not precisely like those I had heard earlier in the village. There was something—I daresay this will seem like the most blatant prejudice—American in it, a controlled and nuanced timbre that spoke of great dignity and education, as well as great privilege.

I bent to pick up my cases, but he stopped me. "Take the candle and go in, sir, for I perceive you have been in this cold too long and are not accustomed to it. I will have a servant bring your luggage."

I did as he suggested and found myself in a great, high-ceilinged foyer hung with colorful tapestries and banners, and with beautiful stained glass fitted into all the casements. The only illumination came from candles set into rather primitive wall sconces, which cast far more shadow than light. To the right of the entranceway, a great stone staircase soared up into the darkness beyond, and I could discern the pleasant contours of an enormous fireplace set into the adjacent wall, and a roaring fire which sent a pleasing heat into the room.

"Go and warm yourself," my host instructed. "I shall have your luggage brought upstairs. We've set up a room for you in the west wing of the house. It is newer than the east wing, which has fallen into disuse in recent years. I hope that is satisfactory?"

"Thank you," I replied. "That is most generous."

I moved closer to the fire and stretched out my hands to warm myself. *Bless the dear old thing*, I thought (at this juncture, having not yet seen his face clearly, I imagined him an old man), *for providing me the creature comforts*. I experienced a pang of guilt then at what I had come here to do. It is always much more difficult when they are civilized. The shapeless, faceless monsters of the pit are the easiest to battle, even though the struggle wearies both the body and the soul. But those beings who can think, who are indeed sentient, and who arguably possess a conscience and a living spirit, these are the hardest of all to destroy, even when the destruction is a kind of mercy.

"Here we are. Ah, I see you have found your way to the fire. I was right. You feel the cold most keenly."

I turned, and what I saw standing before me arrested my attention like nothing ever had before and like nothing ever shall again. Standing in front of me was the most physically striking—handsome is, I fear, too weak a word—man I had ever seen in my entire life. He was tall and slender and beautifully made, with pale skin and dark eyes in which flickered a thousand secret fires. He had a lively, intelligent face, with interesting things in it, and his manner was urbane and wholly civilized. He was youthful in manner and dignity, yet he was not young—I judged him to be at least forty years of age or more. He was dressed entirely in black, save for his white shirtfront, punctuated with diamond studs, and a silk cravat around his neck, of a deep and verdant green. His hair was dark, glossy, and sleek as a raven's wing, and he wore it in the modern fashion, cut short and feathered on the edges, rather like the coiffure of an ancient Roman senator.

He came toward me, paused, and bowed gracefully. "Welcome to my home. Enter of your own free will and leave such happiness as you bring with you. I am Caleb Donnithorn, but please address me as merely Caleb."

I had the curious sensation of existing in two places at once! For it seemed to me that some part of myself flowed out of me and toward him and part of his essence flowed toward me, so that our two selves, or some aspect thereof, met in the middle and not only met but *embraced*. As we flowed together in this manner, I was aware that his touch—the contact of his mind, or whatever it was—had awakened something in me, something that yearned and strained toward him, an eagerness or a desire, the name of which I hesitate to write. This impression lasted but a moment and was gone, leaving me weak, trembling, and as exhausted as if I had run a thousand miles.

"You will want to rest and refresh yourself after your long journey. This way, please." He called for a servant, and presently a slim and diffident young man appeared from the inner reaches of the house. He nodded a greeting, then bent and picked up my heavy cases as easily as if they had been filled with feathers and set off toward the great staircase. "Anton's old bedroom, William, if you please." Caleb gestured vaguely in the direction of the stairs. "Toward the back of the house."

I would have protested his servant carrying all my luggage, but the ease with which the young man accepted the burden was borne in on me most strangely. He was slim and rangy, as if his body had not yet finished filling itself out. The brief glance I had of him revealed a closed and furtive face, a face with many secrets in it. Yet, his strength was equal to the task, and I had the impression that he could have carried twice that weight, had his master wished it.

Caleb ushered me into the drawing room and poured brandy for us both. "You are from London, originally?"

A clockwork sweeper was busily cleaning the many rugs laid down upon the cold stone floors. It came toward us, bumped my foot peremptorily, and immediately turned itself about, clicking angrily. I have often seen such things, but the sight of one never fails to amuse me. They seem so very lifelike, for all they are inherently mechanical, and I sometimes fancy they do indeed have minds of their own. The little sweeper buzzed off down the corridor, its tiny brushes raising clouds of dust as it continued with its appointed task.

"From Maastricht, originally—but I've been living in London for many years." I could not fathom why my origins would interest him. What difference did it make, where I came from? Perhaps he was merely making polite conversation, and I had been too long at fieldwork. His opportunities for rewarding social intercourse were surely limited in this place.

"Ah, yes, Maastricht. Your Brother Inish told me he was sending a Dutchman. How very efficient of him, and of course, I should have known by your name, van Willigen." He handed me a snifter of brandy. "I traveled a great deal in my earlier years, but lately I prefer to stay closer to home." He smiled over the rim of his glass. "Perhaps you will tell me about your country."

I had finished my brandy, and I fear my poorly concealed yawns indicated my readiness to sleep. Caleb asked if I wished supper, but I found my appetite had deserted me. He offered to escort me to my room himself. He led me up the wide stone stairs and down a long corridor that, to my travel-weary gaze, seemed to stretch on into forever. This, too, was illuminated by flickering candles set at intervals along the walls—candles whose light could scarcely pierce the thick and lambent darkness, a gloom that seemed to emanate from the walls themselves.

He stopped in front of a wide wooden door, very handsomely clad in burnished brass straps and with a large brass knob. "My cousin Anton's room, when he chances to visit us. I hope you will find it adequate." Extracting a skeleton key from his pocket, he unlocked the door and gestured that I should enter.

I was gratified to see a large, comfortable bed in a pleasant room, with a great many long casement windows of the sort usual to this part of the world and a fire roaring away merrily in the fireplace. The windows were adorned with heavy brocade curtains, in shades of burgundy and dark blue, and thick rugs, of diverse pattern and design, softened our footsteps. There was a private lavatory off the main room, complete with a bath and all of those other amenities that are welcome to the modern traveler. "William has brought your things." He turned and smiled at me. "In case you feared civility was gone from the world."

"Please thank him for me," I said. I had the distinct impression that he was watching me with some sort of otherworldly foresight—that he perceived my presence with more than merely the five senses God has given man. It gave me an uneasy feeling, as if I were unwittingly revealing myself. *Always remember*—Brother Inish's last words to me before putting me on the train rang a warning in my mind—*say as little as possible. That is always the safest route.* "Thank you. This is perfect." Again I felt the same sensation as before, that some part of me flowed toward him, and I took an involuntary step backward.

"I will have Mrs. Peterson send up some refreshments, in case you wake in the night and find yourself wanting sustenance." He stood by the door, hands clasped behind him. The curious thing was, I hadn't seen him move—but I put this down to my own tiredness and lack of attention. "I wish you satisfying sleep."

Encrypted record, Caleb Donnithorn

I HAVE buried so many. The names of all my blood kin are written on the stones that lie undisturbed on graves so old that there are few alive today who even remember where they are, but I remember. I know all the names, and sometimes when sleep eludes me, I lie awake and I recite them, and I remember them, their forms and faces, their features and the sounds their voices made in life. And I speak to the dead. The dead, I think, keep so very many of my secrets. She, of course, keeps the greatest secret of all, but she will never tell. My darling, my beautiful Elizabeta, who lies cold and still, encased in glass at the lowest level of my fortress, in the deeps of the earth where the course of the mighty Argeş rumbles and groans its way toward the sea.

Her mausoleum I had them build for me, when first this building was constructed: a crystal box of purest glass with brass hinges and a golden handle in the shape of a mighty dragon. At the lower end near her feet there is a grille attached to a network of tubes through which cold air is pumped all day and all night long, preserving her beauty as it was in days gone by. The column of air cycles over and under the corpse, infusing her tissues with cold, and I have been assured by the man who made it that, given sufficient fuel to supply its generator with steam, it will run until the end of time. Sometimes, when it is very late and I am alone, when these others to whom I give shelter have gone their separate ways, I come down and sit with my Elizabeta and talk to her. I lay my face close to hers and press kisses onto the cold glass and caress her icy skin with words. I sing the old songs to her, the tunes we danced to in our younger years, when we were first betrothed. She alone remembers me as I truly am.

I must confess myself surprised by this young Dutchman they have sent me. I expected someone else entirely. He visits me under the guise of offering me the Society's intervention, but I understand why he is here. It was but a matter of some little time before his esteemed Society heard tell of my marvelous machine. Having received intelligence of my unusual device, they are bound to do something about it. This is why van Willigen has come. He, of course, assumes his journey is to rid me of a hereditary curse placed upon my family many hundreds of years ago by the witch Isobel, who, seeking payment for a broken promise, bade my ancestor give her the head of his firstborn son. Popular wisdom and the testament of legend says she interred the head in a bottomless well where it would fall for all eternity, but that is not the entire truth. Isobel was a prodigy of spellwork, able to draw to her the elements of earth and fire, air and water. In me she placed an eternal ache that will never vanish, a thirst that can never be quenched. The premise that I require the help of van Willigen's Society is a useful fiction, the tacit acknowledgement of my particular perversion.

He is young, this scholarly Dutchman, but there is something in his eyes. He guards himself, I think, too well. Were we in another time, I might mistake him for a monk, resolute in his devotion to his deity and in his vow of silence. He has risked, and has suffered by it. He tells himself it is safety to never risk again. I feel sorry for him, if this is what he thinks: the world's sorrows rarely wait for anything as civil as an invitation. But he is educated, this one, and I anticipate any dialogue between us will be most pleasing to me. Shut up here of necessity and without the comfort of those I had assumed were indeed my fellows, I find myself longing for good conversation, and he is a rare one. Given sufficient time and latitude, this young warrior monk will tell me all I wish to know.

WILLIAM WAS waiting when I arrived at the bottom of the stairs. A frown had pulled his brows down, and his mouth was compressed to a thin, hard line.

"I hope you know what you're doing."

I passed by him and headed for the bookshelf. I'd started reading a history of the Plantagenets and wished to resume where I had left off.

"Not going to answer me?"

"William, really—" But when I tried to frame an appropriate response, I found no ready rebuttal.

He came to stand by me at the bookcase, watching as I chose first one book and then another, paged through each, and put them back. "It's past eleven." He glanced at the great clock that stands in the main foyer, and which tolls the hours with its ponderous chimes. "You haven't gone out yet this evening." He reached past me and plucked a book off the shelf: a history of medieval automata. "Shall I call the carriage for you?"

"No… not now." I clenched my fists so hard I felt the nails biting into my palms. The pulsing absence in me had grown since I'd risen, earlier in the evening. "Perhaps later, I might…." Why was I explaining myself to a servant?

"He has come here to destroy us." He moved so that I was facing him, even as I sought to avoid his eyes. "Perhaps he has heard of your quest." He gazed at me soberly, affecting the simple persona of the humble domestic servant, but I knew better. "Your pursuit of redemption."

"William." I wasn't quite pleading with him. "Leave me, now."

I went into my bedroom and locked the door behind me. I could hear the servants scurrying like mice in the corridors, their whispers penetrating even the old stones of this place. I undressed quickly and got into bed, shivering despite the fire, which strove most valiantly to spread heat to all corners of the room. My personal heating pan was where I'd left it underneath the bed, and I leaned down to retrieve it and turned the dials to the hottest possible setting.

My shoulders ached—the old scars pain me most when the weather is cold—and I sought to lose myself in sleep. The last thing I remember hearing is the heating pan's coils clicking as they released a blissful warmth that penetrated to the marrow of my bones. I longed for rest, but the morning's pale light had begun to silver the walls before my eyelids closed in sleep, and my dreams were troubled.

Diary—Jacob van Willigen

HE IS not what I expected. I had anticipated he would be as the others were—similar creatures I had met on previous assignments—but he is not. Clearly our information is corrupted. The dossier given me by Brother Inish is strangely incomplete, and this unsettles me. This man Donnithorn is an American, of good family, educated, perhaps schooled in business, surely well read, urbane, and beautifully mannered. There is more—so much, much more—about this being than we know, and it may be that I am here under false pretences. There is, of course, the possibility that he has enticed me with some spell of his own devising. Such as him are always well versed in the black arts.

He has the appearance of any other mortal man, and his flesh is warm, his hands and eyes accustomed, I think, to great loneliness, an aching time that spans the course of many years. We talked for hours, and with the kind of intimacy that is usually the province of lifelong friends. Indeed, I have the keenest sense that we have met before, and this both disturbs and frightens me. I know the power of deceiving spirits—their ability to change their form at will, to appear as anything they wish, to promise great rewards in return for a man's immortal soul. I must always be on my guard around him.

He is conversant on a great many subjects, but whether he has been educated through some outside agency or whether he is, as I suspect, an unusually receptive autodidact, I cannot yet tell. Nothing we supposed we knew about him stands; he smashes every preconception I had. He is monstrous in his intellect, and his civility, I am certain, hides an animal cunning.

I pressed him to show me something of this land, and he has promised to take me driving in the country. The idea of exploring the mountains by his side appeals, even as I renew my own essential caution. I code and send messages to Brother Inish, using the personal transcripticon he'd pressed on me.

"Take it," he'd urged, slipping the thing into the smaller of my two cases. "You can remain in contact with the Society and update your status if something occurs."

I hadn't wanted it but, looking at it now, I was glad he'd pressed it on me. It was similar in size and heft to a folio, beautifully bound in calfskin, and embossed in gold. By placing a traditionally produced piece of correspondence face down on the transcripticon's flat surface, I am able to procure its exact copy, which I can then send to Brother Inish—or to anyone—through the aetheric or "pneuma" network. That web of silent, extremely rapid communication has lately been made possible by the work of a certain Mr. Hertz, who, I need not tell you, has managed to harness these invisible waves for the benefit of mankind. I tell Brother Inish I am going on an excursion with Caleb Donnithorn, that I will be alone with him, that I will have the opportunity to question him and find out things even our keenest investigators could not uncover. I hope to make him tell me where this machine of his is hidden, so I can begin what I came here to do. I must not fail. I know if he resists me I may have to restrain him; I have with me the means to effect a harsh imprisonment, if such is necessary.

I do not like to think of it, but there are times when such intervention is required. I have done it before—once. A man deep in the throes of spirit possession had screamed, kicked, and fought us for twenty-eight hours, rolling around the floor of a little church near Nuremberg. The twelve demons inhabiting him cursed and taunted us, exhorting us to do our worst. The man had bitten through his tongue and twice had nearly choked on the expurgated contents of his own stomach. At last an exhausted Brother Inish took me aside and pressed a silver dagger into my hand. *Do it. End his suffering.* The memory pulses through me every time I think on it. I especially remember how easy it was to do what I know now was an abominable thing. We laid hold of him, and I pushed the dagger through the layers of his clothing and into his warm, living flesh, and we watched and waited as he jerked and groaned and died. His death took a great deal longer than I would have thought. Would I be able, should it become necessary, to restrain Caleb Donnithorn in a similar manner? With what chains can such a monumental spirit be bound, and for how long?

I am tired. My back and shoulders ache abominably, the scourge of my old sickness. The strong, ancient wine I drank this evening with dinner is working its way through my veins, drawing me into the arms of Morpheus, and yet I fight sleep even as I yearn for it. There is something I must remember, some mental note I made.

Diary, 4:00 a.m. by the clock—Jacob van Willigen

I AM writing this by the light of a single candle, having awakened quite suddenly to the sound of someone weeping. At first I supposed myself asleep, and the sound, a part of my dream. I pinched myself, expecting to feel nothing, but my flesh answered the pinching test and with it came the horrible realization that what I heard was real.

It goes on. It goes on and on and on, beyond what even the deepest sorrow ought to: deep, wracking sobs exhaled on ragged breath. I cannot tell from whence the noise is coming. When first I awoke, it seemed to come from behind me and a little below, as if someone in a lower room were crying and the sound had filtered up to me. Now that I am awake, it sometimes ceases, only to begin again a moment later, painful and violent and lost, a dreadful moaning interspersed with murmured invocations. The voice is a man's voice. A nightmare, perhaps.

I got out of bed, taking my candle with me, and searched all the corners of the room but found nothing. Perhaps, I reasoned, some household servant had crept in here earlier and hid in the wardrobe or underneath the bed, and was now too frightened to move—but I was alone. I crossed the floor and unlatched the great double casement and peered out, wondering if the poor wretch lingered in the courtyard. But there was nothing but the icy night air streaming in over the naked sash and the moon, round and cold and silver, riding silent on the buffeting clouds.

I closed the window and got back into bed, blowing out my candle as I did. I lay there for a long time with the covers pulled up to my chin and my heart throbbing in my chest until my eyelids, heavy with the want of rest, closed of their own accord.

It seemed but a few moments later I awoke with the certainty that someone was in the room with me. It was very dark, the moon having been at last subsumed by clouds, and I could see nothing, but I sensed someone near me.

I was frightened, uncertain if this was a usual occurrence or if some phantasm of the dark had arisen to torment me. I lay there hardly daring to breathe, my whole being in thrall to whomever or whatever had come in to me. I distinctly remembered turning the key in the lock before retiring and then sliding the key under my pillow. I checked, turning the pillow over. The key was precisely where I'd left it, the pillow retaining only a slight hollow where my head had lain. The casement I had likewise closed, although from my window to the courtyard below was a good thirty feet and I doubted anyone could have climbed it. The absurd notion that someone might have come down from the roof occurred to me, but I quickly dismissed it. This may be a strange and esoteric country, and Caleb Donnithorn may be an unusual man (to say the least!), but I am not yet ready to surrender my wits entirely. I must have been dreaming. The previous day's travel and the rigors of my trip from London were playing tricks with me, and I was seeing and hearing things that did not exist.

I waited, wondering if the phantom might not betray its identity by speaking, but there was no sound, and after some period of time, the feeling that I was not alone faded. I went round the room again, carefully searching every corner and finding nothing. I went out into the corridor—black, empty, lit only by the moon and with vast pools of shadow in the corners—and waited, listening. At length I discerned a sound, subtle at first, like the rustling together of a great many papers, but heard from a distance. It gained in volume and sounded now like whispering, as when several people are gathered together in an enclosed space, and there seemed to be a louder, more pronounced noise riding it like a wave. I glanced about me, my candle throwing scant light, but still I could see nothing.

"Jacob."

I whirled around, certain my name had been spoken directly behind me, but there was no one there. I raised my candle higher, hoping to pierce the gloom that lay about me like a shroud. "Who's there?"

"Jacob."

"What do you want? Who is this? Tell me what you want." I fought to master myself. I would do no good to anybody if I dissolved into terror at the slightest provocation. So there were rustling noises— perhaps some member of the household staff had left a window open, and what I heard was the sound of drapes blowing against the wall.

"Jacob… can you hear me?"

I was utterly helpless. My implements were in my traveling case, which was in my bedroom. I considered turning and fleeing, yet feared if I did, whatever—whoever—was taunting me from the darkness would fall upon me and rend me to pieces. I laid the palm of my unoccupied hand flat against the wall and slowly—very, very slowly— began walking back to my bedroom. There was some perfectly logical explanation for it, some atmospheric disturbance or the construction of the ancient house trapped and amplified noise…. There surely was a reason for it.

"I'll grind his bones to make my bread… make my bread…."

My heart pounded so violently I feared it would burst my ribs. I abandoned my candle and ran—yes, ran—to the open doorway of my room. As soon as I had gained the threshold, I shot the bolt and stood for a long time, listening. Presently there was a knock, the kind of light tapping made by one who does not wish to disturb the room's occupants. I made no reply.

"Jacob? Are you all right?" The voice was a woman's voice, of a rich and moderate tone, with a slight foreign accent I could not immediately place. She tapped again on the door, and then it creaked open and a pretty woman, perhaps twenty-five years old, peered in at me. "I heard a commotion in the hall and wondered if you were all right."

This sensible, common exchange of speech, coming on the heels of my terrifying flight down the empty corridor, seemed at once odd and strangely reassuring. Just in time, I remembered my manners and, catching my dressing gown to me, went to greet her. "Madam, forgive me. I fear my imagination has quite run away with me."

"No need to apologize." She was tall, although not as tall as I, and slender, with the kind of graceful carriage one often sees in dancers or those habituated to the stage. Her long dark hair was dressed in a complex arrangement of loops and whorls, entirely impractical but beautiful. Her face was pale, soft, and altogether lovely. "When I first came to this house, I ran screaming—yes, actually screaming—from that corridor. It's a horrible place. I'm not so sure it isn't haunted." She offered me her hand. "I'm Justine Donnithorn. I'm sorry I wasn't here when you arrived, but I was occupied in the east wing." She tilted her head to one side and smiled. "Will you forgive me?"

"Of course—although you have no need to beg my forgiveness, or that of anyone else, madam." I wished I had something to offer her, some brandy or tea, or somewhere to sit down, but the room was bare, and I had nothing but my own goodwill. "You are Caleb's… sister?"

She laughed. "Do we resemble one another?" Her pale, slender hands cradled and caressed her face, as if it were a precious work of art. "They say such things happen, although I've never heard of it." She smiled at me, a luminous glance that seemed to warm the darkness. "I am Caleb's wife. His second wife."

"I see." I was rather taken aback. I'd assumed Caleb's only wife was dead. "Then it is my pleasure to make your acquaintance. I'd no idea the Donnithorn family was comprised of such charming and intelligent ladies." A clock chimed somewhere down the hall. "You keep late hours, madam. Are you a lover of books, as I am?"

"I am. Just now I'm engrossed—is that the right word?—in Bentham's thesis that happiness is to be sought after as the pinnacle of life." She pondered for a moment. "Do you think that's right? I suppose one could consider it a… kind of righteousness." She glanced my way, hiding an embarrassed smile. "Listen to me… talking so freely and you no doubt wish to return to your slumber." She laid a hand on my arm. "Forgive me."

"There is no need." I patted her hand. "Your conversation is charming and I feel thoroughly welcomed."

"Then my task is finished." She dimpled and sketched an elaborate curtsey. "We will talk again, Jacob. Perhaps I can teach you not to fear shapes and noises in the dark. You will like that, won't you?"

I laughed, and the sound of my own laughter was such a relief that I was giddy with it. I turned to light another candle. "Of course I will—and there's no need to apologize. I quite understand—"

The door to my chamber stood open. A swelling wave of great, fathomless horror rose around me like an ocean. I alone occupied the room, yet there floated on the breeze the subtle scent of jasmine and something else I could not readily identify. A thousand tiny voices mocked and whispered, and presently there came a tinkling music, as if a harp was being played or a dulcimer gently struck from far away. I lay awake until dawn began to paint the corners of my chamber and only then, when I saw those first affirming rays of light, did I allow myself to surrender to sleep. I dreamed of a beautiful young woman, and a high wall, and the jagged rocks of the pitiless mountains, and an eternity of loss.

Diary—Jacob van Willigen

I BATHED, shaved, and dressed, and feel a new man for it. The terrors and phantasms of the previous night are gone. I descended to the dining room, intending to breakfast with Caleb if he had risen. I found him in the drawing room where I had seen him the first night, sitting by the fire and reading the local newspaper. The same carpet sweeper I had seen on my arrival, or some precise duplicate, was scouring the rug in front of the fireplace. It backed up and sped past me into another room, and I could have sworn it was fleeing my presence. I do not know what it is about the machines in this place, but every one of them seems to have some great antipathy to me. Judging by what I have seen thus far, my host seems inordinately fond of such devices, for much of the household work is accomplished by the intervention of machines. Of course, the practice is not so odd in this day and age, when even the lowest and poorest home boasts at least one such appliance.

Caleb smiled when he saw me and stood up, extending both his hands in welcome. "My good friend, here you are. I am so very glad to see you." His dress was similar to what he had been wearing the previous night, except his suit was charcoal gray, with a dark blue necktie that featured some repeating symbol done in white. His shoes were buffed to a gleaming shine, and he looked as astonishing in daylight as he had in the dark. "Come into the dining room. My staff has prepared a very good breakfast." The hands that gripped mine were warm and possessed of a manly strength that impressed me.

The dining room was just off the main hall: a large, austere medieval affair whose stone walls and soaring ceilings were hung with tapestries and heraldic banners of diverse types. The table was long and dark and surrounded by a great many chairs, and the large fireplace—a duplicate, as near as I could tell, of the one in the drawing room—boasted a roaring fire to which new logs had recently been added. The walls were decorated with an absolute profusion of mirrors, each one taller than a man. They gave back the fire's reflection, a dazzling kaleidoscope. Caleb bade me sit near him as he poured hot coffee from a self-heating pot at his elbow. They are curious inventions but eminently useful. I had employed one myself during my years at university, although my tiny steel device, with its simple gears and rudimentary heating timer, paled beside the Donnithorn's heirloom silver pot. "Tell me, my friend, did you sleep well last night?"

When he spoke, I had again the curious sensation of being in two places at the same time. As before, something intimately mine—my soul, my essence—seemed to flow outward from me and into him. His query about my sleep caused me to remember a dream I had—a dream that, even now, in the cold light of day, cast its pall of fear around me. After Justine had departed my chambers, I fell into a restless sleep, dreaming of raging rivers and jagged rocks. I woke repeatedly, wondering where I was and unable to reconcile my surroundings with the dark and frightening shapes that inhabited my chamber. Near dawn I slid into a restless state somewhere between sleep and waking, and was tormented by strange and vivid dreams, vivid phantasms that terrified me.

I dreamed I lay alone in a vast meadow—lush, verdant, full of wildflowers of such scent and hue as are never seen in waking life. At the far end of the meadow was a tree next to a meandering brook that shone and sparkled in the sun. I stood and went toward the tree, thinking to refresh myself from the brook, but whenever I drew close to it, my position shifted. Eventually I was able to draw near to it by sheer dint of will, but when I bent to drink, the entire brook receded and I was looking down into a shallow chasm full of bones and disarticulated skeletons. Some of the skeletons were large, as large as a man, while some others clearly had been women. There were a great many children, and some other bones that were wholly unfamiliar to me, but which may have belonged to animals. As I watched, the bones rose up and assembled themselves into roughly their original forms, and a voice, as dry and fragile as old paper, breathed some words into the air. Try as I might, I could not understand them. They seemed to be in some foreign, or perhaps ancient, language.

"You did sleep well?" Donnithorn's voice broke into my thoughts. "Perhaps you awoke too soon?"

A cold thrill raced along my limbs, as if I had been bathed in icy water. The whole of my interior vision was filled with the dream's horrible imagery, and my throat seemed to have closed together at the back. "I... I expect it was the strain of being in an unfamiliar place." I hastened to assure him the room was comfortable and I appreciated his hospitality. I did not wish to give offence, and truly, he had been exceedingly kind to me—so kind that I wondered what he intended. I did not mention my sojourn in the upstairs corridor, and several times throughout our meal I began to tell him of my meeting with Justine but stopped myself. "Brother Inish advised me of your plight." I unfolded my napkin and placed it on my lap. "I am not as familiar with hereditary curses as I'd like, but I can assure you I shall try my best."

"There is plenty of time for that," he said. He reached toward me with the coffee pot and decanted a stream of fragrant hot liquid into my cup. "Would you care to see a little of the countryside today?" He uncovered some dishes that were lying in the center of the table and bade me help myself to whatever I desired. There were cooked meats, omelets, several types of bread, and a selection of fine cheeses, and I found my appetite good and so I was eager to try them all. During the meal, he talked in a desultory fashion, discoursing briefly on the extensive history of the area. This part of the world, I was told, was home to one of the largest wolf populations in the world. He said this proudly, as if he had been somehow complicit—or perhaps I mistake his unusual intonation as evidence of some personal vanity. "I thought we might take a drive, as I had promised you. There are many beautiful places we could go."

As I am eager to see more of this land, my delight at being invited is akin to childlike pleasure. My dream of the night before was merely a dream, and besides, there is the matter of my duty, which I am duly sworn to carry out. I trust Brother Inish and my fellow members of the Society. I am here on a matter of the utmost importance and integrity. I know this. I will do what is right.

Diary—Jacob van Willigen
5:30 p.m.

WHEN I am with Caleb Donnithorn—when I am in his presence, close to him and engaged in conversation—I am most acutely anxious. This sense of uneasiness, allied with his near-irresistible charm, leaves me shaken and off balance. He has never said one unkind word since my arrival, nor has he desisted to provide me with all that I could want, and yet… there is something cruel—nay, something horribly *resigned* to cruelty—in his features. It is not that he is cruel, but rather there is a potential for cruelty in him, not because it is expected, but because it is inevitable.

Before I left London, I spent some time in the Society's library reading whatever material was available about the Donnithorn family. They are a seafaring clan whose earliest ancestor, Josiah Donnithorn, hailed from Devon and who was apparently rich enough to finance his own fleet of fishing vessels. Josiah was a harsh taskmaster, according to those who worked for him, quick with the cat and as likely to beat a man as look at him. Twice a ship of his had run aground and sunk, with no survivors, and rather than pay compensation to the families of the dead men, Josiah kept the matter tied up in court for years, until the widows had died and there was no one left to contest it.

I wondered if Caleb took after his ancestor, but search as I might, I found nothing in any of the records to support my suspicions, nothing except hearsay about the legendary cruelty of the Donnithorns and their rather cavalier treatment of several housemaids who had fallen pregnant while in their employ. The Society's chief archivist, Rani Subramian, was able to locate partial transcripts of the original legal documents, proving the earlier Donnithorn ancestors likely bought and sold slaves and were uncommonly tight with their coin, but beyond that, nothing. It was as if Caleb Donnithorn had stepped through some rip in time.

He took me driving in the countryside today, a trip through an almost magical landscape of surpassing beauty and strangeness, of high mountains and pastoral fields of such pristine loveliness that to see it brings tears to even the most jaded eye. His troika was similar in design to the diligence that brought me hither from my hotel, although much more beautiful. In form it is not dissimilar to the two-man coaches that are so common everywhere these days, with a sealed and covered compartment for the driver and one passenger, and gas lamps at the front and rear for use in darkness. The necessary boiler is mounted at the front, just ahead of the engine, which sheds some of its excess heat backward into the compartment, providing us with blissful warmth for the entire journey. (Mr. Brunel would be wise to take note: I am not an engineer, but I am certain such design could be utilized to provide a little warmth to the northernmost extremities of the tube lines.)

Like the diligence, Caleb's troika was adapted to the mountainous terrain by means of metal treads instead of wheels, and in this way, we were able to climb to significant heights along the narrow roads despite the recent fall of snow. The vehicle itself is fashioned of some sleek black metal and with a surfeit of chromium fitments, which gleam like polished glass. The interior is fitted with leather seats, each the width and depth of the most comfortable club chair, and for the passenger there is even a footstool of the same fine material and furs to wrap around oneself, should extra warmth be desired. The compartment is enclosed by thick glass all around, which is kept clear by the ingenious addition of small rubber wings that appear from the body of the vehicle at predetermined intervals to whisk away any rain or snow which might have chanced to fall upon the glass. Caleb demonstrated this feature for me and showed me how, by means of a brass dial set into the operating console, these rubber wings could be extended or retracted. The troika could be made to go forward by pressing a pedal on the floor, in the same way as our own automatic coaches are driven, and the direction of the vehicle likewise is controlled by means of a wheel, such as ships use.

He seems very proud of his troika, and rightly so. Were I disposed to own personal property, I should waste no time in acquiring such a vehicle for my very own. He must have divined my thoughts, for he invited me to pilot it a little ways up the mountain. At first I demurred, advising him of my rank inexperience in such matters, but he would not be put off. We decided upon a compromise: I would take over the controls, but only if he sat directly behind me, guiding me as necessary and taking over if it appeared I was about to steer us over a cliff. This resulted in much hilarity, as I am slightly taller than Caleb and his attempts to reach round me were amusing, to say the least. I will confess, as well, that I found the sensation of his body pressed so close against mine more of a distraction than I was able to countenance, and I quickly returned control of the vehicle to him.

As we drove, he spoke to me of the history of his land, the legacy handed to him by his grandfather and father, and how his family had ruled this land for centuries. I was fascinated by his stories, which I felt had been constructed for my benefit. I questioned him about the family and in particular his ancestors, but he would only say the family had been founded some eight hundred years before, by a man also named Caleb Donnithorn. This elder Donnithorn had married a young woman from the West Indies, the daughter of an eminent and rich planter. After giving birth to a son, his wife fell prey to melancholy and threw herself into the sea. Donnithorn raised their son with the help of the household servants but never married again, nor did he seek feminine company.

"Your ancestor?" I asked.

"Of course." Caleb smiled—a little archly, I thought. "Surely you can't think I am eight hundred years old?"

For a moment, the possibility that he might be—in this very strange part of the world, anything at all might be!—flitted across my consciousness, but I dismissed it.

The scenery was beautiful, and Caleb a most captivating interlocutor, discoursing easily on a myriad of subjects and showing genuine interest in my own thoughts and opinions. On the way home, we chanced to pass an old woman carrying a load of firewood on her back. She was bent nearly double under her burden, and I asked my host if we ought not stop and help her.

His face assumed such an expression of disgust and outrage that I was taken quite aback. He drew level with the old woman for a moment, and she, seeing who it was at the helm, spat on the ground and made a sign with one hand, which I took to be some sort of guard or charm.

"*Monstru! Strigoi!* Donnithorn, devil." She brandished her fist, and Caleb spun the wheel and we sped off.

It was some time before he spoke, and I perceived he was controlling his anger with great effort. When at last he deigned to address me, he chose to mask his fury by pretending amusement. "You see? They say my name and spit. You wonder what I have done to deserve such blatant disrespect, yes? My family has much history in this area." He chuckled, but not with any warmth or genuine good feeling. It was an ugly sound, a bitter sound. "I am a Donnithorn, Jacob. You had best guard yourself against me."

"I don't understand."

He did not look at me but concentrated on steering the troika. "Back home in London, do they not tell you about creatures such as I am? Do they tell you about the Donnithorn family, our outrageous cruelties, our… legendary excesses?"

I had no ready answer.

Castle Donnithorn

CODED POD, archival. Authorized by Caleb Donnithorn.

William is waiting in the library for me, pretending to read. He, forever fascinated with devices, has sent the walking ladder round and round the top shelves. The noise of it—a frantic, metallic clacking—reverberates down the corridor for some distance. He too is part of this charade, as obligated as I am to play it out to its bitter end. The books and tables are all dusted and the windows gleam, so obviously the servants have been in here recently, which surprises me. The housekeeper, the downstairs maid, and the others dislike him and will scarce tolerate his presence in any room where they are. William has no excess of feeling for them, either. He believes he alone is situated to meet my needs.

"You look sad." He is sitting near the fire, a volume of Dickens in his hand. "Perhaps your new companion is not as… receptive as you'd hoped?"

I have no strength or inclination to fight with him. He has been with me for so long that we are like two halves of one person. "What do you want?"

"When is he leaving?" He rises, laying the book carefully on a small table. It is rosewood, inlaid with cabochon, acquired from a traveler who had passed through Istanbul on his way to the Black Sea. It was to have been a gift for some Eastern potentate, but I intercepted him and took it. Of everything I own, it is one of my favorite pieces.

"William." I do not even command him. I request. This is how our relationship has changed. "When this is over, you may do with him as you will."

His face flattens, the features smoothing themselves down. "And what might that be?"

I want to show Jacob my library. I think he would enjoy seeing it, this enormous cavern filled with books, with newspapers and magazines and periodicals of all kinds. There are deep, comfortable chairs, a fireplace, beautiful rugs, and a sofa. There are ingenious devices for retrieving books from shelves too high for the mortal man to reach. Would he appreciate this room? Even thinking such things is ridiculous. I know his purpose here. Have I been so long without worthy companionship that I would seek succor in such as Jacob van Willingen? "Anything." I draw a breath. "I swear."

"A promise?" He moves to caress my face, but I turn away.

I cannot allow him to distract me, not now, even though he retains all the strength and beauty of his youth.

"A promise."

At first I think he will turn and leave, but he surprises me. He leans close to me, his lips next to my ear, and what he says is for my hearing only: "Are you still crying in your sleep, Caleb?"

He shrieks when I force his arm behind him, the wrist bent painfully. He still has the presence of mind to fear me. "Go. Leave me."

"You didn't answer my question." With that fluidity of limb I have so long admired, he twists away from me. "You never answer my questions." He is angry now and beautiful, but I want more. He excites some primal instinct in me, some desire to crush and torture, to take what is indisputably mine. I hold his arms just above the elbows, squeezing, my fingers digging in cruelly. "Please." He struggles, drops his head back. Oh yes, he wants this. He always wants this. "Don't hurt me."

"Whatever made you think you might speak to me this way?" I move to press his body into the wall with my own. "You ought to know by now, William." I rip away the front of his shirt, baring his naked skin. I lean in and taste him, draw my tongue across his shuddering flesh. He tastes of salt and the discipline I have instilled in him over the years. Yes, it has been years. "You forget…." I fasten my lips to the tender juncture of neck and shoulder. I mouth him like an animal mouths its prey. He is trembling, but not with fear. Never with fear. I have known him far too long to suppose it is anything like fear that motivates him. "I am now and always will be your master."

"Oh God, Caleb, please." He clenches his hands in my hair as I inhale the scent of him, a pungent bouquet of gorgeous odors: sweat and heated skin and that other, elusive quality that makes him absolutely human, perfectly mortal. "Do it."

When I lick his neck, he shivers like an animal in a trap. I allow myself to linger for a moment, right before the act. Hunger for one's sustenance is rare and precious. I hold him carefully, my palm cradling his skull. You must always be gentle. They are so fragile. And then I take him, as I have taken him before.

LETTER: JACOB van Willigen to Brother Coilm Inish, Society for Psychical and Esoteric Research, London W1
Cable code #459-12-A/Eastern European Aethernet via Ragusa hub
My dear Brother Inish,
I had thought to write as soon as I arrived, but circumstances have conspired to keep me from

corresponding as readily as I would have liked. Let me say immediately that my duty to the Society is uppermost in my mind, but I find myself—forgive me!—tormented with doubts.

Believe me when I tell you Caleb Donnithorn is not as we had expected. I fear our information is largely incorrect, and indeed, I would venture that even the most diligent of our researches have failed to uncover the true facts. Everything I know about such things—and you must admit, it is considerable—warns me against too hasty of an action. The device, of course, cannot be permitted to exist, but what of Donnithorn himself? It may be this so-called hereditary curse is tightly bound up within him, and to remove it may cause irreparable damage. What must I do?

I pray you, please instruct me.

J... van Willigen

P.S. Please tell Robertson he may borrow my Carpenter provided he returns it to my rooms unharmed, as it is a first edition. Give my love to Althea and please assure her that the food here is very good, although not as fine as hers.

I had just begun to affix my seal and I suppose I was somewhat careless. A little of the hot wax fell onto my finger, causing a painful—albeit not very serious—burn. I must have cried out, because, before I realized what was happening, Caleb was at my side, had taken my hand, and—most astonishing of all—put my burned finger *into his mouth.* His lips were warm, his tongue and palate moist and gentle against my skin. When I gazed into his eyes, I felt as if I were drowning, and I was suddenly hovering on the edge of tears. I cannot countenance the emotions he arouses in me; his capacity to move me makes him dangerous.

"You must be more careful." He wrapped his clean handkerchief around my finger. "This sealing wax is dangerous. Here, use this instead. It is much safer and I will not need to worry that you are burning yourself." After reaching into a drawer, he presented me with a beautiful silver stylus inset with its own brass reservoir for ink and a second, smaller reservoir containing a supply of sealing wax. He demonstrated how to extrude the wax for heating over any convenient flame. "The barrel of the device keeps the fingers clear of both the flame and the hot wax. Please, use it with my compliments, my friend."

I thanked him profusely and went back to my correspondence, quite forgetting about my injury until some hours later when I chanced to look at my finger—and saw the burn had completely disappeared.

February 6
Diary—Jacob van Willigen

THE SNOW, begun overnight, has continued unabated and is now a howling blizzard of truly frightening proportions. Caleb has ordered fires to be built in each room, and so we are warm and cozy, but I cannot imagine what must lie in wait for anyone unwary enough to venture out in this weather. The wind howls round the battlements and roars down the chimneys like the hounds of Hell; the casements rattle in their frames until I am certain their latches must give way, but everything somehow holds together.

Caleb and I were sitting in his library, reading before the fire, when a young man approached and whispered something to him. As we were seated close together, I could not help but hear the words, but I did not understand them since they were in the local dialect.

Caleb at once laid aside his book and looked gravely at the young man. "Are you certain? It is as bad as you say?" He got up and put his book back on the shelf, then dismissed the servant with a wave of his hand. "My dear friend, I am sorry, but I must leave you and go out."

To say I was surprised is putting it mildly. I wondered whether he might not be risking his own safety unnecessarily by going out in the storm, but he would not be dissuaded.

"It cannot wait. A woman in the village has been in childbed for three days. They wish me to attend her."

This must be some custom of which I have not heard. Why should a man such as the heir of Donnithorn be called to the childbed of a village woman? My confusion must have shown on my face, for he attempted to explain.

"It is the nature of my service to the village, and that of my father and grandfather before me. There will be a death tonight. I must attend."

I wondered to myself if this were not a matter for the local priest, but said nothing. I am merely a visitor to this place and it is hardly my right to question their customs. It may be that he functions as a sort of magistrate, officiating at births and marriages and deaths, as is often the case in some smaller English jurisdictions. Aloud I said I hoped he would be careful of his safety and exercise every precaution on account of the weather—and I asked if he would like me to accompany him.

As soon as I said this, a curious change came over his face: his features softened and something of his seemingly habitual control slipped away. "You would go with me?"

"Of course—if you wish it. I should be happy to help in any way I can."

He spent some time fiddling with his gloves, and when he at last looked up, his dark eyes were suspiciously bright. "It is best that you stay here." His voice trembled a little. "Please, help yourself to whatever you wish. I shall return when the thing is done."

His words made me very uneasy. Later, when a servant brought me a pot of tea, I asked the man what Caleb meant.

At first he pretended not to understand me, but I had heard Caleb speaking English to the man earlier, so this was a ruse he could not sustain for very long. "It is his hereditary duty," the man said. "I can say no more than that. It has always been done this way." When I pressed him for details, he merely bowed and hurried from the room.

The clock had just struck three when I heard footsteps in the hallway near my room. I had fallen asleep some time earlier with a book in my hand and woke now with a start. Caleb passed my open door but did not look up. After a moment I heard his door close, and there was silence for some time. I waited, listening intently, but all I heard was the roar of the wind at the casements.

Around four I got up and put on my dressing gown and went down to the library, thinking to exchange my book for another one. The room was dark, but the gleaming brightness of the snow outside provided a little illumination. Caleb was sitting on the settee, wearing his nightclothes and a dressing gown. He sat with his knees drawn up to his chest, his arms wrapped tight around them, and he was gazing sightlessly into the dying fire. I perceived he was shivering, so I took a warm blanket from the back of the sofa and dropped it round his shoulders. He did not move or acknowledge me as I sat beside him. "Forgive me," I said. "You seem cold." The hypocrisy of my words and actions burned me. I must reconcile myself.

His gaze did not move from the fire, nor did he turn his head. "I wonder if there is some eternal record of lives given and lost, and if so, who is occupied with keeping such a tally. You may be as familiar with me as you wish, Jacob. I do not forbid it."

"Caleb?"

He turned to me and I saw he had been weeping. "I have been keeping such a tally. Would you like to see?" He leapt off the sofa, leaving the blanket puddled on the floor, and went to a cabinet in the wall. Here he pulled down a flat wooden panel to reveal what I immediately recognized as a difference engine—a mechanical aggregator of numbers, able to parse the most difficult equations in a fraction of the time it would take a human to do it. I have of necessity seen such an apparatus before, but this one was beautiful, a masterpiece in mahogany and brass, a miracle of finely honed and elegantly moving parts. "Every one, from the very beginning, I have counted. Each one a tiny little fragment of some ineffable energy, too small to be accurately measured. What is the weight of a human soul?"

His questions made me acutely uneasy. These were not things I would have readily discussed with anyone outside the Society. What did he mean, talking like this? Who besides the Almighty God knew the weight of a soul?

"I fear I cannot ever count them all. From the very beginning, there have been too many." He ran both hands reverently over the apparatus. "When I was eleven, I killed the Turkish soldier who had been sent to bring me in chains to Constantinople at the behest of my father." He traced the Sign of the Cross on a flat brass panel of the machine. "We rode into the city just as the sun was rising, my brother and I tied to the pommels of our horses to prevent our escape. We were noble hostages, you see. One would have thought such might protect us." He gave me a queer, absent little smile. "One would have thought God, to whom we had always professed our faith, would protect us, but He declined." His hands played over the machine, turning the dials so the brass and ivory fitments made a disturbing clicking noise. "This just God, this jealous God, this God to whom all worship so rightfully belongs, turned His back on us"—his voice rose—"just as He turned his back on His only son while He hung on the cross, dying for mankind."

He drew a long breath. "Yet we owe him our allegiance. I believe I said as much to Mehmed, but he was an infidel." He shrugged. "When he approached me in the baths one morning, I ought not to have been surprised. What did I know? I was a child." His fists clenched and his entire demeanor changed. So swift was this transformation that it frightened me. "And when he bent me over the stone and opened me and pressed himself into my flesh while his attendants turned their backs and looked the other way, it was to my God that I cried for mercy and redemption: *Domine Jesu Christe, Fili Dei, mei peccator miserere!*" He spoke—or rather shouted—this last in Latin, and something stirred somewhere in the house, and I perceived the sound of footsteps treading lightly on the floor above. *Lord Jesus Christ, Son of God, have mercy on me, the sinner.* Yes, I knew it well.

"For centuries my family has pledged our swords to God Almighty. For centuries we beat back the infidel invaders. We shed the blood of our young men and of our old men, and gave the purity of our daughters and our sisters to vouchsafe this and many other lands in the name of Christ." He caressed the machine in silence. "When I most needed Him, He was nowhere to be found."

"May I?" I did not extend my hand toward it until he nodded his assent. It seemed to purr slightly underneath my touch, and its mahogany skin was as warm as that of a living thing. "It is very beautiful." I was eager to draw his conversation in another direction. "Did Babbage himself make it?"

"No, not Babbage." He stroked the keys, his expression dreamy in the firelight. "I would have commissioned him, but it was not to be." He sighed and let his hand drop back to his side, his earlier rage gone out of him. "Will you sit with me a little while, if you are not too tired?"

We sat on the sofa together, he with the blanket round his shoulders. "Was it bad? In the village?" My voice seemed unnecessarily loud in the silence. "The weather, I mean. I imagine you had a difficult time going down the mountain. It's not like there's a tube network nearby." The atmospheric railway stopped at the last large town before the road to Castle Donnithorn. Any travel up or down the mountain was by other means.

"It was not the weather." He huddled farther into the blanket. "There are things that I am called upon to do." He turned to me, his dark eyes gleaming. "It was my father, the first time. I was seven years old, and I had been away at school in England. We were called to the house of an old man whose lungs were filling up with fluid. He had been ill for some time and his strength was waning. His family had prevailed upon my father to assist them."

A cold thrill ran up my spine, and my hands clenched themselves into involuntary fists. "Assist them." Why had no one told me? Of course we in the Society know of such things—as abstractions, tales from faraway places or times now lost to the distant past—but if Caleb was adept at such practices, why had no one told me?

"There is a story in the Bible, about the prophet—Elijah, I think it was—who, being presented with a young boy who had recently died, stretched himself upon the body and breathed into the open mouth." Caleb's eyes widened as he gazed, sightless, into the fire. "I had never seen it until that day I accompanied my father. I had only heard it whispered." He nodded. "There is a reason we are no longer welcome." Shaking off his reverie, he moved close to me and caught hold of my hand. "Tell me about your life in London. I have collected many antique maps of England. Should you like to see them?"

I replied that I should like it very much and waited while he fetched them from a cabinet in the wall. The fire burned low, throwing strange and wavering shadows on the wall while the wind buffeted the windows and screamed down the flue. He moved close to me and bent over the maps, the blanket brushing my shoulder. He smelled like vetiver and spice, and his body gave off an unearthly heat that drew me to its warmth. I was glad of him, glad we were sitting close together in this way, glad I was here with him right now, and I had a wild idea that I might circumvent the thing I had been sent here to do. I imagined I could refuse the commission, disobey. I still imagined my will was entirely my own. God! To sit there with him, in close companionship, sharing the warmth of the fire and the wine, and to know—

For pride and disobedience was Lucifer cast out of Paradise.

February 8
Castle Donnithorn

THE WORLD is a white hell, the wind a violence. I have bolted my door from the inside and am alone here with my mirrors and myself, a gallery of endless reflections. Four walls, each wall equipped with four exquisite looking glasses, each glass reflecting me back to myself, an infinity of torment. I once believed the scars would fade with time. I no longer believe this. The two livid weals running from my shoulders to the small of my back are as vividly purple as they ever were and as painful as the day they were made. Consider this, the next time you amuse yourself picking the wings off flies. Imagine, if you will, the pain of having your arms pulled off.

I had just reached my fifth mortal year when my father and a small group of his most trusted aides came to fetch me from my bed. It was autumn, and the October moon appeared, bloated and yellow, above the night horizon, and slender plumes of smoke rose into the still air from the village below. I was sleeping soundly when my father's rough hand fell upon my shoulder and shook me. *Wake up, little man.* The room I shared with my brother Mircea was deathly chill; spikes of frost stood out from the roof beams and glistened coldly on the wooden floor.

I knew better than to question my father. In our house his word was law and he would brook no interference with his raising of us. I had often heard him decry those feebleminded men who allowed their women to admonish them, especially when it came to the treatment of their sons. *I'd be a hundred years dead before I'd let some mother-cunt tell me anything. A boy must be a warrior, not some skirt-clinging simpleton, fed on pap and sweetmeats.* As for me, I'd had no skirts to cling to: I never knew my own mother and the wet nurse to whom my care had been entrusted was sent away as soon as I grew strong enough to take solid food. My education occurred within my father's walls, under the tutelage of many learned teachers, and by the time the first faint black hairs appeared on my chin, I spoke Turkish, Latin, French, and German, as well as my own tongue.

At the age of five, my father and his advisors thought fit to invest me in the hereditary Order of the Dragon, of which my father, like his father and grandfather before him, was a member. I knew nothing of the Order beyond murmured conversations that leaked from under the door of my father's study, sometimes accompanied by raucous masculine laughter and followed by the discreet departure of several dozen cloaked and hooded figures. In later years I would remember that night—the night of my investiture—only in dreams or as a vague feeling of unease upon awakening. I came to despise the necessary evil of sleep, because in sleep, the dreams came, and when I awoke, I felt the presence of something dark and horrible and capable of enacting its own drama, whether I was willing or not.

I remember my father's voice, soothing me as the rough hands of the men held my shoulders down, pressing me hard into the chilly ground. I could feel the cold, drawn upward into me like oil through a wick, and even though they spread a warm sheepskin on the ground, I shivered violently, hard enough to break my bones. There wasn't any fire, no flaming torches held high, no burning wicker effigy, nor candles set afloat on makeshift boats of bark. There was only the cold and velvet night, and the stars pricked out mercilessly above my head, and the setting moon. I was forbidden to make even the smallest noise as the sigils were carved into my flesh, marking me. In time the sigils faded to pale silver and then to nothing, including the dragon rampant on my chest, but I will always feel as if the brands have burned themselves into the marrow of my bones, indelibly.

After the Rites they fed me wine and bread and told me of the hereditary curse that would allow me, like my father and his father before him, to hasten the souls of the dying into the afterlife.

Young as I was, I scoffed at them. *I don't believe you.*

You'd better believe it, young Donnithorn. There will come a time when you will be required to perform the ritual. Only you can usher the dying into their eternal rest, and they will curse you for it. Your name will be an abomination to those who know you. You will be denied the solace of the Holy Mother Church, the refreshment of the Confessional. You are refused the release of Death. Remember that.

Strange that nothing they told me—nothing they did to me—explained the other scars. The scars run, two lurid lines, from the flat blades of my shoulders to the small of my back. Of these scars they said nothing, but no matter: I already knew. The cost of my transgression was my banishing, my exile the price I paid for disobedience. Mortal existence is not for the faint of heart.

The first time I was taken out to hunt, I was eleven years old, on the verge of puberty. The men—my father and his advisors—waited until the night of the crescent moon and then took me deep into the forest. My hands were unbound, the sigils traced on my palms and my forehead in the dark with sticky rabbit's blood, and they urged me forward. *Run, my son, go on.* I was given no particular instruction, told only I had a duty to my father, a duty to the great circle of warriors in whose memory I lived and breathed.

"Find it," the men told me. "Kill it and bring it back to us."

Something had been set loose for me in the forest, a thing whose beating heart I was to locate among all the other beating hearts, all the other life. I understood the nature of such games. I had been made to watch, in order that I might comprehend the frailty of all life and its ephemeral nature.

The previous week my father had taken me out of lessons, and we'd gone together to a monastery on the island in the middle of a great lake. The church was very beautiful, and my father made a contribution so prayers might be made for my soul until the end of time. He had the children brought before us, singly and in groups, so we could look them over. They were the sons and daughters from the local peasant class, sent to the monastery for a rudimentary education. "You must choose one you like," my father said, as though they were a litter of hunting pups, and, when I hesitated, "Do as I say." So I chose a boy about my own age, but there was something wrong with him—he was slow in his wits and my father said he would make a poor candidate. Instead I chose a little plump girl about four years old. "A good choice," my father said, "definitely a good choice, my son." He nodded to the abbot, who had the girl led away. The child must have sensed something wrong, for she began to cry in a most pitiable manner.

I thought about the girl that night as I drove myself onward through the dark forest, my blood singing in my veins. Before we set out I had been stripped naked and had hundreds of tiny cuts made in the skin all over my body. My father and another man rubbed goose grease mixed with extract of hellebore into the cuts, rubbing hard until the muscles began to cramp, rubbing through the pain until I felt like I could fly. It was difficult to stand upright. I wanted to crouch and run on all fours like an animal, slipping through the forest as silent as any beast of prey. I was no longer Caleb, heir of Donnithorn. I could not be named in any human language. The men tried to hold me, but I snapped my teeth and snarled at them.

I found the child under a stand of alder trees, her dark hair in her face. A line of spittle trailed from the corner of her mouth to the ground. She had been drugged. I leaned close to her, my ear at her mouth, listening for her breath, which came slowly, rasping in her lungs. I lifted each of her eyelids in turn, looking for the dark brown iris but seeing only the glistening white sclera. I wondered when she would awaken—if she would awaken. Eventually I lifted her in my arms and carried her to the hut of a woodsman and his wife and left her there.

My father was furious when I finally emerged from the forest at dawn, trailing the child's pink hair ribbon carelessly from one hand. The rabbit's blood had dried on my palms and on my cheeks and forehead, or perhaps I scratched myself on my headlong flight through the darkness. I threw my trophy at my father's feet.

Why didn't you kill it? my father asked, and, *Where is it now?* When I refused to tell him, he slapped me hard across the face with his mailed glove, then had me taken to the cellars and beaten until the blood ran from my scars and the sigils on my body burned like fire.

HE IS polite. He always knocks, unlike the others, who imagine I am eternally available to them whenever they decide. I do not cover myself beyond a simple robe, but he has seen me in this state, this dishabille, before. I, who open myself to no man, have allowed Victor Frankenstein to peer into me as though we were contemporaries and equals. Perhaps it is because I know him to be equally—if dissimilarly—damned. Or perhaps it is because we are both monsters, constructs considered mythical in a world that no longer needs us.

"You've been looking at it again, haven't you?" His fingers are coolly impersonal on my flesh. I watch his face reflected over my shoulder, his studious expression, his soft brown eyes with their long lashes. "I could repair these for you... fix it so they don't show as badly." His mouth curves into a smile. "But you wouldn't like that, would you? Oh, no, you must have your suffering."

"This has nothing to do with suffering." I let my hand linger on his face. "You have no power to efface such marks, nor has any man. These scars run deeper than the bone, Victor, and can never be erased." Truthfully, I don't know that I would wish for their erasure, since my scars are all I have to remind me of what I once was, and what I am now, and how far I have fallen. Strange, then, that I, who have been both antagonist and exile, should choose as my confidante a mere anatomist. Yet, it is Victor who soothes me when I return from the performance of my duty in the village, Victor who sits beside my bed, laying cool cloths on my fevered brow, Victor who—occasionally— allows me to kiss him.

He allows it now. His mouth is hot, his tongue a glorious intrusion. Of all my brides, of all the lovers I have ever known, Victor is my favorite.

February 9
Diary—Jacob van Willigen

I HAVE not seen Caleb all day, and I am curious as to where he has gone. I am certain I said nothing during our conversations to insult him—but feelings are a peculiar thing, and it may be that I let slip some imprecation that to the Western mind is nothing, but which causes enormous offence to one such as him.

I was awake until quite late the previous night, poring over the notes I had brought with me and making some preliminary sketches of the castle, as well as I can. I would very much like to venture outside and circumnavigate the entire fortress, but the winter's cold is formidable, and even accustomed as I am to weather, I fear the deadly chill as I have seldom feared any other thing. Our intelligence about Caleb Donnithorn is less than I thought, and the Society's archives contain very little information about Castle Donnithorn. As far as anyone can tell, it was built in the thirteenth century, during the era of the Basarab rulers, of which Caleb is a descendant. This fortress—I hesitate to call it a "home"—is disturbingly like a labyrinth in its interior construction, which consists of many narrow stairways leading to dark corridors, themselves letting into small rooms that lack any casement larger than an arrow slit. Many of the rooms on the castle's north side are empty and appear to have been uninhabited for a long time. Caleb and such servants as I have seen occupy the south side of the building, a fact which puzzles me. Why leave so much of a building uninhabited? Is there structural damage? If so, what kind and how was it caused? Are there regions of the manor that even Caleb does not know about?

I have moved from my notes to a volume of a famous theological treatise when there is a light tapping at my chamber door. "Come in." I resent the intrusion, but I do not want to appear unfriendly. I am a guest here, after all.

Justine slips into the room and pushes the door shut behind her. Her expression is grave, and if I knew her better, I might suspect some misadventure. "Jacob, forgive me." She smiles, and I see there is a dimple in one side of her face. I didn't notice this the last time we met. "I apologize for disappearing the other night. I thought I had quite forgotten my fear of that room, but it appears I was mistaken." Today she is wearing a deep green gown of silk velvet and adorned with ribbons. There are green ribbons in her hair, chasing each complicated loop and whorl around and around, circles fading into circles. The hair has been meticulously styled so there is no starting point, no ending. She comes to where I am and leans over my shoulder. "What are you working on?"

"Just reading." I show her the spine of the book and its title. "Justine, how is it you know Caleb?"

She doesn't betray herself, does not even blink. "My father was an old friend of the family." Her smile is almost genuine, and so I ask her why no one lives on the south side of the manse. "The south side? I don't know." She is lying, of course.

"I find it odd." That side of the structure faces the mountains and a deep ravine plummeting some four hundred feet to the surging river below. There are ancient pines rising some two hundred feet into the air, their outstretched limbs dusted with snow. The vista from that side of the house is stunning. I say as much to Justine.

"Oh dear." She rubs a section of her dress, pressing her fingers to an invisible spot. "Now, how on earth did I...?" As I watch, the place where she is rubbing thins, turns red, and exudes a scarlet liquid, a spreading stain.

"You've hurt yourself." I snatch up a handkerchief and move toward her, but she retreats, suddenly afraid of me. "Justine?" Her mouth works soundlessly, lips opening and closing on empty air. "What is it?" I ask. She is behaving as I have seen madwomen behave, locked for eternity in the cold hell of some asylum. "May I fetch someone for you? A servant?"

She tilts her head, as if in wonderment. "Why did they send you? You, of all the others they could have sent. Why?"

"I don't understand."

"You are the only other...." She clutches the hem of her dress, gathering the stained fabric into a hectic ball. "You are the other." She turns and flees.

I have a sister, so I know women suffer their monthly courses. I don't follow Justine, knowing that in her discomfiture she will seek solitude.

You are the other. A curious thing to say.

I reclaim my book and am deep into a chapter on moral responsibility when I become aware of someone looking at me. It is the servant, William. He has come soundlessly into my room. He is wearing an apron like a grocer wears and carrying a wooden toolbox. He is quite handsome—or would be, were it not for his expression of perpetual contempt.

"You ought not to talk to her."

I'm curious, and I ask why.

"Because she ain't there."

I can't quite place his accent. Like Caleb, he is an American, but I'm not sure if his broad, flattened vowels are New England or the South. The top two buttons of his shirt are open, displaying the strong column of his throat with its faintly present Adam's apple. I have a sudden vision of him in Caleb's bed, his pale skin slicked with sweat, mouth open—

"Of course she is."

He shifts his feet, and the contents of the toolbox clatter. "You ought to know better, from what I heard." He shuffles away, rattling like Marley's ghost.

Below the fortress is the mighty Argeş River, into which Caleb's young wife, Elizabeta, is supposed to have plunged to her death. Search as I might, I can find no trace of Elizabeta in this dwelling—not so much as a single portrait, not a lock of hair, an earring, a fan, or a handkerchief. It is as if the woman had never existed, so firmly has she been consigned to the past. Caleb, for his part, never speaks of her, which leads me to believe there was no great love between them in their marriage. The only signs of a female presence in this house are, of course, Justine's. Are there others? While lying in my bed at night, I have heard light footsteps from the room above mine, and sometimes, on the edge of sleep, I have detected what sounds like the timbre of female voices. Who these women are is a mystery. I have never seen them either inside the castle or anywhere about the grounds. Had I seen them, I would not hesitate to ask the location of Caleb's wondrous machine, which is surely hidden somewhere under this roof. In time my navigation of the castle will lead to its discovery, wherever it may be secreted.

In my youth, I was once given a key by an aged woman, a singular stalk of rusting iron that to my knowledge opened nothing. She lived by herself at the end of our street, and my father often pressed me to perform small tasks for her. Since she was very poor, she had no access to small luxuries the rest of us consider inevitable, and she would ask to borrow certain appliances—can openers, large wooden spoons for mixing bread dough, a clockwork sweeper every spring to brush the winter's accumulation of dust out of the sitting room drapes.

She kept a very odd bird as a pet: bright red, the size of a robin, with a circle of turquoise-colored feathers at its throat, like the jewel of a necklace. The bird supposedly could speak, but I had never heard it utter a word. Whenever it saw me, it would squawk disdainfully and fluff its feathers, as if I had somehow offended its dignity by being in the same room. My father was fond of roasted sunflower seeds, and whenever I went to the old woman's house, he would give me a bag of seeds to bring to the bird, whose name was Jaap. Antje, the old woman, would open the door of Jaap's cage and offer the seeds one at a time. The bird would eat them from her hand while it regarded me with one round, shiny black eye. *I know you,* it seemed to say. *You are a liar.*

The iron key came into my possession one November afternoon, when the day's small measure of light was fading rapidly in the west. I had called upon the old woman to reclaim a clockwork scrubber my father had loaned her. She said she wanted to give me something for my trouble. Being venal as all children are, I readily accepted, thinking my reward would be some money or a rare book (I was a bibliophile, even then) from her late husband's collection. My disappointment when she handed it to me must have shown on my face. The key was a pitiful, rusted thing, misshapen and old. What it was good for, I had no idea, and I briefly considered handing it back, except I knew it would hurt her feelings.

Antje pressed the thing into my palm and curled my soft, childish fingers around it. *You think this is nothing.* She held on to my hand so hard the key cut painfully into my palm. *You think I am giving you nothing. You'll see.*

I tried the key in many locks since then, but it opened nothing of any import. A year or two ago I chanced to spend a week in Edinburgh, and on one of my frequent walks around the city, I came upon a walled garden at the end of a narrow close. A wooden door, arched at the top in a vaguely gothic design, stood open to a descending passage, deeply walled and terminating in a gloom as absolute as the grave. It occurred to me that I might descend with it, and the more I pondered this possibility, the more alluring it seemed. I stood for a moment or two, regarding the passage set before me.

When I next came to myself, I was standing before a wrought iron gate set into a stone wall. I had traveled some distance from my initial starting point—indeed, the entrance was no longer visible to me—but whether this was a question of proximity or a trick of the light, I didn't know. The passageway was lit by small, gas-fed lanterns set at intervals along the narrow corridor. There were no doors or windows that I could see, and I was hesitant about traveling farther down. Few persons of even my intimate circle know I am dreadfully panicked by enclosed spaces, and I have no reservations about screaming like a frightened schoolgirl should I find myself in a vault or cellar or otherwise enclosed. When I was at school, this was the subject of many not entirely kind jests at my expense, and I am somewhat ashamed to confess I did nothing to silence my critics.

At the apparent terminus of its length, the passage turned abruptly to the right and continued for some distance, passing through an arch and stopping at another iron gate. This one was more heavily constructed than the other and fastened with a rough and unwieldy looking padlock. It occurred to me that my strange key might open it. The idea so amused me that I tried this, but the lock refused to admit the ancient metal. Antje's image swam into my mind: *You think this is nothing.* I stood there for a long time, holding the key, but nothing happened. When I emerged again to street level, it was night. I stood alone in a gloomy place suddenly full of tiny noises and subtle movements.

I SLEPT late and, upon coming down to breakfast, found a young man waiting for me in the dining room.

He had begun already to break his fast but rose as soon as he saw me and extended his hand. "You will forgive me, please. I ought to have waited, but I fear I am not as continent in my appetites as I ought to be." His accent and manner of speaking were English, even if his name was not. "Victor Frankenstein. I am very pleased to meet you. Caleb has spoken of you."

I took my seat opposite and accepted a cup of coffee. "*The* Victor Frankenstein? *Doctor* Frankenstein?" The Society had collected volumes of intelligence on Victor Frankenstein, from his earliest forays into anatomical study to his disastrous—some would say blasphemous—attempts to reanimate a human corpse. Such cases so often come to our attention through the intercession of good Christian women and men who, having borne witness to such abominations, wish them forever curtailed. One, who had been at university with him, forwarded a packet of letters which had purportedly passed between Frankenstein and an unnamed male correspondent, identified only as "L." The content of the letters ranges from a quotidian blandness to expressions of sensuality so frank that Brother Inish has forbidden them to the younger members of our order. I myself have read them, although the task was onerous and not one I would willingly undertake. The passages in question are invariably penned by "L" and describe— in excruciating detail—things he wishes them to do when next they are together. The merest contemplation of such lurid passages was sufficient to send me into paroxysms of shame even as my curiosity yearned to know who "L" was.

"I see you have heard of me. Yes, well...." His dark eyes rose to meet mine. "Don't believe everything you hear, van Willigen."

I replied that his researches into methods of extending the natural lifespan of man were renowned around the continent and, indeed, the entire world. "I think it is a great thing you are doing." I hesitated to add that most of the civilized world wondered nowadays what had become of him, for the name of Victor Frankenstein was not merely renowned but also somewhat notorious. All reports indicated he had fled England after it was revealed that he had a penchant for grave robbery, doubtless as a means of culling the raw materials necessary to make his blasphemous homunculi. "I attended one of Luarch's London lectures several years ago. He suggested that your theories about the origin of the soul were the most revolutionary he'd ever encountered, on a par with Johannes Eckhart, I heard him say."

"You flatter me, van Willigen. Eckhart was far more mystical in his approach, and I am at bottom a scientist." He smiled, a nervous smile. Indeed, his entire person seemed to resonate to the plucking of some invisible string. "We receive little news this far east, but I have heard of you and the work you have been doing for the Society."

"The Society." I tried to keep my expression neutral, but I was shocked. No one has heard of the Society. Until they recruited me— rescued me, as it were, when I was tossed upon their shores—I had no idea they even existed. The idea that they were the subject of common conversation in such a place as this was astounding to me. "I fear you mistake me, Doctor."

"All right." His smile didn't waver. "I shall play along, then." He let the subject drop, something for which I was grateful, and we passed the meal in enjoyable—if somewhat desultory—conversation. Under any other circumstances I would have found him a charming interlocutor, but there is something odd about Frankenstein, something *missing*. How shall I best describe it? I made use of his distraction during our conversation to touch his mind, and there are definite gaps there—places in his memory where things have been removed and replaced by other things. These erasures have been undertaken gently. His mind is rather like a patch of landscape where once a building stood: the structure has not been removed forcibly, but rather systematically dismantled a piece at a time and taken away. When I rose from the table, he bid me good morning and invited me to come down and see his work if I was so inclined. "I keep a little workroom down below. Caleb has been kind enough to furnish me with everything I need, and I think you might enjoy seeing the progress of my research." He winked, the impish gesture of a mischievous schoolboy. "We can even visit the Lady if you like."

"The Lady?"

Frankenstein bit down on his bottom lip and drew me close to him. "You mean he hasn't told you?"

"About?"

"His wife, the Lady Elizabeta. Not her real name, of course. It's just what he calls her." As he spoke, he drew me out of the dining room and down a narrow hallway, from which branched other passages leading into the castle's innermost regions. "She jumped. From the window in the tower, just over there." He pointed at the wall, but I gauged his meaning clearly enough. "It was the dead of winter and she was quite disconsolate. A straight plunge, you know, into the Argeş River. It was frozen, but the force of her fall, coming from that distance, shattered the ice like glass. He climbed down himself to retrieve the body." Frankenstein shook his head. "A dreadful business. I expect her neck was broken at the very least." He drew my arm under his and clasped my hand in a filial manner. "That was all before I came here, of course. Ah, here we are."

We stood in front of a thick wooden door, bound with iron straps and fitted with a large brass ring just above the keyhole. The corridor in which we stood ended abruptly at this door, which had apparently been erected for the sole purpose of closing off that part of the hallway. Victor Frankenstein took a skeleton key out of his pocket and, fitting it into the keyhole, turned it thrice about. A subtle groaning could be heard, the sound of metal clashing against metal, and then the door swung inward, revealing a set of stone stairs leading down into a murky blackness.

My heart beat faster in my chest and I wondered if here, at last, was the monstrous machine I'd come to destroy.

"Follow me closely." Frankenstein took a small gas torch from his pocket and struck a vesta to light it. "This way."

I did as he asked and kept close behind him, following the blue glow of the torch down into the darkness. So complete was the obscurity around us that I at times fancied Frankenstein had vanished, leaving me alone with naught but a faint blue light to guide me. My eyes, unused to the darkness, strained to see where there was nothing to be seen, producing sudden flares of brilliant but fragmentary light and queer, revolving patterns. Curious scenes enacted themselves in my mind's eye, so powerful and real that they unsettled me. It seemed I stood at the edge of a vast and ruined plain, over which were strewn forms of a similar likeness to men, yet were not men. Then I was lying broken and bleeding on some stairs leading into a high stone building whose many windows glistened in the early sunlight. *In paradisium deducant te Angeli*, a voice whispered, masculine yet wholly gentle. *In paradisium deducant te Angeli.* As is so often the case in my nightmares, I had the sensation of falling.

"Here." Victor Frankenstein reached for my hand and drew me forward into a chamber filled with golden light.

At first I took the luminescence to be the reflected rays of the morning sun, somehow filtered and channeled into this dank and airless space. As my eyes adjusted to the light, I saw a veritable pantheon of candles had been lit and placed in niches on the walls. We were standing in an underground cavern, a complete cathedral in miniature, hewn from the living rock. I could only stand in awe of it, gazing about me with the rapt admiration of an acolyte in the presence of some minor miracle. "Astonishing."

Frankenstein seemed pleased that I liked it. "Isn't it? He made it for her, what some might call a shrine, but I personally think that word far too ironic for what it truly is." He smiled. "Come. Let us visit with her." He beckoned me to the front of the chapel where, just behind the altar, there stood a device whose form reminded me of a communion table. It was not quite six feet long, and its width being no less than three feet at its widest part, but narrowing toward one end. It was roughly as high as a man's waist, and as we drew nearer, I saw it was beautifully embossed with intricate spiral patterns not unlike those found on ancient Dacian ornaments. The whole of it was held in place by a huge brass claw which held the box as an eagle might hold a small object in its talons. A whirring emanated from it, a sound like the thrumming of a million insect wings.

"Good God," I breathed.

"Look," said Frankenstein. "Isn't she lovely?"

The glass box was a coffin, yet this unadorned word can hardly suffice. A monstrous brass wheel protruded from the ceiling and was attached by metal chains to a boiler apparatus, which now and then gave out puffs of steam. Frankenstein explained the boiler was fed by coal, which kept the engine running; what I had taken for a claw was in fact a rudimentary ventilation conduit whose terminal end vented outside the castle wall. The pipe drew in cold air and caused it to circulate inside the coffin while a clockwork device discreetly attached to the underside of the lid (here, he pointed out) timed each cycle to the second, so the air need never grow stale. As fascinated as I was by this marvel of engineering, it did not hold a penny torch to the creature lying in the coffin, and seeing her, I understood why Caleb allowed no portraits of her to hang anywhere in the castle.

She was beautiful, if a mere word could suffice. Her skin was waxen pale, yet her lips in death retained their crimson blush. Her dark brows arched over silken lids whose inky lashes were as finely drawn as the scales of a butterfly's wing. Her dark hair lay massed in a profusion of small ringlets, and her forehead was decorated with a gold and ruby diadem. Yet all these things notwithstanding, it was the expression of absolute sweetness that affected me most powerfully. I could not in truth imagine such a lady leaping to her death from the castle's highest parapet.

"Didn't I tell you?" Frankenstein's voice was hushed, reverent. "She is lovely, is she not?" He laid a finger on the glass just above her mouth. "If you look very carefully, you can see how the circulation of the air can fool one into believing that she breathes."

I bowed my head and made the Sign of the Cross. "God grant her eternal rest."

Frankenstein's gaze was suddenly opaque, and he seemed to regard something I could not see. "If there is any such thing as Paradise."

February 11
Castle Donnithorn

I SPENT the greater part of yesterday in solitude, lying in the silence while my body restored itself and the strain of performing my duty began to fade away. It is never an easy task and becomes increasingly more difficult as time continues. There is no discernible effect on my physical being—I am, after all, ageless—but each act wears away a little of my soul until I fear there will be nothing left of me. I shall thus pass eternity as an empty shell, through which all winds blow, a hollow thing made of brittle bones and memory. The dubious gift of my mortal ancestors resides not in blood or bone, but in the invisible auric field that cloaks the human form. Because of it I am able to usher the dying into eternal light by a simple exchange of energies. The procedure is not without risk and certainly not without pain, and the performance of the Rites causes massive etheric weakness. Thus I am required to rest for some time afterward, until the body can restore itself.

The woman was far gone by the time I arrived, just as I knew she would be. They never call me until it's much too late, and then they hide their faces from me when I enter, and make the Sign of the Cross and spit. They fear the Evil Eye and my malignant presence, even as they desperately need me.

The room was full of blood. The child, they said, was trapped in the birth canal. The village doctor came to meet me as I entered, his hands red to the elbows. "She has been laboring for three days and there is nothing. The child is dead and still we cannot pull it free." He had been trying: I saw the bloodied forceps and other such instruments of torture lying in a pan beside the bed. A mechanical cleaner whirred busily underneath a table, sucking dirt and moisture. I pushed it out of the way with my foot. The filthy bed linens stank of blood, of feces and the peasant woman's unwashed body.

The villagers were crouched in a huddle in one corner of the room, whispering amongst themselves.

"Tell them to go."

When I bent over the woman, she opened her eyes and smiled at me. "Thank God, you have come at last." She clasped my hand and kissed it, her tears falling onto my skin. "Thank God you have come."

I told her the child was dead. I laid my hand on her distended belly, and the child passed out of her, macerated flesh and broken bones flowing like water. I held him in my arms and blessed him, then laid him on her chest.

Her swollen breasts leaked milk as she cradled him and sang to him and touched the lids of his closed eyes. She could not cease thanking me, weeping and clutching at my hands, and blessing me. The storm battered the windows and shook the house to its foundations. The doctor came back into the room, and I told him to leave. I opened my bag and removed the small wooden box I carry with me. Her eyes widened when she saw it, but she mastered her fear. "You are merciful," she said. "Yes, you are the god of mercy." Always at this juncture, they inevitably mention God. I would smile at it, except for too long I have seen the way such mortals die and there is, I fear, nothing to smile about. "You will be gentle with me?" She clutched her dead child to her breast.

"You will feel nothing." I laid my hand over her eyes. "You will fall into a peaceful sleep." I kissed her brow, her lips, the hollow of her throat, and the skin over her heart. I laid the bread and the salt and poured the wine. I spoke the ancient words, then laid myself prone upon her, hand to hand, head to head, and finally, my lips upon her open mouth. She breathed twice more, and then life was extinguished utterly. I stood, drew the covers over her and over the dead babe. "I give you rest and easement. I pray you, walk not after death." I lingered for a while with the death still in me, and then I breathed her soul into the open air, where it would find its way to Paradise. To the modern mind, with its sustenance of Science and Reason, the idea of a world after death is ludicrous, but I know and, worse, I remember.

When I went out into the hallway, the doctor was waiting with some villagers. He offered me the dead cake, which I refused as I have always done, and gave me a golden krone, which I accepted. It was snowing hard when I left the house, with violent winds out of the northeast, and I should have taken my automatic coach, but always at the performance of my hereditary duty I prefer to walk. It is the principle of the thing: the act must be accompanied by suffering. The suffering is usually my own. By the time I reached the castle, I was chilled and shivering, my clothing soaked to the skin, and my scars sore and aching.

Victor was waiting for me, had filled my bath with hot water and stimulating salts. "How was it?"

"I took it too quickly this time." My lips were trembling so violently that I could scarcely speak. "I feel quite unsteady."

He chafed my wrists and helped me undress. The water was deliciously soothing. Victor lingered for a moment, hoping I would invite him to join me. When I did not, he went away quietly, not bothering to hide his disappointment. He is too attached; his devotion may yet prove problematic. His initial purpose was to research the means by which the machine might fulfill its purpose. I erred in making a friend of him. It is an error I make all too often these days, and yet I need Victor Frankenstein as much as I need the others. In this he is invaluable to me. Because I can take into me a human soul, it stands to reason I might be able to retain it, without the ill effects—the disorientation and the bad dreams such mortal remnants often cause me. I am adept at capturing the souls of dying mortals only insofar as it involves my hereditary duty to the village—what would happen if I captured one and kept it for my very own? Would I then be mortal, human, able to feel? It is a question Victor and I have often pondered, even since our early days together. It is the reason I sought such minds as his to create my glorious machine. It is why I will never allow anyone to deprive me of it.

He has not said so, but I know this is why Jacob van Willigen is here. The Society would never dispatch such a one as him for anything except the direst need, and yet I wonder if he understands the purpose of his presence here. What lies have they told him all these years? That he is an arbiter of justice? That he is the hand of God extended? That he lives to abolish evil? They would never tell him the simple and unvarnished truth: that it takes another like me to destroy me. I doubt he even knows. No, I am sure they have not told him. The Society would keep him ignorant for fear of what will happen once he understands the truth of what he is.

The death took too much from me; I am weak with it. I hate to do it, especially since I have just now sent him away, but I must. I summon Victor, and he is at my side immediately. He is such a good boy. He knows the things I need. He strips himself and climbs into the water, and I go at once into his arms. "You waited too long to summon me." He holds me up. His breath is warm against my ear. I turn my head and take his mouth, and for a moment, I forget myself, but only for a moment. "Why do you draw away?" His gaze is tenderness itself. "Take from me what you need. I beg you."

"No. It isn't right." I am lying to him, but perhaps I am also lying to myself. His naked body is pale and smooth, with lean muscle just under the skin. Looking at him causes the hunger to grow until I can hardly stand it. "I would not hurt you for the world." It isn't quite a lie. I turn my gaze to the wall of mirrors opposite the bath. We are reflected, he and I, multiplied.

"Please." He is trembling. "I would like you to."

I watch us in the wall of mirrors, watch my hands as they reach to cradle the back of his head, hold him close to me. I breathe his scent, leaning close to taste the moisture on his skin. He makes a small noise deep in his throat and his hands clench into fists behind my back. "In ancient times my embrace was known as the kiss of God." I mark his shoulder with my mouth, leave the purplish imprint of my teeth there on his tender flesh. "Do you know, Victor, I will never be permitted to enter Paradise?"

Already he is voiceless, inarticulate, and mute. His swollen member throbs against my belly. I cradle his skull and raise his mouth to mine, and then I drink deep from the fountain of his life, until I am sated and strangely whole again. I lift him from the water and carry him to my bed and cover him, and then I stoke the fire to a roaring blaze.

He will need the warmth if he is to recover, and I want that for him—I need it.

It isn't blood we take. I have never tasted blood.

February 15
Diary—Jacob van Willigen

I HAD hoped, with a change of atmosphere and the excitement of traveling to a foreign country, that my old affliction might leave me in peace. In this, as in so many other things, I was mistaken. Usually I slept comfortably, bedded down in the room Caleb had provided, and I was untroubled by dreams.

Yet on subsequent nights, my dreams returned with force, and I was scarcely able to close my eyes without being immediately precipitated back into the surreal landscape of my imagination. I dreamed of death and skeletons, of dry bones horribly reanimated to speak and sing. I dreamed I was walking in a wide green meadow, beside a river flowing peaceably into the distance. The meadow is full of flowers, some of which I recognize and others which appear so strange and otherworldly that I cannot conceive of their existence on this Earth. Near the edge of the river is a large tree whose spreading branches cast gentle shadows on the ground. As I approach this tree, a figure steps out from behind it. As soon as I see this figure, I am filled with an overwhelming joy—the mere memory of which now, in my waking state, brings tears to my eyes. I break into a run and, reaching this figure, I throw my arms around him and embrace him. He is my dearest friend, the companion of my soul, and I am delighted to see him. Almost as soon as I discover him, the scene begins to fade. The meadow, the tree, the flowers, the placid river, and, worst of all, my dear companion, vanish—and I am falling, falling, hurtling to earth.

Inevitably I awaken in tears. This dream has troubled me for as long as I can remember and, during my novitiate, so distressed me that I went to Brother Inish to ask his spiritual counsel. He listened to me with great compassion, and when I had finished, said, "I cannot say for certain what this experience is, Jacob. I only know it is unusual." I debated whether to say what I was thinking, but finally remembered my courage and blurted out that I believed I was remembering Paradise. As soon as I said this, I realized I had made a grave error, for his face changed—tightened, somehow, closing in on itself—and he rose from his chair. He paced toward the window, his hands clasped behind his back, then suddenly turned to me. "I regret I have another appointment. You will please go now." His reaction was so jarring to my sensibilities that I never again confided the subject of my dreams to anyone. Yet my dreams are not the only uncomfortable nocturnal experience I have lately had.

I had just drifted off to sleep last evening when I had the overwhelming sensation that I was not alone in the room. I raised my head and immediately perceived the figure of a young woman seated at the small writing table in my room. She wore a dark dress with lace at the collar and cuffs, and her hair was pulled back into a bun. There was nothing remarkable about her: she was no particular age, neither old nor young, with dark eyes that seemed to burn out of an uncommonly pale face. She was writing rapidly with a pencil and didn't look up when I inquired as to what she was doing in my room. At first I thought it might be the elusive Justine, come for one of her nightly visits, but this woman had nothing of Justine's beauty. She was thin, ascetic looking, and her burning dark eyes—which I could barely make out in the pale moonlight—betrayed a hint of madness.

"I prefer to write in here," she said. "The light is so much better than in my own room."

This, of course, was a patent absurdity, seeing as how it was pitch black save for a thin beam of moonlight coming through the window.

"How did you get in here?" It was the obvious question—the other being why on earth would she suppose it appropriate for a young woman to enter the sleeping chamber of a gentleman without either his knowledge or his consent.

"Far too easily, I expect, but if I were to tell you how or why, it would frighten you. He wouldn't like that." She wrote without ceasing, the pencil seeming to fly over the page. "Has he said anything about us?"

I confessed aloud that I hadn't the slightest idea what she meant. This made her laugh, a full, throaty laugh, with her head thrown back. I confess, I thought her either dangerous or perhaps a little mad. "'Us'?"

"The other brides—Ada and Victor." She was then sitting on my bed, nearly on my pillows, and yet I had no clear idea she had even moved at all. "Has he told you anything about us?"

Victor.... Victor *Frankenstein*? "No. Nothing." I pulled the covers up around my waist and immediately felt foolish for having done so. In the moonlight she appeared like a statue of a woman, an imagined figure from a dream or fairy tale. Her eyes gleamed with an unearthly light, and as she leaned toward me, I was afraid....

...and yet I was fascinated. I have seen so much here that is far from the ordinary, even to one such as myself who has been trained to disregard the ordinary as merely a veil erected over all the potent truths of the world. Her skin was pale as marble, and yet her lips were the most lustrous red I had ever seen, gleaming darkly in the moonlight. I imagined what a kiss from those lips would feel like, and suddenly I wanted her to kiss me, wanted her to fasten that red mouth onto my body and draw cries of rapture from me.

There was a stillness in the air, as if we were the only living things inside those castle walls. I reached to untie her hair, but she stayed me and unfastened the clips that held it bound, allowing it to cascade around her shoulders. "You have only to speak." She touched my lips with the palm of her hand, and a thrill ran through me, dark and savage. I felt as if I were moving in a dream: I reached for her and pulled her toward me.

The door to my chamber flew open and Caleb was there. I have never seen him as angry as he was then. He seemed to reach across some great chasm as he caught the woman by the shoulder and pulled her from me. "How dare you?" he hissed. "How dare you touch this man? How dare you cast eyes on him when I have forbidden it? This man belongs to *me*."

The woman drew back, eyes blazing with towering hatred. "You?" Her laughter was as unearthly a noise as I had ever heard in my life. Were I to live one thousand years, I should never again chance to hear a sound of such tinkling, hellish gaiety. "You yourself have never loved. You never love. Who are you to forbid me anything? There was a time—"

Caleb seemed to grow—that is to say, his physical being seemed somehow to enlarge itself—until he towered over the woman, the bed, me, and everything in the room. "I have loved. You have seen it yourself." And there was something infinitely sad and lonely in his voice, the same something I had heard before, as if he were bent with the weight of this untold grief. "Yes, there was a time when I, too, loved." There was a long silence, and in the silence was some dark emotion, stretched out wan and quivering under its own weight, a sorrow drawn impossibly thin by the passage of so many cold and uninviting years. "Mary." Caleb reached out to her, and there was such appeasement in the gesture. "I beg you, do not torment him. He knows nothing." He drew a ragged breath that to my ears sounded like the unholy passage of an icy wind through some ancient charnel house. "I remember when I went all the way to London looking for you, Mary."

She drew back from him, her body taut and quivering as if she would spring at him, but she only stood quietly against the wall, her slim figure in its dusty black dress a mere shadow among shadows. "Yes," she said, and she laughed again, that horrible, tinkling laughter that had so chilled my soul but moments before. "Yes, you came all the way to London, Caleb. And what did you do in London once you got there?" She raised her small white hands, and I saw the fingers were contracted into claws, thin talons of hate striking at the empty air. "Yes, Caleb, you came to London, and you and your—"

"Please, do not speak of him." Caleb put his hand over his eyes, as if to shield himself from some unpleasant phantasm of the imagination. My eyes had by now adjusted to the darkness, and I could clearly discern the two figures standing there before me. Caleb looked tired, as if he had not slept for many nights, and this strange conversation seemed to drain him of his spirit and his will. I found myself wondering why the woman named Mary hated him so much, or seemed to hate him. What had he done to her? Or had she, in her turn, done him such a grievous injury that the memory of it lay between them now like an ancient rancor?

"Oh yes, I will speak of him!" She advanced on him, her slim figure trembling with rage. When she again spoke, it was with an atavistic growl. "I will speak of Victor Frankenstein, the third of your Brides, your favorite diversion, the all too willing companion of your bed."

Caleb's right hand was a pale flicker in the darkness as he lashed out at the woman, and striking her in this manner, dashed her to the ground. She lay there in silence for some time, Caleb looming over her, waiting for her to rise, doubtless so he might strike her again.

Everything in me protested against this malicious brutality, this vile abuse, but I was so terrified by the spectacle before me that I could do nothing but watch. God preserve my sanity! Why on earth was I sent to this place? To deliver justice, a warning? What I had thus far witnessed in this place only confounded me further. What sort of a man was Caleb? A heretic and a blasphemer, surely, but wicked as well, immoral? Who was this woman he called Mary who saw fit to invite herself into my bedchamber in the middle of the night, who laughed like a wanton, who mocked him? The room was cold and silent, and in the silence, I could hear her laughing. She laughed as she raised herself from the cold flagstones; she laughed as she brushed the dust from her dress; she laughed as she went away, departing into an icy darkness.

Caleb exhaled slowly and came to stand before my bed. "My dear friend," said he, "I am so very sorry that you had to witness such as this. Between Mrs. Shelley and I there is a long and tortuous history. Given another hundred years or so, I am certain we could make right our differences." He extended a hand toward me but did not touch me. "But we are not in England now, and I fear you will find our ways rather unlike those to which you are accustomed. I hope what you have seen here tonight will not unnecessarily prejudice you, for I would count you among my friends, were you amenable to that."

I believe I stammered something about his impeccable manners and the supremely flighty nature of the modern woman. Whatever it was I said, it must have sufficed, for Caleb bowed gracefully to me and, turning on his heel, left the room.

I lay for some time with the covers drawn up to my chin, shivering as one in the throes of a deadly fever. What sort of a place was this? What in God's name was I to make of such bizarre outbursts? I did not care for Mrs. Shelly's opprobrium of Dr. Frankenstein, nor her insinuation that he and Caleb were engaged in some sort of perversion.

The tiny clockwork cleaner bumped the door and pushed itself into my room. The appearance of the little machine was so sudden and so unexpected that I cried out, my heart hammering furiously against my ribs like the unsprung gears of some deranged mechanical engine. I watched it as it made its way around the room, buzzing softly in the corners, drawing up the dust. It was a small, ordinary thing, the sort of unimportant little machine that one sees almost every day, and its presence calmed me and allowed me to pass the rest of the night in something that was almost sanity.

March 24
Diary—Jacob van Willigen

IF I feared my bad dreams were to be the only source of my nocturnal torment, I was wrong. Already I have had an unsettling introduction to the woman Mrs. Shelley, and last night I encountered another of Caleb's houseguests. Caleb and I sat up until very late, talking before the fire. Caleb, as I have already said, is a charming and intelligent interlocutor whose conversation covers any number of stimulating subjects. Not forgetting the purpose of my mission here, I had hoped to entice some information from him. At length I grew tired and, seeing me stifle a yawn, Caleb rose and insisted I go to bed.

"My own sleep, my dear friend, is such that I can subsist on only a little, whereas for you a proper night's rest is as needful as air. Go now into your bedchamber and we will continue this discussion in the morning." He took both my hands in his and bid me good night.

I had no sooner opened the door to my chamber when I perceived the figure of a young woman lying on my bed and wearing naught but a dressing gown. She was perhaps thirty years of age, with dark blue eyes and light brown hair, which she had ornamented with all manner of beads, baubles, and even feathers.

"So you are Jacob van Willigen." She smiled lazily, as if my coming into the room had only just awakened her from the sleep of centuries. "Caleb can hardly stop talking about you. I wonder if he knows your purpose here is to destroy him?"

I strove to contain my shock at seeing a woman in such a position as she had chosen to adopt. "Madam, I would beg you leave my bedchamber immediately. This conduct is not worthy of a lady."

She laughed—that same tinkling, musical laughter I had heard from Mary—and pulled aside the hem of her gown, exposing the full length of her legs. "I've heard you come from an order of warrior monks, van Willigen, and that you have lived in the cloister for a thousand years."

"Hardly that, madam. I am scarcely forty years old." Her legs were fair and slender, but the sight of them seemed so unwholesome to me that I was repulsed and wished her to cover herself immediately. "But tell me, are you also a guest of Caleb's?"

She was convulsed with laughter. "A guest? Oh, my dear boy, I am his bride. Did he not tell you?"

This was not the first time I'd heard the word "bride" spoken in relation to the master of Donnithorn Castle. "Caleb is married?" A violent heat leapt into my cheeks, and I perceived that even the tips of my ears were burning. "Madam, forgive me. I would have properly addressed you, had I only known."

"Caleb is thrice married, if you must know—but I see by your expression that such things are never done in England." She rose from the bed, the silken gown trailing off her shoulders. "You may call me Ada." She raised her hands, parted the garment, and dropped it onto the floor behind her. She now stood as nude as Eve before me. "What do you think of me, van Willigen? Am I to your liking?"

I should have averted my eyes, not wanting to look upon her shame, but found myself curiously powerless. Her flesh was pale as wax and looked as cold and still as marble, and the curves of her body appeared to have been milled by some great machine rather than formed in the softness of Nature. "Madam I beg you, cover yourself. This behavior is not seemly."

"Look at me, van Willigen. Does my woman's flesh instill desire in you?" She pushed herself at me, her breasts raised in her hands. "In life I was entirely a creature of the intellect. See now what he has made me."

I turned away and made much of arranging some papers on my bureau. "I am only interested in his machine, by which he purports to create monsters. The Society has charged me with its destruction."

"His machine?" She laughed. "Which one, sir? For there are many, and in stricter terms than that which you and I speak, we are all machines of varying complexity, each capable of our own strange intercourse. Has he shown you the difference engine? Do you not think it beautiful? A thinking machine, my dear monk, capable of storing a sequence of operations as well as the data generated by those operations, but only if the user chooses carefully. Precision, my dear monk, is all." Her words belied a truly monstrous intellect, one capable of astonishing works beyond the imagination of most mortals.

"I'm not a monk," I told her, "not exactly."

"Yet you turn from the delights of the flesh."

"I have pledged my life to the preservation of good and the death of evil."

"The death of evil?" She flung her naked arms about my neck. "Can such a thing ever be, my dear?" Her mouth tasted like wine, like sin and chocolate, and the unearthly heat of her body burned through my clothes. Had I wished it, I could have had her then and there, in any manner I pleased.

I shoved her away from me. "Please, Madam, I beg you. I have sworn certain oaths." This was not precisely true, but I had chosen to devote myself to academic study rather than pursue the pleasures of the flesh. I wiped my mouth on my sleeve. "I would ask that you respect them."

"You will succumb." She was angry but covered it well. She bent and retrieved her garment from the floor. "You will not be the first." The door fell shut behind her, although in truth I did not hear her leave.

I moved quickly to shoot the bolt across, wondering if her assault might continue on another front. I had given her no motivation, had not responded to her caresses, but her questions, couched as they were in such frank and forthright terms, haunted me. *Does my woman's flesh instill desire in you?* I had resisted her. I, who had taken no vows of chastity, had been entirely unmoved by her— and when I contemplated the nature of desire, I did not see the luxurious softness of a woman, but an altogether harder form of sinew and bone and battle-hardened muscle.

THE MORNING is chill, and I was loath to venture from my bed, even though the sun has long since risen over the mountains and the world seems full of golden light. I descended in a foul humor, resolving to contact Brother Inish at the earliest opportunity and request a cancellation of my mission.

Caleb was waiting for me in the dining room, and the sight of him drew my gaze as a lodestone draws iron. Today he was wearing a dark blue coat, the color of a mountain stream in summer, and dark trousers, and a ruby-red silk cravat with an exquisite gold pin. His hair was glossy, shining with a dark fire, as he also shone. He is truly the most splendid creature I have ever seen and I cannot forbear looking at him.

"My dear friend, come and tell me how you slept." He rose from the table and grasped my forearms warmly. "Is your room comfortable? Is everything to your liking? If anything is lacking, you must tell me. I insist upon it."

I wondered if it would be appropriate to ask about the women—Ada, Mrs. Shelley, and Justine—but I feared it would seem discourteous to my host if I began prying into his personal affairs, and so I remained silent on the subject.

Caleb rang for hot drinks, and in a moment, a maidservant appeared bearing a pot of chocolate and two cups on a silver tray. She brought, too, a message for Caleb, sealed in a tiny envelope. He took up the envelope and examined it, and all at once his expression of good cheer changed to consternation. "I had been afraid of this" was all he would say, and I did not dare press him on the matter. I had no doubt he will advise me of its contents when and if he desires to do so. With an effort he addressed himself to me. "You are not unduly discomfited by remaining here with—beyond your appointed departure?"

I had the keenest sense that what he meant to say was "with me" but at the last moment stopped himself. What is it that prevents him from acknowledging the trust—nay, the budding friendship—which exists between us? Is he afraid of something? And yet our discourse these few weeks has been amiable beyond compare. Daily we grow more and more familiar, and it may be that this familiarity will in time yield up valuable information.

"Indeed not," I replied in answer to his question. "I should like nothing better. I only hope you will allow me to examine your difference engine again." My duties to the Society would be best accomplished with guile. Caleb has no reason to fear me or the Society, and absolutely no need to bow to our wishes. If I intend to find and destroy his blasphemous machine, I must needs make a friend of him and gain his trust. Eventually, Caleb will have to be brought to complete submission in this matter. I did not relish the idea of deliberate deception, but I am expected, I know, to bring him to heel quite permanently. If he does not relinquish the machine, I am required, under the aegis of the Society, to eliminate him. Brother Inish was quite explicit on this matter.

We require that you curtail the activities of Caleb Donnithorn and especially the series of experiments he has lately undertaken in the company of Victor Frankenstein of Geneva. Do you understand, Jacob van Willigen, the nature of your commission?

As custom dictates, we were both standing beneath the Great Arch, each with a hand on the Guidance Stone. The late-afternoon sun filtered through the ancient windows and threw colored jewels onto the floor. I was barefoot and wearing only a simple novice's robe. Brother Inish was, as usual, resplendent in his scarlet cassock.

I understand and I obey. Such simple words, yet so powerful in meaning. How many times, in my years with the Society, had I spoken them? How often had I, like every other acolyte, stood here underneath the Arch and swore again my fealty to the Society? In how many ways had I seen my faith in Brother Inish and the Society redoubled and repaid?

And do you understand, Jacob van Willigen, that if Donnithorn cannot be effectively contained, you are hereby charged with his absolute destruction?

I understand and I obey. I knelt to receive his blessing, but even as I did so, doubts were churning in my mind. That day, kneeling under the Great Arch, my conviction was absolute. Where has my assurance gone?

All throughout our conversation I noticed Caleb was unable to keep his mind away from the little envelope. He took it up and handled it, then put it back on the tray. He poured chocolate for us both, forgot he poured it, then poured it again, nearly overflowing both our cups.

Finally I was unable to stand a moment more of this distraction. "I really do believe you ought to open your letter. I can remain awhile in the anteroom if you wish privacy."

"No." He waved his hand, indicating I should remain. "No, my dear friend. Please, stay where you are." He broke the letter's seal with his finger and drew out a sheet of fragile-looking paper. The handwriting was as tiny as the envelope, thin and spidery, and had evidently been produced by a shaking hand.

My curiosity, never easily tamed, now fairly twanged. He was clearly much affected by the message, for he crumpled the paper in his hand and hurled it at the fire—then, standing abruptly, he went to the window, and I assumed he was thinking until I heard the quiet but unmistakable sounds of weeping.

This alarmed me more than I can say. Seeing Caleb cry was like watching some great colossus crumble into dust before one's eyes. I was at his side in an instant, my arm about his shoulders while he convulsed with sobs so violent I feared for his safety. I murmured such healing imprecations as I know in an attempt to soothe him, but he would not be comforted.

"I can only blame myself," he says brokenly. "I persist in making friends of them, when I know—*I know*—how fragile they are, how mortal, how… temporary." He moved to the settee, his features wild with grief, his body trembling in the grip of some unknown sorrow.

I saw a vision with my mind's eye: I stood on a great, stony plain with the jagged peaks of unknown mountains in the distance. The scene was brilliantly lit now and then by violent bursts of lightning, and the roar of thunder shuddered the ground beneath my feet. I was beset by savage pains in my body and a curious, bone-deep ache in my shoulders. The muscles of my arms writhed, twisting themselves into agonized spasms. A quiet voice emerged from the chaos: *It is time for you to go.*

The reverie passed as swiftly as it had come, and I was sitting with Caleb. We were silent together, listening to the roaring of the fire. The little clockwork timer on the chocolate pot clicked over, emitting a tiny burst of steam as the pot turned dutifully to reheating itself. Caleb raised his face to look at me, tears drying in salty rivulets on his skin. "An old man," he explained. "An elder of the village below, he has for some years been very kind to me."

I could not prevent myself. I reached out and brushed away his tears. "He has died?"

He shook his head. He was a warm and subtle presence in my arms, and I thought my flesh would remember the sweet weight of him long after this embrace had passed. "He is dying and I must go to him. His son will presently arrive to summon me. It is time."

"*In paradisium deducant te Angeli.*" I said. For some reason the unsmiling visage of Brother Inish swam before my inner eye: *We cannot expect such mercies for the unbeliever.* I pushed the vision away.

"Is that what they are intended for, these angels?" He laughed shortly, as if I had said something amusing. "To usher one into heaven?" His dark eyes glittered dangerously. I sensed that anything I might say would be the wrong thing. He stood and straightened his clothes, a series of fitful movements. His back was ramrod straight and the movement of his hands was quick, undisciplined, and jerky.

"I suppose." I shrugged. "Is that not what the Church teaches?"

"I wouldn't know." He dusted the sleeves of his coat angrily. "I find that I am unwelcome in the local church, as unwelcome as I am in many other places. This old man, this friend of mine, he has suffered for his decency to me. For the sake of me, he has made himself a pariah in the village, an unclean thing." His face crumpled and he bowed his head. "Now, and at the hour of our death."

I was shocked to see him make the Sign of the Cross. My blood turned gelid in my veins at the sight of it. Even the devil could quote Holy Scripture. Even Lucifer was once revered among the angels.

I imagined I was standing in an icy river, my body turned against the flow of the current, fighting it, albeit uselessly. I wore heavy garments, which, sodden with the freezing water, pulled me under. I struggled to move some bulky object to the shore, but it refused all my efforts to displace it. These were not my memories. I have no memories. "Let me go with you."

From somewhere in the castle, there was a tapping noise and footsteps. A tall manservant I have never seen before ushered a young man into the dining room.

Caleb moved to receive him, shook his hand, embraced him, and kissed him on both cheeks in the European fashion. They spoke rapidly in the native language for several minutes, and Caleb translated for me: "He says that his father has a tumor in his throat which has grown so that it is pressing against his windpipe and cutting off the supply of air. For some time he has been slowly choking to death. He is asking me to go to him now." Donnithorn spoke to the young man, who nodded, bowed, and was suddenly gone. "He will go ahead to prepare for my arrival." He hesitated. "Are you certain you wish to go with me? Or perhaps academic curiosity compels you."

I answered truthfully that I was interested and would like to assist him in any way I could. I recognized this was an opportunity to learn more about him and to discern the strange practices he and the villagers obviously believe in. He consented and, as I watched, prepared a leather satchel with certain items I assumed were central to the procedure he would enact once we reached the village. Most of these I recognized but strangest of all was a small, hollow glass sphere with a tube projecting from one end; this he placed in a silk-lined box and secured it with leather ties.

Since Donnithorn Castle was situated on top of a mountain, we were unable to walk all the way to the village, but were obligated to take a water-driven funicular down to the valley. This was a curious device which Caleb himself had designed and engineered. The ascending car was driven by the descent of a similar weight of water, and this principle worked in reverse as well, so if one wished to descend the mountain, the weight of the ascending car was replaced by water. I had seen such machines in use elsewhere in the world but none as elegant as Caleb's, with its gorgeous wrought-iron cages forming shapes as beautiful and fragile as a snowflake.

When I complimented him on its construction, he told me he had it built for the people of the village, many of whom feared to travel up the mountain by the usual road, which they believed to be haunted by formless entities and the spirits of the dead. "Because my family has long been prominent in this area, we believe those who live below are our responsibility. I have the means to make their lives easier, and I encourage them to look upon me as their patron."

The old man's dwelling was located at the edge of the village. In years gone by, Caleb told me, the old man had committed some sin for which the local people cast him out. Except for his son, who had a wife and children of his own, the old man lived a hermit's life without the help of anyone. The house was little more than a filthy hut with a dirt floor, and the old man's dying bed merely a pallet of rags. He lay there half insensible, his surroundings lit by a stub of candle that flickered dangerously in the cold draught continually admitted by the broken door. The tumor in his throat had perforated the flesh of his neck and ran with blood and a foul putrescence. So bad was the stench that I was forced to hold my handkerchief over my mouth and nose. Only the interposition of this scrap of clean linen saved me from vomiting. The state of the old man's health, the meanness of his surroundings, and his lack of company both saddened and angered me. Surely if one as elevated as Caleb can lower himself to offer comfort to a poor old peasant, his fellow villagers, themselves Christians of the Eastern church, ought to do no less.

Caleb regarded the old man for several moments, his head on the side. The man's eyes moved ceaselessly in his head, rolling back and forth, and I imagined he was taking the final measure of his surroundings before departing the earthly plane for (it is hoped) a better place. Caleb gestured at the son and spoke some words in the local tongue, whereupon the son immediately left the hut and went outside.

The morning sun climbed higher over the mountains as we stood together in the poor old peasant's home, and so incongruous was the situation that I found myself inwardly marveling at it.

As I watched, Caleb opened his satchel and took out the instruments of the ritual: a small square of bread, wrapped in silk; a portion of salt in a glass bottle; a measure of red wine in an earthenware jug; and the curious glass sphere which I had seen earlier. He bowed his head as in prayer and, laying the bread and salt upon the old man's dying breast, spoke some words before quickly consuming both the bread and the salt. I recognized the ancient ritual of "sin eating," which is still practiced in certain areas of Europe and the British Isles. Perhaps Caleb's ancestors passed this down to him in their lore, or perhaps he was trained in the art during his early religious instruction.

The old man, speechless as he was, reached out and clasped Caleb's hand in both of his and kissed it over and over, and that quite fervently. When he had done this, he lay still, as if waiting. Caleb, laying aside the instruments of his rite, leaned closer and—astonishingly—placed his opened mouth over the old man's. The prone body shuddered, the back arching as if in the throes of an epileptic seizure, and there was the choking, gasping sound of the old man's death rattle. Caleb inhaled deeply, seeming to grow larger even as the old man's body shriveled; his entire being was lit with some interior glow that gained in presence and brightness until I was forced to turn my eyes away.

The hut filled with the noise of a thousand voices whispering at once in dizzying profusion, and then, as quickly as it had come, the noise vanished. I perceived Caleb's presence at my side and turned to look at him. Tears stood in his dark eyes as he held the glass to me. "Witness this, Jacob van Willigen: a human soul. A single, precious soul that, had I the means, I would take into myself and thus be worthy of redemption." There, suspended in the glass, was a tiny spark, an infinitesimal point of the purest blue light. "As I am, I will never be permitted to enter Paradise."

With that, he waved his hand over the glass and the light grew suddenly bright, flared like a dying star, and disappeared. The hut was again merely a dirty hut at the edge of an indifferent village. The old man was a hollow shell of flesh and bone. We went outside and Caleb summoned the son and embraced him. We traveled back up the mountain with the morning sunlight bright on our faces and in our eyes.

Only when we reached the gates did I find the courage to ask, "Is that why you are building a machine? To capture a human soul? Why would you do such a thing?"

"I must rest, my dear friend." The procedure had exhausted him. There were deep lines under his eyes and his handsome face was gaunt and strained. It was, I thought, as if something of the old peasant's death had clung to him, working its way under his skin like morbid ink. "Please, let us discuss this matter later in the day, when I am better rested."

If Caleb is evil—as Brother Inish believes—he would not sacrifice himself so readily to ease the pain of others. Why am I now more frightened of him than I have ever been?

March 31
Diary—Jacob van Willigen

I WAITED nearly half an hour for the water-driven funicular to make its way back up the mountain to where I was, and by the time it arrived, I was nearly frozen solid. The calendar indicates spring is imminent in other places in the world, but it is hardly in evidence here. I was obliged to wear my warmest woolen clothes and a scarf. I had wanted to see the village that lies at the bottom of the mountain, but, remembering my initial journey to Castle Donnithorn, I did not relish having to negotiate the steep switchbacks and sharp turns of the rudimentary road. It was hardly my place to tell Caleb the most efficient way of going up and down the mountain—but, were I left to my own devices, I might well have borrowed Caleb's personal engine and gone down that way. Caleb's servant William told me there are excellent roads accessible to motor vehicles which make the trip down into the village a pleasure. The villagers, of course, despised and feared the road, insisting it is bedeviled by evil spirits and the souls of the unbaptized dead, but such talk was the stuff of nonsense. Caleb insisted the villagers appreciated the convenience of the funicular—that they made use of it whenever they wished to present their petitions to him. Given what I have seen thus far, I suspected otherwise: the villagers despised and feared him, and they would only ever breach his steadfast mountain keep to set it—and him—on fire. Only with flames could demons be driven out.

The matter of Caleb's machine grew ever more curious. The glass coffin in which his dead wife lay was no great secret, nor was it *the* machine the Society wishes to destroy. No, Caleb was making quite another machine—rather, his geniuses, as he calls them, were making it for him, or trying to.

It had been Frankenstein who unwittingly gave the game away late one evening while we sat playing whist. We had been discoursing on the nature of life and death when I asked where Caleb was. I hadn't seen him all day, and his personal study stood empty, casements open to the evening air. "Perhaps he considers an infusion of fresh air necessary for health," I said. I laid down a card and allowed myself a small groan. I had no luck with cards.

"Who?" Victor asked and blushed most charmingly. "Beg your pardon. My grammar has always been abominable." He took a sip of brandy from the glass at his elbow, choked, coughed violently, and recovered.

"Caleb. I haven't seen him all day, and he's not in his rooms. He's left all the windows open." I wondered if he had been called down to the village to minister to some poor soul in the throes of their final distress.

"Oh, he'll have gone looking for an experimental donor." Victor turned over a card and smirked. "He does quite a bit of roaming around when he needs another one. Believe me, we might not see him for days."

"Experimental donor?" My scalp prickled, and a keen thrill chased along my spine. "Donor for what?" Inexplicably I was reminded of the hollow glass bulb I'd seen him using the day we'd visited the old man with the throat tumor.

"For the capture cylinder I'm working on. Hasn't he t—" He broke off tersely in midsentence. "No, he wouldn't have."

"What the devil do you mean?"

A clattering in the hallway heralded the arrival of a small cart bearing refreshments, what is nowadays called a servitor. The smaller models are clockwork driven, but I have seen their larger cousins in use at public events, and those run on steam. This one bore a pot of tea and a rack of freshly made toast dripping with butter.

"Victor?"

"I don't…." He sighed, reaching for the pot to pour for us both. "You mustn't tell anyone." In front of him, I swore such oaths as I knew and promised to keep silence. Whether he believed me or not, I didn't know, nor did I particularly care. "You've seen him... what he does to them, when they're dying." I indicated I had. "He believes it's possible to capture a soul at the moment of death."

I shrugged. This was nothing new. I had seen him perform his rites over the dying, and Caleb had told me himself that he intended to harvest a soul as soon as a way could be found to successfully contain it. Did Frankenstein think he was offering me something new by telling me these things?

"There are hardly a sufficient number of deaths—for the continued experimentation the device requires. He goes down into the village at night." Victor sipped his tea and made a pleased sound. "In order to test his hypothesis."

"His hypothesis?"

Victor shook his head. "There must be souls to capture, my dear Jacob. As there are not sufficient deaths...." He shrugged. "Sometimes one is obliged to... you know, give progress a little shove in the right direction."

He goes down into the village at night.

I FOUND William early next morning in the library, with books and papers spread before him on a table and a small gas flame burning at his elbow. It was a cold day, with heavy clouds and a vicious wind out of the north, and I had thought to borrow a volume or two. So deep in thought was he that I was loath to disturb him, and so I stood for some time and watched him, another scholar absorbed by the pursuit of his life's work to the exclusion of all else. No sound passed between us save the scratching of his pencil, the amiable hum of the little lantern, and the occasional noise of pages being turned.

I might have passed unnoticed from the room, or so I thought, but he dispelled this notion, saying, "Is there something you want, van Willigen?"

"You've known Caleb a long time."

He raised his head and regarded me wanly. "And?" His eyes, I saw, were the pale brown of brandy, with lighter flecks of gold. He was not unhandsome, and I could see why Caleb retained him.

"What is it that you do for him? What duties, I mean."

"I perform such duties as he requires." He turned back to his work, effectively dismissing me.

"Why do you stay?" A particularly vicious gust of wind buffeted the house, rattling the casements in their frames. "Surely there are many other places you might go. A man of your youth and ability should—"

"Please, I beg you. Do not pursue this line of inquiry any further."

I looked at him more closely. His face was unnaturally pale, his features straining against some momentous inner effort. "Have I said something wrong?"

He rearranged the papers on his desk, opened and closed a large book and then a smaller one, and ran his fingers through his hair. His gaze rose to meet mine, then quickly slid away. "You're wondering why I don't leave." He laughed mirthlessly. "I cannot."

"But surely you aren't a prisoner here." I glanced around me. "I see no bars on the windows, no great locks on the doors. You may leave anytime you wish."

"If I were to leave this place—and believe me, Mr. van Willigen, I very much want to—it would mean not merely my life in this world, but my existence in the world hereafter." He swallowed with what seemed like a significant effort. "He would see to it that I suffer eternal damnation."

It struck me as wholly ridiculous. "No man has that power."

"I am under a kind of… *geis*." He seemed to be forcing himself to go on. "Do you know this word? It means a spell of obligation." He clenched his fists, as if desperate to make me understand. "I am bound to this place until such time as I am released from my vow, the vow *he* fashioned and imposed upon me."

It was a dangerous thing he did, telling me such truths, and yet I knew there was no other way. To whom might he confess? I may well have been the only visitor they had seen for months. "A *geis* is a taboo, either of obligation or prohibition, placed upon a person by one who desires to make the subject enact his will."

"Then you understand that I am a prisoner here." He picked up a pencil and began writing something on the papers in front of him.

"I wish you would invite me to sit down."

"Please." His tone was faintly ironic, and he seemed to be mocking me. "I beg you, sit where you wish."

I chose a narrow wooden chair with a high back, a grotesquely ornamented thing with dragons carved on every surface, lolling and twining, their serpentine tongues coiled into complicated knots and torques. "He has bewitched you." I clasped my hands together on my lap. "Suppose the only way to break the enchantment is by killing him."

"I couldn't do... that." And, when I asked why, he said, "The *geis* encompasses and encircles the village, the mountain, and some little distance beyond. He wished me to have room to roam, to stretch my legs as well as my mind."

"Does he exercise this sort of control over others, or just you?" I couldn't imagine someone allowing himself to be thus manipulated. True, the Society required its binding oaths, but there was nothing preventing me from leaving, if that was what I wished.

"What would you have me do?" He raised his hands and let them drop. "Shall I drive a wooden stake through his heart, as the old texts describe? Or perhaps I ought to shoot him with a gun that has only silver bullets in it." He got up from his chair and walked to one of the long windows that overlooked the valley, hands clasped behind his back.

I moved swiftly, noiselessly, seeming to appear beside him out of the air. It never fails to shock someone when they see me standing suddenly beside them, but we of the Society have our little games as well. "Ah," I said. "You hide your consternation well. I think you would be an estimable opponent in whist or any other game."

He turned his unfathomable gaze upon me. "If you stay here, he will destroy you."

I drew a slow breath. "You are being held against your will? You are a hostage. Is this correct?"

"He will suck the life from you," William said, "just as he takes it from everyone. Have you seen him, then? In the village? Have you seen him—" His voice rose, as if he no longer cared who heard. "Have you seen him as he drains away the death, ushering them into the next world as would a god? Have you ever wondered what replaces the fleeting soul he takes from them? Do you not think that darkness draws more darkness to itself? God!" He turned away, his fists clenched at his sides.

"I came here only to find and destroy this blasphemous machine Caleb has made, by which he intends to supersede the will of Almighty God. Victor Frankenstein has revealed it to me, and when I assess the time as right, I will destroy it."

His features sharpened with interest and curiosity. "What do you mean?"

I waved my hand. "A slip of the mind's tongue, William. No more." I turned to go, but found my arm was clasped about the elbow.

He drew me back into the room. "Tell me what you mean. What machine? What blasphemy?"

I slipped easily from his grasp and made my way back to my rooms.

April 1

Donnithorn Castle

Encrypted record, Caleb Donnithorn—coded archival pod

SHE WAS the first genuine error I made, the first in a long time. When the idea of my machine initially occurred to me, I knew I would have to wait—wait until the world and the civilization of man had advanced so that such knowledge was not merely possible but commonplace. I needed to enlist the assistance of minds that intuitively understood the nature of my quest, minds that could make the leap from possible to probable to absolute. And so I waited out the great Renaissance as it produced myriad works of genius, and the Age of Reason with its ideals of equality, fraternity, and justice. I amused myself among the upper classes and the lower, now and then dispensing advice where it might do the most good and allowing myself the occasional *liaison dangereuse* when it suited me to do so. As a member of the nobility, I was welcome wherever I went, and I went everywhere.

Eventually, having tired of Continental delights, I chanced to find myself in Britain, an island I had not ventured to visit since Plautius was governor and Caligula, the madman rampant, ordered his men to attack the sea. Much had changed in England since, and London especially commended itself to my notice. I took a suite of rooms at an appropriately lavish hotel and resolved to enjoy myself.

This was not difficult to do. Purely by chance, the hotel I had selected was a favorite of society ladies for the taking of late-afternoon tea, to which they were sometimes escorted by their handsome, full-grown sons. The daughters I was less interested in. Most English women, especially the upper class ones, were pale and vapid creatures, engaged in an endless display of wealth and breeding, forever trolling the dark waters of society for a suitable husband. I once made the error of introducing myself by my hereditary title, after which the daughters and their enterprising mammas all rushed toward me, clamoring for my attention, pressing visiting cards on me, and begging me for an invitation. They talked of nothing except teas and dances, and the dresses they hoped to have or the ones they already had, and whether or not the current mode of styling the hair enhanced their features. Their idea of conversation involved the repetition of society gossip, interspersed with their own insignificant opinions, cloaked in giggles and weighty glances.

One such affair occurred at the home of the Earl and Countess of Maynouffe in late November and, having exhausted the city's supply of museums and galleries, I decided to attend. At worst, I reasoned, the evening would comprise a couple hours of abject boredom in the presence of English nobility. At best I might compel some glorious young stallion back to my rooms for the night. I duly presented myself half-past the appointed hour and was ushered into the salon of a very large house in Kensington. The hostess pressed on me a cup of weak punch that tasted as if it had been flavored with a lady's eau de toilette, and now and then a butler circulated with a silver tray upon which had been placed some small circles of pastry I assumed were food.

The entire proceeding made me smile, remembering as I did the grand feasts of old, when my father would return victorious from the hunt and our household would eat and drink for days in the great hall, seated at long tables from which servants came and went all day and night. The walls were lit by great torches and there was music and dancing, and the colorful banners of the family hung from the rafters alongside the captured battle standards of our enemies. The whole village would turn out to be fed and feted by my family. My brothers and I were permitted to stay up as long as we wished, partaking of such amusements as appealed to us, whether watching the jugglers as they cavorted among the tables or following the fire-eater through the castle. Musicians and an entire troupe of dancers were retained for the occasion, and Roma children, slaves of my father, waited on us and did as they were told. But it wasn't merely dancing, music, and play: the feasts were an important part of my father's rule, and during the festivities, he and his intimates would discuss important matters while my brothers and I watched, listening carefully to their congress, knowing in time we would be expected to conduct ourselves as his rightful heirs. Times were different then, and the world a more primeval place. It was this quality of knowledgeable talk that I missed during my evenings in London.

She was standing at the far side of the drawing room, discoursing in a manner both charming and voluble. I had rarely seen such a striking woman, for all that, she was so small: dark hair, dark eyes, and burning cheeks. She glowed from within, animated by power and arcane energies. I made my way across to her, passing groups of men holding glasses full of their English brandy, cheroots clamped between their teeth, discussing politics, religion, and the government. I lingered by the fire, and for a while, I listened solely to the sound of her voice. It soared over all the others, a subtle and confident music.

"...I declare that the problem of electricity shall be easily solved by the introduction of fluidic magnetism." The speaker was a tall man with ginger hair and whiskers who lingered over her—or should I say loomed, for he was exceptionally tall.

"Fluidic magnetism?" She laughed musically. "Oh, dear Lewis— now there is a notion, indeed!"

The group around her shifted apart and I was able to make my introduction. "I am Caleb Donnithorn, madam." I pressed her delicate knuckles to my lips. "Your servant."

"Much better you should be my vassal," she whispered hotly, her lips touching my ear. "Or my chaperone, to sweep in and rescue me from this crowd of dullards. You're an American, aren't you?"

"In a manner of speaking, madam." I had bent to kiss her hand and I imprisoned it still. The fire of her being pulsed through her veins, but beneath this, something had already begun to weaken. Perhaps I was only just in time.

"Then let us in some manner speak." Her smile came reluctantly, a favor she did not readily mete out to strangers. "You must tell me more about yourself."

"Madam, anything I would say should pale utterly beside the poetry of your voice."

And so you stoop to flattery, her eyes seemed to say, but she merely smiled again, indulgently.

We lingered for a while afterward, sipping cups of mulled wine before the fire, talking about thought and literature, God, and politics. I enjoyed the myriad of turns her mind could take and how it could hold several ideas at once. She was adept at conversation but not facile, a rare combination in a woman of her class and times. Her eyes in the firelight were dark blue with impossibly long lashes, and twin spots of hot color burned high up on her cheekbones. Her bosom rose and fell in a hectic rhythm, and I could hear a quiet sound underneath the beating of her heart, a subtle error in her body's essential rhythms.

"I believe I know who you are. What you are." Her eyes lingered on mine and on my mouth. She wanted me to kiss her—yes, she secretly wanted that very much, and more—but it was a desire she would never articulate. Not this woman, not in this age. In another time, another place, perhaps—a woman of my old life, five hundred years before, she would have made her desires abundantly known to me. We were less civilized then, and far more free.

"Who am I?" I reached for her hand and held it loosely in my own. Her flesh was warm, moist, her pulse hammering in her fingertips. The brilliance of her mind glowed like white-hot coals, illuminating her fragile body from the inside out. She reminded me of a candle in an airless atmosphere, burning all the more fiercely because it would soon be extinguished forever. In the midst of all these self-important dullards, her intellect marked her out, distinguished her. More than even that, I saw and smelled and felt the blooming death in her, the rot forming on the perfect rose.

"You're him, aren't you?" She held my gaze, a slight smile playing about her lips.

I leaned close, my attention trained on her entirely. "Tell me."

"Death." The word escaped her in a gasp. "You need not shield me, sir. The doctors have been evasive with me. They employ a great deal of euphemism. I would that you be as clear with me as crystal."

"Then I will give you the dignity of truth. Have they told you how long?"

Her smile was sudden, and I saw the effort of her courage pained her. "Their opinions vary. Some say months. Others feel it is a matter of weeks." She clasped her hands together, gazing down at her small, white fingers. "Is there anything you might do for me?" She raised her eyes, but her gaze kept sliding away from mine, as if there were something else she wanted to say but did not, could not.

"Yes."

"How?"

"I cannot tell you. But believe me—"

She stood. "Do it now."

Blood rushed to my face so sudden it left me light-headed. "Madam, I regret—"

"You said that you could do it. I insist." Her eyes burned with tears. "Do not make me beg you."

I stood slowly, the room seeming to tilt on some unseen axis. "I would not be so discourteous." I wondered if she understood what she was asking. I wondered if I cared.

"How is it done?"

I told her. To her credit she did not flinch, but I saw her shoulders shake a little, a barely perceptible shudder.

"Madam, I would not expect…. That is to say…."

"We will do it now. My home is but a short distance away. Should that be a suitable location? If not, I shall make alternate arrangements."

I held her wrap for her and helped her to fasten it. A carriage was waiting beside the door, its engines emitting tiny puffs of steam that rapidly dissipated in the cold night air. I helped her into the vehicle and tucked a lap rug round her. She was smaller now, nestled against my shoulder, and her dark blue eyes glittered in the scant light that lay in cold pools on the doorstep and the pavements. The rich façade of Kensington flashed by, more quickly than I would have thought possible. I had chosen well. I was certain of it. She would make a fit companion for me—no, more than that, a *glorious* one.

The ritual was simple. I explained this to her as we ascended the stairs. The servants had all gone to bed and the house was dark. Here and there a lamp burned low, its flame guttering in the sudden draft from the open door.

"There will be no pain."

She strove to master herself, her shoulders quivering under the strain of her emotion. "The doctors give me laudanum for the headaches, which come a lot more often these days, and sometimes my vision leaves me. This won't—you must promise not to hurt me." She blinked. "Caleb."

"There will be no pain." I drew a deep breath. "There will in all likelihood be ecstatic, overwhelming pleasure. I am told the act is quite… erotic. Forgive me."

"Erotic." She held my gaze. "I am intrigued."

"Madam, you as a woman of great sagacity and wit must know that nothing in this world comes without price." There was no easy way to broach the matter. I had come to England searching for the minds I needed to undertake the building of my machine. Certainly I would take her death from her, but I required something from her in return. It was important she understand that.

"Of course." She reached for her reticule and was in the act of opening it when I stopped her.

"Not money." I smiled gently. "As the only surviving member of a noble family, I have access to my ancestors' fortune. There is something else I would like, something which I believe would benefit us both, were you disposed to provide it."

"Then tell me what it is you wish, sir, and I shall take whatever steps are necessary to secure it for you."

She listened intently as I argued my case, and when I was finished, she nodded slightly. I could tell my proposal intrigued her. "Your wish to secure such a device is admirable, although some would call it foolhardy. Those who believe in Reason would dispute your claim that the soul even exists. To attempt its capture is akin to stalking the Minotaur."

I smiled. "Then you shall be my Ariadne, madam. With the thread of your intellect, success is inevitable."

It was almost too simple. I ought to have known better.

"I KNOW what it is you intend to do." She lay beside me, one slender leg about my waist, her dark hair streaming unconfined around her white shoulders. Yes, she was beautiful. I think I loved her even then. "Bysshe was of similar mind."

Of course, Percy Bysshe Shelley, the poet and dead husband. For how long, I wondered, had she been widowed?

"What do you mean?" Pleasantly sated now, I knew if I closed my eyes I would be instantly asleep. The exchange had gone well: in that brief moment just before the crisis, I had taken some small portion of her life force, a particle of her essential self so tiny she would never know its loss. I had replaced it with an equally infinitesimal atom of my own, which would reside forever in her cells, endlessly replenishing her mortal body until the end of Time. In essence, I had given her eternal life—but this meager description does not suffice, cannot suffice. The exchange is so profound a thing. There are even those of my kind who do not truly understand it.

"My late husband was a practitioner of the natural sciences." She lay on her back, her body full of small tics and shivers, her skin growing ever paler by the moment as the small particle of my being enacted its full potential inside of her. "He believed in such things, that the fundamental atoms of existence could be altered by means of electricity. What is it? Galvanism. Mesmerism. The agency of fire, Caleb."

I was aware now of the passage of time, and my impatience became an urgent thing. "Come with me," I urged. "Come home with me—now, today. We can go on the train, or by sea if you prefer."

"Why?" She stroked my forehead and the bridge of my nose. "Of course I will go with you, but why now? Why this day and not some other? Why is this such a suddenly urgent matter?"

I deliberately avoided her gaze. "Haste is always best at the outset of a journey. I should like to get away from London as soon as possible. I will need to wire ahead to my servants, to alert them that I am bringing my... bride." Yes, that word would do as well as any other. The newest Lady Donnithorn, Mrs. Shelley.

"You are facile with language and with other things, I would allow." She rose and pulled on a gown and went to sit at her dressing table. "I will go with you. Today, if you deem it fit." Her reflection turned its gaze on me, and I detected the same predatory presence in her eyes that I had marked at our first meeting—except then I had named it intelligence. "But measures must be taken.... I cannot merely evaporate into the ethers with you."

She would go with me; she would go. "Then let us go quickly."

In the matter of the death of the great authoress Mrs. Shelley, a corpse was found in her bed that morning, nude and still warm, with a faint flush dying along its pale cheek. The official cause of death, as enjoined by such medical minds that attended, was a longstanding tumor of the brain.

WE SAILED to France on the newest of the White Star fleet, the airship *Tantalus,* under cover of darkness, as I was eager to get home. From Paris we took the pneumatic train to Munich, passing through the beautiful Alpine countryside. Mary wished to stop, but I dissuaded her.

"It is vital that I return home. My servants have all in readiness for your arrival. They will be disappointed if we delay."

She did not believe me—I knew this—but she said nothing. When we pulled into the tube station in Munich, she descended the short flight of stairs ahead of me, her skirts held in one small hand, her traveling case in the other. I had already advised her that the pneumatic tube companies retained porters to carry one's luggage, but she insisted she would carry it herself and she would prefer, moreover, I not interfere. I wondered aloud what there was inside—surely an item of such paramount importance that she could not trust its conveyance to an employee of the pneumatic company. At this, she shot me a look of pure venom, a glance so full of hatred I recoiled from it.

For the first time in all my ancient years, I knew—I was convinced—I had made a fatal error. She was beautiful, willful, violent, sensual, and brave. I had not counted on her being dangerous, and yet she was. She was more dangerous to me now than she had been mortal, more dangerous to me than she would be five hundred years from now, when her altered nature had matured the wild edges off of her. I ought to have known better than to choose a woman who had not only given birth, but who had lived to see the products of her body wither and die away. A mother's grief is the hardest and most enduring grief of all. As before, with my poor drowned darling Elisabeta, I had been a fool for love. I had chosen unwisely.

The Lady is dead. The news had come to me by way of Joshi, an extremely old man who had been one of my own father's loyal servants. *She has leapt out of a window.* Such was his wisdom that he did not attempt subterfuge but told the tale just as it was.

With a group of trusted men, I climbed down to the foot of my fortress, to that treacherous spot where the icy river gnaws its way past stone, and found her. The fall had shattered her spine, and on the way down, she had struck her face on several sharp outcroppings of rock. I waded into the water and pulled her body out onto the shore. Her once-beautiful visage was now horribly disfigured and she was bleeding from her ears. She was bleeding from the ears and mouth—and she was still alive.

Caleb, let me go. It's time I went into the river.

Like my beautiful Justine would do, three hundred years later, Elisabeta had already done. What was it I expected to do, I wondered, sitting there with my dead wife in my arms. Would I do as my father and grandfather had done and breathe the breath of life again into her lungs? There were some who said that snatching someone back from death was anathema, that doing such a thing tore them from the hands of the Almighty. I have always believed the Almighty could stand the loss, considering what he has taken from me. Justine, the blade poised at her throat, could not bring herself to commit the act that would sever her from her God forever, and so jumped to her death. Like Elisabeta, she offered herself to the Argeş, and the waters received her sacrifice.

Mary landed at the foot of the stairs and plunged into the crowd that had gathered on the platform. I tracked her by the waving feather on her cap. Near a newsstand she paused, looking about her as if searching for something.

I moved silently to her and caught her by the arm. "Stop this. You must stop this at once."

"You think you can control me." Her smile was cunning. "He thought the same thing. And now here we are." Her voice rose, and I realized, with a cold thrill, she was speaking German, a language she had never learned.

"Our train will be leaving. Please, you must come with me."

"Remove your hand from my arm or I will scream this station down."

I returned to the platform alone. Alone I waited until the final whistle blew, and alone I boarded the train. I listened in a horribly contented sort of discontent as the pneumatic pumps engaged and the long string of cars rose off their metal pads, each individual car lifted and borne aloft, its metal sinews creaking and straining. I watched out the window as loved ones waved to departing passengers, some of them weeping openly while some others seemed rather more glad than was proper.

Where was Mary? I imagined her wandering—no, running—through the *Centralbahnhof* wildly, her hair about her shoulders like a madwoman. She would be taken up as such and confined in an asylum, and she would live forever, shouting about the things I had told her, the things I had done to her.

It could not be permitted. I would have to find her. I would have to hunt her down and dispatch the wretched woman or else....

I ultimately found her in a small back room of the station, seated upon a tottering pile of other people's luggage, her reticule in her lap and such an expression of fixed determination upon her face that I was tempted to laugh aloud. I did not. "Come down from there this instant."

"I know what you are." She clasped her hands together, one over the other. "I can see now. I wonder why I never noticed it before."

"Because you were entirely mortal before." Really, this was becoming an extraordinarily dull game. "Now you see with eyes made bright by the gift I have given you." I reached out a hand to her. "Come. We depart within the hour, and I would rather not be late."

She regarded me narrowly from atop her perch of luggage. "My purpose is only as you have stated—no more and no less?"

"Precisely. The machine is of paramount importance. All I want from you, Mrs. Shelley, is your brain."

She placed her hand in mine and allowed me to help her down. "Merely a brain. That is all I am." She tilted her head to one side and peered at me. "How bizarre a thing it is, to construct a functioning simulacrum from parts of other men and women. Have I ever told you about my novel? Oh yes, all of it is real. That is the thing no one ever recognizes. Victor Frankenstein exists, Caleb. I have met him. I know Victor Frankenstein as well as I have known even my own husband."

Her smile was chilling, and all throughout the trip, I kept stealing glances at her, trying to ascertain what had taken place during the transfer to make her suddenly so hostile. When we arrived, I took certain precautions. From her sleeping head, I drew a single hair and tied one end to her bedpost. Then I took the other end between my thumb and finger and began to walk. I walked all around the castle and out into the courtyard, down the mountain and into the quiet village, all the time stretching the hair to a preternatural thinness and spinning it out behind me. By the time I was done, it was nearly daylight, and Mrs. Shelley's hair had been wound three times around the village, its cellular signature impressed upon the landscape so she might go that far but no farther.

In this way, I guaranteed her attendance and compliance. There would be no headlong dash toward the nearest precipice, no artless fall into the waiting arms of Death. She would not be another Elisabeta. She would not be Justine. Only I can break the thread that binds her to me.

April 1
Castle Donnithorn

I FIND him in his room, sitting by the window, his case open on the bed. For a little while, I watch him in silence. He has a most noble profile—he may be one of those magnificent warriors who once ruled these mountains—and yet there is something vulnerable in him, something eminently sad. He cannot know the things he longs for are true, but also entirely out of his reach. He will live out his impossibly long existence striving to regain his place at the left hand of a God who cares nothing for him.

"Jacob." He doesn't turn around when I speak his name. "Will you come with me?"

He rises wordlessly and follows me without question. I lead him out of my house and up onto the mountain. There are no markings here, no extant gravestones, nothing to indicate anyone at all is buried here, except for a plain, wrought-iron fence enclosing a square of ground. The winds today are cold, and yet he stands here with me, shivering and coatless. He is of fine mettle, this one. Inish was correct to send him. I suspect he will complete his task in whatever way seems best to him. Yes, I am certain of it.

"My father is buried in this patch of ground. Your history books tell you otherwise. They tell you how my father's ship was scuttled by the men who sailed her, men who had sworn allegiance to him alone, and how he was brought back to his homeland in an iron cage."

For a long time there is nothing except the sound of the wind between us. Jacob van Willigen raises his eyes to mine. "You know they sent me here to—"

"Yes." I wonder if he is willing to do it. "My grandfather is buried over there. The rose bushes were my grandmother's idea. The woman was forever putting herself forward." I did not remember her. She had died long before I was born.

He moves closer to me, close enough that I could reach out if I wanted to and touch him. He is not averse to touch. The day I learned of my dear old friend's death, van Willigen took me into his arms and held me. What possesses such a man? The memory of being held by him has become a palpable ache and pervades my dreams as well as my waking hours. Until he came, I had not realized how lonely I had become.

"Yes." It is her face I still see sometimes in nightmares—her face, contorted with rage and hatred. *I know the monster you are! I know the things you do! God will punish you. God will send his angels to take you into everlasting fire.* "Yes, I was married." A tiny purple flower grows near the foot of my father's grave. I bend and pluck it. "Twice, as you know… neither was not a happy union."

The cold wind pulls at van Willigen's hair and flaps the tails of his coat. His expression is somber. "It's because of the machine—the machine you're making, you and Victor Frankenstein. The Society isn't willing that such a device should be used for evil purposes."

I hold the flower to my nose. I am not thinking of the machine, nor of van Willigen's precious Society. My mind is free to roam the centuries: I am lying on the belly stone under the shadowed dome of an Ottoman bathhouse, languid and content. "Evil purposes," I muse. I hand him the flower. "Let us get out of the cold wind, hm?"

One of the first things I did when I took possession of this house was to install an extensive network of piping, boilers, and automated cisterns required to supply a proper bath. I cannot lie and say my time in Turkish captivity was pleasant, but it did instill in me a love of hot water. Scarcely a day passes that I do not immerse myself, and if something troubles me, I find succor in my bath. I do not retain a masseur—that aspect of the hammam has never appealed to me—but my bath is outfitted with every other ablutionary necessity. It includes a hot room, with its large circular stone to lie on, and the not-quite-Turkish stone pool, in which I like to linger, soaking blissfully, continually refreshed from the huge brass cisterns I had installed to heat the water.

"A Turkish bath." He gazes at me, astonished. "Have you brought me here to drown me?"

I cannot help laughing. "If I wanted to kill you," I say wryly, "you would already be dead." I tell him I would like him to join me in a bath, but his gaze is wary.

"Just a bath?"

"Just a bath." I lay my right hand over my heart. "I promise."

There are no *tellak* here, and so we wash each other, laughing like schoolboys. He yelps when I pass the rough cloth over his chest and belly, and I turn him round so I can wash his back—

My face is burning; my eyes are full of blood. My heart is thumping so hard in my chest I can feel its pounding in the bones of my back. I can only stand and stare at what I am seeing. Of course I had suspected, but to be confronted with such patent proof is almost more than I can bear. There are scars—long purple scars, scars that are the exact replica of my own—extending from his shoulders to the curve of his waist.

He senses the direction of my gaze and all the blood drains from his face. "What is it?"

I turn my back and wait. His shock and disbelief are nearly palpable. "You are going to say it is not possible." I am shaking so hard I can barely speak. Is he at all cognizant of what they mean, these scars? "Please, I assure you it is. I remember—everything that went before." He wants to speak, but I forestall the interruption. "I remember also my mortal life: my childhood, my confinement in a Turkish prison, the death of my brother." It is hard now to draw breath. I am gulping air as though I had run a hundred miles. We stare at each other and I am cold, cold as the dead.

Jacob speaks, with some difficulty. "I don't understand." He reaches out and fastens his hands on my upper arms. "What made them? How came you by these marks?

I drag him after me into the hot water and we immerse ourselves. "Did you know, when Brother Inish sent you? Did you realize that this was the case? Or did Inish himself tell you?" My heart squeezes with sorrow and a bitter recognition. "Do you know what you are, Jacob van Willigen?" I exhale on a sob, my face burning. "I believed I was the only other one. I believed I was alone."

"No." Jacob's eyes are huge, dark with shock, and glistening like black water. "I don't... I'm not...." He is sitting so close to me, so close. I can see the tiny flecks of gold in his dark eyes. "I fear you are mistaken. You... you cannot know this."

"Yes." I perceive his anguish as a tangible thing, and yet I force myself to smile. "The scars on your back—did you never wonder what made them?"

His voice is hushed. "I thought they were from...." He blinks. "I did not know what made them. I assumed I had been born with them."

My dear van Willigen, you were never born as mortals are. I deliberately hold back the things I most want to say. I have sworn no oaths, taken no vow of silence, but neither can I be as cruel as this— I, who have learned to make cruelty an art. "I cannot believe the Society did not tell you." He has probably been with them since the very beginning. In some curious twist of happenstance, he may have fallen on their very doorstep. "I cannot believe they kept this from you."

His expression is unfathomable. "Come closer."

Scarcely have I moved when his hands are in my hair, his long fingers tugging and stroking so that I grunt from pleasure. His mouth is hot and the kiss he gives me is sloppy and unpracticed, and yet it thrills me to the marrow of my bones. I reach for him and fold him into my arms, holding our naked bodies together, and I sweep my tongue into his mouth, tasting him. It has been so long—ages, eons, surely centuries—since I allowed myself such indulgence, and God knows he is worthy. I want to lie on him and kiss him slowly, slowly, until our skins melt together with the sweat of our exertions. My body tightens, my senses aroused to the reality of him, my cock full of pulsing blood. "Jacob... beloved."

He is out of the water so quickly, his body a mere blur of movement.

"Van Willigen! Jacob—"

He dashes away, his bare feet pattering on the stone floor, his naked skin a pale shadow.

I have failed.

April 2
Diary—Jacob van Willigen

I HAVE failed.

I admit I conducted myself poorly, but his assertion that I am something other shocked me so horribly. For some time now, I have been aware of the unnatural impulses within me, but I have never imagined anything like what he suggests. I had always assumed I was born with them, or perhaps my scars came from some childhood injury, something so painful and traumatic I had put it from my memory. I have had a mortal life, the same as anyone. I was born in Maastricht to Julia and Vincent van Willigen. I was sent to school at the usual age and tutored in the usual subjects. I drew trouble to myself in measure equal to that of other boys my age. At sixteen I entered the university, intending to read philosophy, theology, and the law. My mother died young. These facts are irrefutable, and yet....

On what street in Maastricht did you live? The voice in my mind is like an imaginary prosecutor, inspecting the facts of the case. *Can you recall the number of the house in which you grew to manhood? Describe, if you will, the objects in your childhood bedroom, your mother's kitchen, your university common room, the church where you made your first Holy Communion.* Of course I remember: the street was.... There was a tall oak at the end of it, just before it.... No, that was in another part of town, closer to Frau Besser's house, my music teacher, the one who taught me how to play the violin.... I didn't play the violin. I had never played the violin. Clearly that was someone else.

My heart begins to hammer in my breast and my palms are sweating. I take a piece of paper and immediately draft a message to Brother Inish: *Request immediate details of*—Of what? How on earth could I phrase such an appeal? *Greatly fear I am misremembering the details of my own life. Request clarification.* Attempting to compose such a request makes me seem like a blithering madman. Of course I had been born in Maastricht; of course I grew up the son of Julia and Vincent van

Willigen; of course I was put to university and ultimately emerged with degrees in theology and law. Eventually my studies had commended me to the notice of the Society, whereupon I was drafted by Brother Inish. Surely there were records kept, somewhere. Surely I exist.

I remember once, some years ago, when I was still in my novitiate, I was invited by Brother Inish to accompany him to the home of a woman who believed herself in possession of the wrong soul. Her parish priest had contacted the Society, worried because this formerly healthy young woman had suddenly become gravely ill and, furthermore, was on her deathbed. Normally such cases—last confessions and the dispatching of the soul into Heaven—were the responsibility of the local church. In this case Brother Inish had decided to intervene because the woman's admission of her sins included a confession of murder, allegedly committed one hundred years prior to the current date, when she lived in Capua and was a man by the name of Luigi Capone. She demonstrated to Brother Inish and myself an astoundingly precise memory of names and personal details, as well as the geographical proximity of Capua to other local sites of note, the name of the parish priest officiating at the local church a hundred years before, and other things.

Brother Inish, always skeptical of such stories and wondering if the woman wasn't perhaps under the thrall of a demonic entity, sent me to examine the local records for the past one hundred years. There had indeed been a Luigi Capone living in Capua at the time. He had been a stonemason by trade and had been apprenticed to one Giovanni Mollari, but had stabbed Mollari to death during a feast. Conscious of his crime, he had promptly fled Capua, taking a ship to Ireland, but Mollari's kinsmen, discovering the details of Capone's flight, were waiting for him. They dispatched him and threw the body over the Cliffs of Moher into the sea.

The point of this narrative is that our personal histories are not always as clear and precise as our memories might make them seem. Hidden within the crypts and folds of any mortal brain are myriad points of view, many of which are at odds with the accepted version of events. If indeed this woman from Capua in truth believed she had somehow captured the soul of a man long dead, a man named Luigi Capone, then perhaps her supposition was correct. There are more things in heaven and earth, as the Bard has said, than are dreamt of in our philosophy.

Shortly after my return from Capua, I planned to pay a visit to the home of a man whom I had known well in my school days. I hadn't bothered to mention my excursion to Brother Inish, since he did not know the man and would probably have no interest in my extracurricular forays in London. He was of Irish extraction, named Cantwell, and he had been living in London for some time, pursuing postgraduate study in the field of medicine. I hadn't seen Cantwell for nigh on twenty years, but I believed, as people do, that until I heard otherwise he was still engaged in the practice of medicine, still studying in London, still precisely where I had left him, living above a chemist's shop in Harley Street.

I remembered my previous visit very well. It had been a warm day in early April, and there were purple crocuses blooming in the window box in front of the shop. I had worn a light overcoat and sturdy shoes, as Cantwell had promised to take me on a tour of his neighborhood. He was engaged to be married, and so I brought my wedding present to the couple in a pretty box tied up with a satin ribbon. I ascended the narrow stairs beside the chemist's shop and rang the bell.

Almost at once my hail was answered by a thin, adolescent girl, her hair done up at either side of her head in braids. She was wearing a pinafore and her sleeves were pushed up above her elbows. "Whatcher want?" I advised her I was seeking Harrison Cantwell and was he at home? The girl stared at me as if I'd only then sprouted from the wall. "Ain't nobody here by that name." Then she shut the door in my face.

So great was my shock and astonishment that I stood there for several minutes, wondering stupidly when the door might open again, revealing my friend Cantwell. On my return to the Society motherhouse, I explained the entire adventure to Brother Inish, especially the part where Cantwell seemingly did not live where he'd said he had. I remember Brother Inish and I were in the library, and he was engaged in collating some early Rumanian religious texts that had been donated to the Society by an anonymous nobleman of that country. *I think perhaps my memory is much affected lately*, I said. I remember I said it in a jovial way, as one does when one seeks an answer but does not wish to be perceived as too aggressive. *I went to see Harrison Cantwell in Harley Street, but he wasn't there.*

Inish simply stopped. His entire body froze in place, the muscles of his back stiffening under his carmine robes. *Harrison Cantwell?*

My dear friend Harrison Cantwell. I knew him when we were boys. His father was an Englishman who worked for the Dutch East India Company. He was stationed in Maastricht for a time. I must have told you about him.

I don't recall what Inish said, only that his entire manner was most curiously affected. The next day I went to the City of Westminster's depository of public records and searched out Harrison Cantwell. I found not a single entry. Fearing some mistake or error on my own part, I searched again, thoroughly combing all and any records to which I might gain access. Still there was nothing. I began to worry that I had made some horrible mistake, that I had mistaken the time and date of our assignation, and that Cantwell was waiting in vain for me. The idea began to press on me so that I became quite worried, then ill. By the time I boarded the six o'clock tube rail for the motherhouse, I was feverish and shaking. Brother Inish met me at the door and ushered me inside. Sometime during my expedition I had gotten caught in a downpour and my clothes were soaking wet. My head had begun to pound in a most disagreeable manner, and everything about me appeared queerly bright. The last thing I remember is three novices peeling my wet clothing from my limbs and putting me to bed.

When I awoke several days later, Brother Inish came with the Society's resident physician, Dr. von Hohenheim, and told me I was suffering from pneumonia. Yet, prior to my second journey into Westminster, when I went to investigate the records, I felt strong and well and demonstrated not even the slightest inclination toward illness. How had I become seriously ill in the course of a single afternoon?

I had never questioned the origin of my scars but always assumed their existence was attributable to natural means. Now I am no longer certain of anything. If the condition of my body is—as Caleb supposes—the result of some wildly unlikely scenario, then my entire existence is equally questionable, and that is not the worst of it.

Where Caleb is concerned, I can no longer trust my own impulses. The longer I stay here, the more strongly these impulses assert themselves, and I think it but a matter of time before I succumb to them. This afternoon, in the bath with him, I came very close to giving myself over, body and soul. I have never to my knowledge indulged in carnal pleasures, but if Caleb had indicated a desire for sensual congress, I would have acquiesced. I desire him. Desire is something I have not felt for a long time, and in me it is an emotion always coupled with love. I fear I am falling in love with Caleb, and I cannot! I cannot allow my personal feelings toward him to cloud my judgment of his unholy mission.

I lay awake last night, turning such things over in my thoughts even as I strove for sleep. At last, convinced I would find no rest, I got up and went into the library to find something to read. I thought I might peruse some staid volume and hopefully bore myself to sleep, but I saw I had been anticipated: Victor Frankenstein was already in there.

"Oh, it's you." He was standing on a ladder, his arms full of books, and I reached to help him. The volumes he had chosen were mostly engineering texts, full of detailed diagrams, as well as a book on moral theology and another on the nature of the soul. "I'd have thought you'd be asleep by now. Insomnia? Yes, well, you'll get used to that soon enough. Caleb keeps very odd hours, and the rest of us have learned to adjust ourselves to him."

I asked whether he was working at so late an hour, and he indicated he was. Would I like to see the laboratory?

"Is that permitted?" But then I remembered how Caleb had shown me his difference engine—had seemed very proud to show it off, in fact. "Perhaps I'll leave here and tell the world about your fantastical inventions."

"Oh, don't be silly." Victor tucked the stack of books under one arm and took my hand. "As if such a thing were even possible. Come on—we've just to go downstairs." A wide wooden door was set flat into the wall opposite the library. Victor opened it and we went in, and I saw a flight of narrow stone stairs descended for some distance into darkness. "Keep hold of my hand." Victor glanced back at me. "At least until the lights come on." No sooner had he spoken than tiny sparks began to appear before my eyes as if by magic, and I saw miniscule lights had been embedded in the stone walls and appeared to illuminate themselves as we passed. "Just bulbs, old man. Don't pay them any mind. I use a mixture of several inert gases, electrically excited to produce light."

At the bottom of the stairs, we found ourselves in a wide, low-ceilinged room with wooden ceiling beams arching gracefully away into darkness. The room must have been immense, occupying the castle's entire cellar space, and every inch of it was taken up with fantastical machines whose purpose I could only guess at. "Please don't touch anything." Victor drew me into the center of the room, where a cheerful fire was burning in the massive fireplace. "It takes ages to get supplies up here, and many of these things are very fragile." He laid the books on a table and pulled on a long white coat such as laboratory assistants wear. "I've been working on this particular one for ages." He gestured to a huge, gleaming mass of glass and metal. "Deucedly difficult, I can tell you." Two brass arms protruded from one end of it, and to the ends of these were attached flat metal plates, their distal surfaces covered by pads made of some soft cloth, probably wool. "The induction is easy enough—God knows, nature takes care of that—but capturing the product after the fact?" He threw his hands out in a theatrical shrug. "There's never enough time, not really. It disperses into the ethers before you can say boo."

I wondered if here, at last, was the heinous machine. It didn't appear as I might have supposed it. At the very top of the apparatus were four glass bulbs with long, thin necks. These terminated in four brass tubes that fed into the body of the machine. Just beneath, a piece had been cut out and several dials had been inserted, on which were stamped various numerical values. "We got one—just one, mind you—last winter, during the influenza. I managed to sustain it for five days, five entire days." He shook his head, his lank blond hair falling over his forehead. "And then it simply… evaporated." He fetched a screwdriver out of his pocket and began tightening screws all over the instrument.

"What did?"

"The soul. They're bloody hard to capture, I can tell you."

My skin prickled. *Anathema. We declare him anathema.* "Did you say…?" The room spun weirdly, and I clutched at the edge of Victor's workbench, and the wounds in my back leapt into fiery life. *The dragon and his angels fought, but they were defeated, and there was no longer any place for them in heaven. And the great dragon was thrown down....* "The dragon."

"Good God, man, you don't look at all well." He caught hold of me and shouted for a manservant. I was lowered onto a settee and a cold, damp cloth was pressed against my face. "Next thing we'll be mopping you off the floor."

I threw the cloth off me and started for the stairs, my whole mind turned toward escape. At the top I fumbled with the knob, cursing as it resisted me, until finally I felt it turn and I was out, running down the corridor. Pale moonlight illuminated the great, wide hall with its banks of silvery mirrors, and I saw myself in these mirrors as I fled, my arms pumping at my sides, my expression wild with fear. I reached the front door and caught hold of the great iron ring hung from it—

The sensation was akin to ice-cold water being dashed into my face, and I felt as though I'd just awakened from a dream or nightmare. I stared at the door, at my own hand clutched around the ring, and I wondered what it was I'd been trying to do.

"Jacob." Caleb's hands settled onto my shoulders and his voice was at my ear. "You are walking in your sleep, my dear. Come. I will put you back to bed."

And then I was looking up at him as he drew the covers over me, his every gesture a tenderness, and it seemed as though a great sadness welled up in me. I felt my face wet with tears.

"Oh, Jacob, my darling." Caleb lay beside me on my bed and drew my head down onto his shoulder. He must have been sleeping himself, for he wore a long nightshirt of black silk and his lustrous dark hair was much disheveled. He smelled like lavender and pine, and his body was inhumanly warm, but it was important I get up because Victor was doing something.... There was something in the cellar. There was something.

Caleb turned my face and captured my mouth, and my body surged toward him. I felt myself woefully untutored and I was ashamed, but he didn't seem to care about that. His arms were tight around me, and we lay together for a long time, kissing. His hand slipped into my nightclothes and rubbed each of my nipples in turn until I was groaning and pressing myself against him like a wanton. "Jacob, my beautiful darling." We were naked together, but I did not remember taking off my clothes. It hardly mattered anyway: this was what I had wanted from the first moment I had seen him. His body was lean and pale, his flesh as white as virgin snow, his skin smooth and very nearly hairless. He reached for my prick, swollen so that the skin was tight as a drum, and worked the flesh in an agonizing rhythm until bright sparks burst behind my closed eyelids.

I turned and sank my teeth deep into his shoulder as my crisis took me, burning through my belly and my chest in great, lashing waves. I came to myself with the taste of blood on my tongue—his blood, I realized. "I'm sorry." I drew back and saw, to my shame and horror, I had left the vivid imprint of my teeth in his flesh. "I'm so sorry."

"It's nothing. My darling, it is nothing." He touched the wound, smiling at me a little painfully, and when he removed his hand, I saw the imprint had almost gone. "You are enthusiastic in your pleasures, Jacob. That is good. Yes, that is very good." He was still unsatisfied, I saw, and I reached for him and was stayed by the gentle pressure of his hand. "Tell me," I murmured. I was becoming weary, and soon I would have to sleep. "Tell me why."

"Why?" His mouth touched my temple, the lobe of my ear, the side of my neck. "Because you are beautiful, my darling Jacob. Because you and I are so much alike."

"That is meaningless," I said.

"Sleep." He drew his fingers over my eyes, and I was immediately exhausted.

There was something I meant to remember, something about Victor Frankenstein and an iron ring, but I slid suddenly into a sleep as profound as the grave.

April 5
3:30 a.m.
Caleb Donnithorn, Castle Donnithorn

I WAS careful to leave his bed before he woke this morning. I am hardly ready to answer the questions he would no doubt assail me with, had I remained in his embrace.

Ada was waiting for me when I returned to my room. She sat on my bed, wearing a fussy nightgown with a great many frills and flounces and no less than three bows tied under the chin.

"Get off my bed. I'm tired."

"Had your taste of him, have you?" She was reading Montgomery's treatise on evoked particle potentials, a glass of Tokay resting on the nightstand. "Was it as good as you expected?" I stared at her until she stood up and closed the book. "It will never work, Caleb. Such a plan is madness. I'm surprised you even thought of it in the first place." She regarded me through narrowed eyes. "It isn't like you to be so foolish. You were always… particular. Careful about things, about people." She tilted her head, standing before me with that stillness that is always and forever a reminder that she and I and Mary and Victor are not as we once were, and never will be again. "He isn't like us. What do you hope to gain from it?"

I ignored her and concentrated on turning down the covers on the bed. "Leave me. I am weary."

Let it never be said that Ada Lovelace, feminine genius and woman of science and mathematics, gave up easily. She came to where I was and pulled at the closure of my dressing gown until it parted. Her fingers found the faded imprint of van Willigen's teeth. "He bit you."

"How very perceptive you are." I slapped her hand away. "No doubt history will regard you as a genius."

Her eyes are a clear, dark blue. She is a beautiful and brilliant woman, my equal in every way. Because of me, Time no longer holds any power over either her body or her mind. Because of what I have given her, she will remain just as she is for all eternity.

I suppose I ought to be grateful.

"You allowed him to bite you." Her little hand is cool against my cheek. "What if he—"

"He won't."

"You allowed yourself to love him?" Her hand slips around to caress the back of my neck.

I listen to myself sighing, relaxing into the presence of this strange, cool woman. Yes, this coolness is the very thing that has always attracted me: being near Ada was not unlike taking shelter under the spreading limbs of a great, pliant tree. "No."

She drops the book onto the bed and both hands are under my hair, kneading in a delicious rhythm. "You pleasured him." Her thumbs press into the base of my skull and her touch is almost cruel. "It hurts you, doesn't it? Your neck? I suppose that's inevitable when one has had his head cut off."

"That was a long time ago, Ada."

"Yes. A long time ago." She smiles, not unkindly. "Caleb the Unholy. What a dreadful soubriquet they gave you, your enemies."

"Are you my enemy, Ada?"

"I have more reason than most to hate you."

"Get out." I take her by the arm and put her out of the room, then shut the door behind her. She is the boldest of my brides, but even Ada knows to respect a closed door. I must be alone for this, alone with my contemplations. My whole being is in a state of sensual torment, and for some time, I twist around on my bed, wondering if I ought to seek self-pleasure, wondering if it's worth it.

Toward dawn I drift into a light sleep, dreaming of Jacob van Willigen. I see him rising naked from the water again and again. I see him disappear without a single backward glance. The long, purple scars on his back and shoulders are the same as mine. There is such history between us.

I awaken with a start and the awareness of a warm, masculine body in my bed and a tousled blond head resting on my shoulder. I look down into dark eyes and a clever, pointed face: Victor Frankenstein.

"It won't be long at all." He draws my face close to his. "We are nearly there."

I breathe in the clean scent of him. Something taut and unpleasant uncoils inside of me and drifts away. "Oh, Victor." There ought to be some endearment left for him, some verbal caress, but there is only urgency and lust.

His strong thighs press hard on either side of my waist, holding me, and his fingers tug cruelly at my hair. He strains my head back and sinks his sharp teeth into my skin, and my desire swells until it fills the world.

Diary, Ada Lovelace
April 5, Castle Donnithorn
4:00 a.m.

I PREDICTED it would not be long before Caleb's amorous fervor landed on some other... I didn't honestly believe it would be a sunburnt scholar with ink on his fingers, a common dullard whose perception of the world rests on the demented ravings of some desert-dwelling Judean madman. Caleb cannot seem to see past him, is obsessed with him, and I fear he is determined to bring the plodding Dutchman into our midst and keep him here, whether we are in agreement with this plan or not. What Caleb wants with him, I cannot imagine, although it almost certainly has something to do with the machine. Everything has to do with the machine. It consumes the whole of his existence. He forgets that without my help, the machine cannot exist. He assumes incorrectly that I am sanguine about being tossed aside. He cannot imagine that, scorned as I have been, I might withdraw my willingness and my aid, and leave him with his precious machine.

I did not truly expect him to indulge me. It has been a very long time since he's sought the pleasure of my bed and more and more these days his passion turns to Victor, who appears to satisfy Caleb's most primal and atavistic desires. I did not care for being turned out.

Perhaps he imagines I might be easily put aside, as a child discards an unwanted toy. If I were a man, I would challenge such presumption at the end of a pistol.

April 15
Diary—Jacob van Willigen

"TELL ME why." We were walking near the castle, Caleb and I, taking advantage of the warm spring weather to stroll companionably arm in arm. The mountains at this time of year were truly spectacular, with every tree in a beautiful state of forwardness. The scents of all the flowers filled the air until I felt myself quite intoxicated with their fragrance. How easy it was to forget oneself in a place such as this.

"Why?" Caleb smiled. I have grown used to his smiles, rare and precious as they are. In my hubris I imagined I can decipher their meanings and divine one from the other.

"Why do you want this machine? Will you at least tell me that?"

"You were sent here to destroy it. I know this. Why the sudden interest in its meaning, its function? Enlighten me, Jacob."

I swallowed the rising lump in my throat. I knew he could be formidable. I knew he could remain quiescent or explode into a murderous rage. I did not fear him—at least not physically—but I was loath to spoil the peaceful mood that permeated our discourse. "The Society believes your use of the machine is to create… abominations."

"Abominations." He nodded. "I see." The corners of his mouth turned up, and there was a playful light in his eyes. "You no doubt have done your research. Knowing as you do that Doctor Frankenstein is among my assistants, you have concluded that my machine is a natural extension of the good doctor's earlier work."

"Is it?" I clutched his arm. We had been walking across the lower slope of a magnificent mountain, our feet treading paths that had in times past been trodden by Caleb's noble ancestors. He was in good spirits, conversing volubly and well with me at breakfast, and after we had eaten, he himself escorted me down to Victor Frankenstein's laboratory where he received a full report of the doctor's progress.

"No."

"Caleb, I can but be true to my calling, true to my God—" At this his eyes flashed, and his features settled into lines of hostility. "I have been sent here to destroy the machine and to prevent any further work of this sort. It is the will of the Society. It is the will of Almighty God."

He turned and caught hold of my shoulders. The freshening breeze from the valley ruffled his dark hair. "Almighty God." He nodded. "Let me tell you a little story, Jacob."

He had been born into a mortal body and raised at the court of a certain European nobleman. As a child, he and his two brothers enjoyed every advantage. Compared to the villagers around them—many of whom lived in utter squalor—the young Donnithorn had the best food and drink, the finest books and clothing, and the attention of several highly learned tutors. "It would seem, Jacob, my friend, that I lived what is now called 'a charmed life'." He stood for a moment gazing out over the valley, hands clasped behind his back, his gaze fixed on the distant hills. What he was thinking, I could not say.

"All that changed when my father received a missive from a certain Eastern potentate, advising him that tribute was due. My father owned and controlled all that you see before you, but how could he extract gold from the soil? He did the only thing he knew, and I went with my younger brother to Constantinople—as noble hostages, of course, but hostages all the same. This you already know. You may not know that if my father betrayed his vow, the ruler of that country had the right to end our lives." The words rang with a finality that made me shudder. "To vouchsafe my father's loyalty, we were treated as honored members of the court. My brother and I received an excellent education, and after a time this ruler began to look upon him with... favor." Caleb's eyes narrowed and he kicked at a clot of earth. "Before long, he was beloved by the sultan and I was simply the remnant. You must understand how things worked: the sultan could not kill me, even though he had no further use for me, because to do so would invite my father's retribution. He was duty bound to keep me alive, and he did—after a fashion."

I felt as though sand had been poured into my throat. "How?"

"I was imprisoned for... a period of time. You have to experience a Turkish prison to truly appreciate the tortures of the damned. Because I would not relent and because I repeatedly attempted escape, my captors punished me most severely. I was often whipped until the blood ran—this was usual for them. When I still would not submit, they withheld my food and water. I was made to crouch on a stone pillar in an oubliette—do you know this word, Jacob?—for several days at a time. When even this failed, they resorted to other measures. Even strong as I was, it undid me. Rape is a powerful weapon in the hands of a conqueror. I am sure you have heard this before." We had reached a flat stone large enough for two men to sit side by side. Caleb sat and patted the surface beside him, indicating I should sit. "You remember my father had initiated me when I was still but a child, calling forth my native abilities. This service that I perform for the people of the village, I attempted similar with my captors. I had the naive idea that I could somehow kill them by draining their life force. This only works, however, with those who are already dying, and there are certain unpleasant effects." He turned slightly so he could look at me. "The memories of all those I have... 'helped' remain with me, in the repository of my own mind: the love, the pleasure, the guilt, and pain that these mortals have experienced, it lives in me." He searched my gaze. "Do you understand? I am their final judgment."

I experienced a sensation akin to an icy breath against my neck and shoulders. "I had no idea." I wondered how much Inish really knew, and if even he understood the nature of Caleb's dubious gift. "So you are building the machine to take your place."

"Yes. In a manner of speaking." He rose to his feet. "And I hope, in time, to capture a soul that I can use—that can be implanted in me."

"A soul."

"Yes, Jacob. A soul of my own, if you must." He clasped his hands behind his back. "Does this constitute blasphemy? I don't know—a theologian I am not. Is it possible? I have searched the world for the minds that I believe can create such a mechanism. If this particular iteration fails, there is always time to make another and then another and another until I am successful." He leaned close to me and murmured, "I have eternity at my disposal, Jacob. Eternity. I am in this wretched, soulless state because of your Almighty God." Something below caught his attention and he straightened. "A messenger."

We espied a young man approaching from a distance and at great speed. By the time he reached us, he was out of breath. He stopped before us, panting heavily, flushed, and excited. Caleb laid a hand on the young man's shoulder and offered him a drink from the flask of *palinka*—a fiery plum brandy—he habitually carries with him. "What is it?"

At first I thought something had gone horribly awry, and I imagined some terrible tragedy had befallen some member of Caleb's household—either that, or Brother Inish had sent someone from the Society to enforce the decree.

Happily, I was not correct: the young man had come running to invite us to his sister Katja's wedding that afternoon. I confess, I was caught off guard by this unusual request, and I initially sought to avoid what must surely be an intrusion on this young couple's nuptials, but Caleb assured me everyone in the village and all the inhabitants of his castle would be expected to attend.

"That does include you, my dear Jacob. Our host and hostess would consider it an insult if you did not attend." He advised the boy that we would be there, and with that, hurried me down the mountain, our earlier conversation seemingly forgotten.

I have since bathed and shaved, and am trying my best to dress myself in the odd assortment of clothing I found laid out on the foot of my bed: dark trousers, made of the finest lightweight wool; a fine white shirt beautifully embroidered with intricate designs; and over it all, a colorful, hand-woven waistcoat of deep crimson, reaching nearly to my knees. I do not imagine I look anything besides ridiculous and I can hardly peer into a mirror without wishing for a long moustache to twirl. In addition to all this, there is a pair of Caleb's high, black boots I am instructed to wear. I am heartily glad none of my old Society fellows can see me in this outfit. I should be sent to Coventry if even a whisper of my sartorial sins were known in London!

[…]

Caleb was waiting for me at the foot of the stairs, similarly attired, although he is much better suited to it than I. He reached out a hand to me and gripped mine firmly, and I perceived he was much affected by the sight of me in native dress. "You are—" He bowed his head for a moment. "—glorious, my friend." He cupped my face in his hands and gazed deeply into my eyes, and I wondered what was causing him to behave in this manner. "You are… beautiful."

I have not forgotten how he pleasured me, bringing me effortlessly to my crisis. I cannot now look at him without recalling the incident. I confess I do not know what to think. It would seem I have utterly abandoned my mission. I cannot find it in me to care.

We took the funicular down the mountain, and I watched in fascination as the large vessel containing the water rose up toward us, in perfect counterpoint to the vehicle's descent. Caleb was in a state of barely suppressed excitement, pointing out various features to me as we descended. At the bottom of the mountain, we were met by a procession of villagers, all dressed very fine, the girls with flowers in their hair.

"Come." Caleb urged me forward with him. "We go to the church."

The church was built of stone and very simple, as well as heavily fortified. Caleb explained to me that, in times past, the villagers would barricade themselves inside, in the event of enemy invasion.

"Did you ever hide in there?" I asked, my smile a little sly. I confess I was curious to hear what he would say. There is still so much about Caleb I do not know.

"Mm, once." He slanted his gaze at me. "All right, twice." He tried not to smile as I burst into gales of laughter. "But I was very young."

"Perhaps it wasn't an invasion so much as inclement weather," I offered.

Caleb glanced at me, then quickly away. "In inclement weather I was made to stand outside in the courtyard—a test, to see how well I could withstand the cold."

The frivolity I'd been about to utter froze on my lips. "Outside?" I could only gape at him, astonished. "In wintertime?"

"This bothers you." We had been walking with the villagers toward the church, but now Caleb stopped and allowed the procession to go ahead without him. "Why does this bother you?"

I could not answer him.

"Because I was a child?" He linked his arm through mine and drew me forward. "Our notions of childhood are rather different from yours. When I was a boy, it was customary to expose children to the elements. It is how we test our offspring, to see whether they have the necessary fitness to withstand the harsh realities of life." He looked at me searchingly. "I see by your expression that you think this practice is barbaric."

Again I said nothing.

He stopped, turned me to face him, and held my shoulders. "Then what is it?" His voice was very gentle.

"You were a little child," I said.

His hands tightened on my shoulders. "The day is beautiful. The weather is fine. I beg you, put it out of your mind. Today we celebrate love, hm?"

I remember little of the ceremony, except the bride and groom were young, and beautiful, and their faces shone for one another with an obvious joy that was perhaps tempered with a little anticipation. The church was entirely empty of pews, but beautifully ornamented and filled with a gorgeous array of sacred vessels, icons, and holy pictures. Instead of sitting, as we would in an English church, we stood and watched as the patriarch blessed the union with the traditional crowning of the bride and groom. I turned to glance at Caleb and—had I not seen it myself, I would not have believed it—there were tears glistening on his dark lashes. Immediately following the ceremony we proceeded— again en masse—to the reception hall, which had been beautifully decorated in advance by the young ladies of the village, with fresh flowers and baskets of fruit. A band of local men had been assembled to provide the music, which they did with great gusto and skill, and there was much dancing. I was amused—but not surprised—to see Caleb inviting several women to dance, all of whom graciously accepted, with the exception of one.

The elderly woman who had declined a ride in Caleb's coach all those weeks ago, and who had spat at us on a deserted mountain road, saw Caleb approaching and made a disgusted face. She said something to him I couldn't quite hear, but which I assumed was intended as an insult. Caleb drew back, his smile becoming quite fixed, almost frozen in place. As I watched, the old woman made the Sign of the Cross and pointed two fingers at him before turning her back.

I hurried to his side. "What was it?" I laid my hand on his arm, and he started, staring at me like a man coming out of a stupor.

"It is nothing." He blinked. "Come, they dance the *perinita*."

In the interests of scholarship, I will attempt to describe this most beautiful wedding dance, although I fear my narrative powers are hardly equal to the task. The *perinita* is the traditional Romanian wedding dance, known colloquially as the "little pillow," although in truth, when I have seen it, a handkerchief or shawl has most often been used. The dance begins with all the women dancing in a loose circle, holding hands, usually to the music of accordion and fiddle. A man, holding a handkerchief in his hand, approaches the lady of his choice and makes much ado, waving the cloth over his head, announcing his intentions to the assembled onlookers. He then drapes the shawl or handkerchief, whichever is the case, over the shoulders of his lady, using it to pull her toward him, and they kiss. In a shockingly modern interpretation of this custom, the women do it also, in precisely the same way. Needless to say Caleb found the shawl more than once about his shoulders as one lady after another pulled him close and kissed him, albeit decorously, on the cheeks. Whoever is kissed then takes the shawl himself and chooses the one he will kiss. This goes on until everyone in the gathering has been kissed at least once, or the master of ceremonies calls a halt.

It was well past two in the morning when the newly married couple departed and the wedding guests dispersed. Caleb and I walked arm in arm through the village, in no particular hurry.

"Did you like it?" he asked me.

"I liked it very much."

We rode the funicular up to the top of the mountain, and within moments, we were back at the castle. I bade Caleb good night and went to my room, intending to undress and go immediately to bed, but a small movement at the periphery of my vision halted me. Caleb was standing in the doorway, wearing his dressing gown and a silk scarf draped around his neck. Twin spots of color burned on his cheekbones and his face was unusually somber. "Jacob."

I turned and spoke his name, but my voice sounded strange to me, as if I were speaking across a great distance. "Caleb."

"Will you dance the *perinita* with me?"

My entire body trembled as I drew near, reached past him to close the door, and turned the key in the lock. The silk slipped around my neck, and he pulled me to him and held our bodies together. I could feel the hard bulge of his erection against my belly. I slipped my fingers into his hair and held him by the nape. He gasped aloud as I drew my thumb down his cheek, and I leaned in to claim his opened mouth. We were spinning in a maelstrom like Dante and Beatrice, whirled inexorably into some other plane where Time was meaningless.

The night shattered into a series of images, fleeting glimpses of hands and lips and skin. He made to pleasure me again, as he had done during our previous congress, but I prevailed, holding him down and drawing aside the flaps of his dressing gown.

"No!" He threw me aside as if I weighed nothing; his strength must have been prodigious. "You must not!" A moment's pause while he withdrew from the bed, righted his clothing, and assembled his composure. "My darling Jacob, you must not." His chest rose and fell, his breathing tremulous. "I will explain. I know I must, but... not now. Not... yet." He paused for a moment in the doorway, one white-knuckled hand gripping the knob. "Not yet. Not now."

From the diary of Caleb Donnithorn
Undated

THE WINTER of 1850 was cold, unseasonably so they told me, for England. Accustomed as I am to the long, frigid winters of my homeland, with their deep snows and sudden, violent blizzards, the temporary chill of England was but a pleasant respite, and I have seen so many winters. Upon my arrival, I went to the dean of _____ college, a small university located but a short distance from London, in the sort of quiet village where people who see much but say little resided. I told him I had come to England with the idea of studying the English language and intonation, as well as some great works of literature, and I would be greatly indebted if he might advise me as to a suitable institution. I hinted that my resources were nigh unlimited and I was willing to pay handsomely for the privilege of sitting in on lectures, should he deem it appropriate. I suggested—but did not say outright—that I would make it worth his while to accommodate me, and I spoke of my ancient and noble family, of our revered lineage, of my ancestors who had for so long been a friend to England in times of peace and in times of war.

In truth, I was looking for something—a very particular thing for which I had come all the way to England. I did not tell him this, of course, and I was careful to couch my request in the most diplomatic language possible, lest I give offence. Thus I was duly accepted into the university and given lodgings.

The man with whom I was rooming was a silent sort of creature, much disposed to study and contemplation. He spoke only when absolutely necessary, and I seldom saw him elsewhere in our lodgings. He desired no friendship with me, nor I with him, and so I sought the company of my fellows elsewhere. The dining hall was a place I often commenced to visit, sometimes spending hours there in study and contemplation. I usually brought some book with me, so as to appear occupied should some less than desirable companion attempt to engage me in conversation. There were three or four other scholars whose society I sought, and whose companionship assured the pleasant passage of long, rainy winter days. It was one such day when a friend drew my attention to a solitary student, a young man who appeared to have no friends at all, nor did he desire any.

"SEE THAT fellow over there? No, by the wall." He indicated a thin, blond fellow who was seated by himself, drinking what I assumed was ale, with a sheaf of papers spread on the table before him.

"Is he a friend of yours?" I asked. We had just dined on the most tender saddle of beef I have ever had the pleasure to taste outside of my own country, with an ample sauce in the French "au jus" tradition and tiny potatoes. I had considered ordering a bottle of Tokay but ultimately surrendered the idea, fearing my companions would think me the bragging type. I chose instead an ordinary Chambertin, of the sort Napoleon the Great was said to favor, and we supped quite amiably on it.

"Him? Good God, no." Geert, a medical student and one of my favourite companions, drained the last of the wine from his glass. "He's Swiss, that one. Extremely clever—as far as anybody can tell—and completely mad."

"Hm." The Swiss had a pile of books before him, and now and then he would open one and page through it quickly, then discard it back onto the pile. "He doesn't look particularly mad."

"Wait."

I watched a serving girl walk by, then three students from the nearby college, already drunk as lords and singing some incomprehensible tune about carriage wheels. The blond man seemed to notice nothing, his gaze fixed on some indeterminate point in the distance. I half-expected him to start up and call a greeting to a friend, but he did not. Instead, he nodded sharply, then again, as if in agreement with some unspoken attestation, and began to speak—aloud, in a slow murmur—to the open air.

"Do you see?" Geert's breath was warm against my ear. "Absolutely barking."

No, not mad, I knew—merely the first mortal I'd ever seen who had managed to harness the power of a djinn for his very own. It was said Mehmed the Great, during one of his campaigns, had captured a demon whom he accurately named, thus enslaving the demon to him for eternity. "What's his name?"

"Frankenstein." Geert had abandoned any pretense of laughter and was now watching the Swiss as intently as I. "Victor Frankenstein."

I chanced to meet young Frankenstein again—indeed, I could hardly fail to encounter him, seeing as how our paths so often intersected. If I went to the dining hall to take sustenance, I saw him sitting by himself, inevitably in the midst of a great pile of books, talking aloud as he so often did, and gesticulating to the air. When I attended chapel with the others (the first rule of a foreigner in a foreign land is, of course, assimilation—and my family had always made our obeisance), I saw him on his knees, seemingly lost in the willing self-surrender of devotion, eyes turned upward to the chapel's ornate ceiling as if he expected God or one of the lesser angels to materialize there. His rooms were a floor below mine, adjacent to the common room, with its deep, comfortable chairs and its huge bay windows overlooking the street with its bustle and squalor, but I rarely saw him there.

Sometimes in the evening, Geert and I would sit together before the fire and talk of our studies in a wandering fashion, touching on many subjects but lingering on none. Geert was much disposed to discuss the world in terms of its endless possibilities and especially the hidden knowledge he allowed existed in the natural world.

"Whirlwinds, Caleb—tidal pools, snowstorms in winter, the burning sands of Africa! Think of the myriad potentials hidden in a common drop of water or the power of a lightning strike. We may one day discover that such things have eminent power to sustain or even create life out of nothingness." He followed my gaze. "Good God," he said. "Truly this is a momentous day." He nodded at the door where Victor Frankenstein stood, blinking like a captive newly led into the light.

I was pleased, although I did not dare show this. I had called him and he had come. "Herr Frankenstein." I stood, indicating he might sit with us. "Please draw in by the fire, for I perceive the evening is cold—but you must not mind, with your fine Swiss constitution?"

He moved to where we were but continued to regard us both with a weather eye. "Good evening, *Lord* Donnithorn, Herr Geert."

I poured a measure of brandy from the flask of Ţuică I habitually carry with me. The tips of his fingers and his nose were blue with cold. "Are your rooms unheated, Herr Frankenstein?"

"I dislike complaints as much as the next man," he said with a grin. "And yet I fear to show my people as less tolerant of cold than the Dutch"—he nodded toward Geert—"or the Transylvanians. However—" He took a healthy gulp of brandy, choked, but carried on manfully. "—there is something the matter with the flue in my fireplace. It will not draw."

I knew for a fact that a flue will fail to draw when it is stuffed with soiled rags. Yes, I knew this very well indeed, and he was a handsome one. I had chosen well. I liked the flush of his pale cheeks and the way his blond curls tumbled over his collar in a style made popular by the poet Byron. There was indeed something poetical about him, most beautiful, and I was eager to engage him; that his preliminary research into the extension of human life had already gained him the approval of the academic community did not escape me either. I asked him about his homeland, the great mountains there, and the beauty of the land in springtime, and he answered me in kind while Geert sat quietly, smoking a thin cigar and regarding me through narrowed eyes. When at last we parted for the night, I was flushed with triumph. There was much yet to do, of course, but already so much progress had been made.

"When did you do it? And in the name of God, why?" Geert shrugged out of his topcoat, slung it over a chair, and began to untie his neck cloth. It was his habit to wash himself every night before retiring. I enjoyed watching him undress, although he had never allowed me to see him entirely unclothed. Every night he would disrobe and take the candle into the other room, where I could hear him splashing about in the basin and watch his shadow move and gesture on the wall. "I don't know what you mean." I went to the fire and stirred the embers into flame.

"Don't demur." Geert called from the other room. "You don't even bother to deny that you somehow engineered this. For what purpose, I cannot tell." He stirred soap into lather and applied the froth to his face. "I confess, I cannot think why you should want to do this. Frankenstein is mad. He is avoided by everyone. Why should you seek out his society?"

I folded myself down into the chair by the window, suddenly weak. The rain had begun in earnest now, lashing the windowpanes with fury. I felt like my essential force had been somehow drained away from me. "Perhaps I am merely interested." I wanted to go out. It was raining, true, but the urge was growing in me, had been growing for many days, and now—especially now—I could no longer ignore it. Against my better judgment, I rose and pulled my coat on.

"You're going out?"

I let the door fall shut behind me, pretending I hadn't heard the question. The rain fell steadily—a heavy, lancing cold with a thousand needles in it—and I hunched my shoulders, my head drawn down into my collar. I had no real idea where I was going, but it didn't matter. I no longer heeded the dictates of reason, but something older was driving me onward, something infinitely deeper, something as old as the primordial blood throbbing in my veins.

I found myself in a tiny room, crouching with some other people at the side of a woman's bed. The smell of blood was strong, and her breath came in great, labored gasps. Oddly I was not out of place, and the other mourners accepted my presence among them as if I belonged.

With a start I realized why: my dark topcoat and hat might have marked me out as a visiting undertaker, come to prepare the dying woman her inevitable place. She was younger than I had first expected, but her physiognomy was much wasted by her illness and perhaps the rigors of her life. Her surroundings were unhealthy in the extreme, dank and unwholesome, lit only by a guttering oil lamp.

I remembered my father's words: *You will haunt the bedsides of the dying. You will be the final face they see. This is what it means to be of the family. This is what it means to be a Donnithorn.*

"HOW OLD were you?"

I was somehow back in my rooms at the university, sitting close before the fire with Geert, a volume open on my lap. It was raining very hard—still—and I was unsure of the hour or how I had come to be there. "I was five when they took us as hostages to Mehmed. My brother Mircea—" My brother, whom they had buried alive, his eyes burned out. Yes, my brother. "The light hurts my eyes." I was overtaken by a curious languor. Yes, I knew it well.

My father and those others like him had always told me to take care—that a worthy companion was never chosen lightly, but cultivated, brought carefully along like a tender vine. *It should take months, if not years.* My father's friend, one Radu Ionescu, the man for whom my youngest brother had been named, had said this to me at my own induction ceremony. *It has always been done this way.* Was that my intention? I wasn't entirely sure if Victor Frankenstein was what I wanted in a companion, yet every man takes a bride and I was well past the age.

Victor Frankenstein kept a small office on the library's upper floor, in a secluded corner under an eave and close by a stained-glass window depicting the metaphorical triumph of Knowledge over Superstition. I had often seen him there, sunk deep in thought with his head in his hands and his usual sheaf of papers spread around him. I think he looked most beautiful when he was in just such an intellectual reverie as this.

"I believe you might find this useful." I laid the volume on the desk. That it didn't actually come from this library hardly mattered.

"What?" He pulled himself away from his work reluctantly, his eyes full of thought. "Herr Donnithorn, I…." He smiled. I was suddenly hot and cold together, dizzy, sweating, trembling like a man in the throes of a violent fever. "As you see, I tend to lose myself in my research." He took the volume up and caressed its binding reverently. "Oh, my." He examined the title and paled perceptibly. "Do you…. Are you aware…? Of course. You would know, but this library does not have a copy. There are only two copies of this extant in the entire world." His voice rose excitedly and he stood up, his work forgotten. "Where ever did you get it?"

"I regret I am unable to divulge such information." His eyes, I decided, were some shade between blue and dark gray, shimmering like sapphires. "I would…." Some syllables hovered on my lips and fell unspoken into the air. I was making a fool of myself. "Herr Frankenstein, I wonder—"

He stood so close to me that, had I desired it, I might have laid a hand against his cheek or kissed his parted lips, but I had sensed no movement in him, so fixed and held was I by his mere presence. "Yes." He smelled like mountain water and deep pinewoods.

"You haven't even heard what I would ask."

"Whatever it is." His fingers were warm against my wrist. "Anything."

Oh, my dear one, you cannot imagine…. "Would you dine with me this evening? I should very much like to hear—" I turned my hand, captured his fingers, and held him. "—about your work."

"I must profess, I cannot think what I have done to warrant such a generous gift." The little volume lay on the table between us. Now and then Frankenstein would reach a tentative hand to caress its leather binding—gently, sacredly, as one caresses the flesh of a lover.

"I knew it would be an aid to your research." I stopped just sort of addressing him by his Christian name. To be familiar so early suggested vulgarity, and I had no wish to appear crass. I hoped—by my choice of venue, by the wine I had purchased, by the location of our table, by my careful attention—to convince him of my seriousness. I was wooing him, as I myself had been wooed, as my father and his father before had been elegantly seduced. It was absolutely necessary for the continuance of our kind. We were required to make the *ispăşire*, the atonement. Yes, I was wooing Victor Frankenstein.

"But Caleb—" Victor caught my gaze and colored, a delicate spill of blood beneath the skin. Tonight he was dressed in a dark blue topcoat that caused the irises of his eyes to flare a deep sapphire. On the little finger of his left hand, he wore a gold signet ring engraved with his family coat of arms, a helm and casque atop a flag. When he leaned close to speak to me, the scent of vetiver and lavender rose from his clothing.

"Tell me," I said, as casually as I could manage, "about your research."

For a moment I thought I had perilously overstepped myself. His elegant nostrils quivered slightly and his pupils dilated until his eyes looked black. "My research." He laid his napkin down. "Well, considering your gift…." Again, he caressed the book, his long fingers lingering on the spine. "I should think you at least have a working knowledge."

"You are…." I glanced around the room. The hour was late and most of the other diners had long since gone. The only other occupant was a man in a long dark coat, wearing a hat whose brim obscured his features. He had been sipping from the same glass of brandy for an hour. "You are studying the limits of mortality."

"I am seeking a means by which life may be extended, yes." His face closed down.

What are you not telling me, I wondered. "And the rekindling of that fire?" I probed. "After life has been extinguished—what about that?"

His face emptied of all expression. "Only God Almighty can create life. It was Christ our Savior who raised Lazarus—"

"That is no longer true." I raised my glass, my manner sardonic, knowing. "You, Victor Frankenstein. You have done this thing. Yes?"

"No." He sipped his wine, then sipped again as though his throat had suddenly gone as dry as dust. "No one can do such a thing."

Obviously you have never heard of the Order Draconis, I thought, *or you would not be so secure in your faith.*

HE HAD done nothing to alert me or to alarm my sensibilities, but the silent man sitting by himself sipping brandy unnerved me. There was something vaguely sinister about him, something strange and out of place. Some infinitesimal fiber of his being resonated with my own as if, at some level, we knew each other.

He reminded me of an encounter I had once had in Prague, when I was a younger man traveling with some older members of the Order Draconis. Our business required a visit to one of that ancient city's great libraries. There, seated by myself, high above the central courtyard, I saw him: a lone figure in black garb that I at first mistook for a priest's cassock. He was not, as far as I could tell, engaged in any sort of scholarly research. I thought to amuse myself by watching him, but he turned and, as if divining my intention, gazed upward to where I was hidden, raised his hand, and pointed to me. It was as if he had not only seen me but had heard my thoughts, which was absurd. Only saints and angels, and certain other noncorporeal beings have such power. Such was the intensity of his gaze that I shrank back and, descending the stairs at speed, hastened to find my chaperone. For months afterward I bolted out of sound sleep, a gasp frozen in my throat and the image of great black wings seeming to hover over me in the dark. It could not, of course, be the same man. In any case he would have to be either immortal or several hundred years old. He would have to be as I am.

"Thank you for this." Frankenstein clutched the book to him, his pale features luminous in the lamplight. We stood outside our common lodgings, neither of us willing to go in. A light snow had begun to fall, tiny flakes drifting slowly down out of an ink black sky. "Come here." He beckoned me to him and caught hold of my coat's lapels in a deliciously familiar fashion that warmed and thrilled me. "I fear you now have the advantage of me, Caleb."

"I seek to press no advantage," I murmured. His skin was so fine I could barely make out the tiny pinpricks of his pores. His eyes were huge, dark blue, and with lashes far too extravagant for a grown man. His lower lip was pink, as though he'd been biting on it.

"I rather wish you would."

His mouth was hot and wet, his lips open, his tongue slipping past the barrier of my teeth. As quickly as it started, it was over and he was disappearing up the stairs, leaving me alone. I moved out into the street, the fire of that kiss singing in my veins. Yes, he was magnificent and I wanted him—God, how I wanted him! He would make a fit companion for me. I hesitated for several moments, weighing my options, and then I turned and plunged into the darkness of the stairwell. I had planted the seed. The trap, once sprung, would yield my prey to me. Once that had been accomplished, Victor Frankenstein, I knew, would follow me anywhere.

A week later my supposition proved correct. A vaguely worded communication from Frankenstein requested the pleasure of my company and directed me to an address some distance from the town. I took the precaution of hiring a horse and carriage, and at the appointed hour, I drove myself to the house Frankenstein had designated: a shambling stone farmhouse at the far end of a patch of muddy ground, set about with unfamiliar trees of an impossible height, trees which sheltered it from the road and the glances of any curious onlookers.

I pulled my rented carriage up close to the front door and spoke some gentling words into the horse's flattened ears. Beasts are the masters of the natural world. They sense sounds and vibrations far too faint for mortal ears, and they are much more closely attuned to the terrestrial pulses. *"…e în regulă."* I smoothed her silken mane. *"Nu faceti griji."*

There was no porch or gallery attached to the house. The front door appeared to open directly into the structure itself. I mounted the stairs and rang the bell but heard no attendant sound of footsteps from inside. Fearing I had arrived at the wrong house, I turned to go. The sound of an opening window caused me to turn.

"Your Grace!"

I looked up. Victor Frankenstein's head protruded from an upper window and he was smiling broadly. "Doctor Frankenstein. Is this where you conduct your researches?"

He waved a hand. "It is indeed. Do come up. The door is unlocked."

I followed a winding interior staircase and my preternatural senses to the upper floor and found myself in one of the most curious rooms I had ever seen. The walls were lined with shelves, some of which held books—ancient tomes on subjects many and various— while others were crammed with strange jars and vessels. I recognized an alembic, a crucible, and a series of retorts, as well as a beautiful gold cupel, that repository for the rendering of precious metals. In addition to these more traditional tools, there were machines of a modern hew, many I did not recognize, but which appeared to harness the power of electricity. One such device resembled a physician's examination bed, but with added extensions for the head, the arms, and the feet. This latter was easily some nine feet long and nearly four feet wide—much, much larger than the dimensions of a normal man. It was fitted with stout leather straps whose joints were studded with brass. These were made to buckle together across the width of the bed and resembled restraints commonly in use in lunatic asylums.

"So glad to see you." Frankenstein took both my hands in his and squeezed them. He appeared to have been working steadily for some time. His face betrayed a pale shadow of beard and the clothes he wore were hopelessly rumpled. "I am so very excited about it. I wanted you to be the very first to see it, above all others."

I couldn't help but laugh at his nervous excitement. "I see. And what is it, this latest? Further proof of your intellectual prowess?"

"You must see for yourself. Come, it is just out back." He caught hold of my arm and led me out of the house and into a stand of trees some little distance away. "You will be astonished."

Presently a structure loomed out of the darkness, a sort of shed or purpose-made outbuilding, constructed out of wood and stone and squatting on the landscape like a wayward toad. Frankenstein lit a small torch as we went in, and I saw this building was arrayed differently from his laboratory. Instead of metal tables and various alchemical apparatus, there were handsome rugs, a pair of sofas, a chaise, and a deep, wingback chair beside which had been set a lamp, obviously for reading. A fireplace, so large a grown man might stand upright inside it, was set against the far wall, and to either side of it there were bookshelves, filled with a selection of titles by the most prominent authors of the day. There was a small dining area, I saw, into which had been placed a table and a single chair. All of this was in no way unusual except for the outsized scale of the things, which I have not mentioned. Everything in the hut—the bed, the table, the chairs, the lamp—were at least twice as large as those a normal man might want.

"It's all to scale, of course." Frankenstein grinned at me, his whole being fairly vibrating with excitement. "As you will see, a larger vision was required." He clasped his hands together. "There's not a few wretched murderers and lunatics gone into him, I'll tell you that." His laughter rang like a child's. "Should you like to see?"

It occurred to me then that we were not alone here, he and I. The realization that some creature, some *thing*, was resident in the structure made my skin crawl. Was it true? Were the things I'd heard and read about Victor Frankenstein actual fact? Had he managed where so many others before him had failed? "Of course."

There was a staircase set against the far wall, which presumably led to some higher part of the house. Frankenstein ascended three or four of the steps and called out, "Darius! Darius, will you come down?"

We waited, and then something stirred as if rousing itself from sleep. From above there came a noise like the dragging of chains, and slowly, furtively, a creature appeared. In form and figure, it was roughly human but monstrously large, at least nine feet tall and of a comparable width. It descended the stairs with great deliberation, placing one foot firmly before moving the other, and as it came toward us, I saw it was grossly misshapen. The eyes were spread much too wide on the skull, with one—the right—drooping toward the ear. The nose resembled little more than a set of paired holes, the result of using insubstantial materials or those in which the processes of decay had already begun. The lips, too, were as grotesque as the rest, flattened and liver-colored and, as with the eyes, one side of the mouth drooped lower than it ought to have done. The prodigious hands, easily four times the size of my own, swung ponderously by its sides, and the great feet, shod in leather boots, were like the hooves of some appalling animal. Yet for all this, the creature lived: it breathed and moved about.

"My God…." I wanted to go to it, to touch it, but felt as if I were rooted to the floor.

"Darius, this is my very dear friend, Caleb Donnithorn."

The monster inclined his head and held out one massive paw as I approached. I allowed it to shake my hand; the sensation was akin to having one's appendage encased in a huge, padded mitten. "I am very pleased to make your acquaintance, Caleb Donnithorn. You are quite well-known in your own land and, indeed, beyond it."

I stared, astonished beyond the power of speech or even comprehension.

"Yes, Herr Donnithorn, I can indeed speak—and think and reason, if you hold such things in regard, as my dear father does." The creature—Darius—inclined its head in Frankenstein's direction, and I understood, with a pang of horror, that it regarded Victor as not merely some undistinguished progenitor but as its father.

"Darius has had the very best education." Frankenstein, still on the stairs, moved to place one hand on his progeny's shoulder. To do so he was required to stand some three steps above it, so lofty in stature was the creature. "The most learned tutors were procured from all the great nations of the world." He smiled benignly upon the monster. "It was my wish that he be as fully realized a man as you or I. Of course, given the unique circumstances of his birth, Darius cannot move about the world the way you or I do."

"Except at night." The creature's voice, too, was melodious, so at odds with its grotesque appearance that, if one were disposed to meet it in the dark, one would imagine it an angel or a god. "Then, I am free to roam where I will." It extended a hand toward the table. "Come, let us take tea. Shall I amuse you with tales of my origins? Most people are born into this world through ordinary means. I myself was born through extraordinary means indeed."

For more than an hour, we sat with the creature Darius, while it poured tea and pressed small cakes on us and told astonishing tales of its nocturnal wanderings, which seemed to take in the length and breadth of the city, leaving no street or lane unexplored. Dressed in a dark cloak and hat and with its face concealed behind a veil, the creature was able to attend theatrical performances and lectures (albeit, while seated at a remove from the other patrons) and roam the city's parks at will. Long after the great libraries and museums had closed for the day, it crept in and explored, sampling all manner of mortal knowledge. It went about with astonishing stealth. It had never been caught nor even suspected and was careful to leave no trace behind. In this way, it enjoyed a relatively normal—albeit nocturnal—existence.

"You are truly a master." I took my leave of Victor at the front door. "I am in awe of what you have achieved, my dear friend." I glanced around to see whether we were being observed before I kissed him. "Now I know the extent of your talents, I am certain there is nothing we cannot do together."

Yes, I had chosen very well. Victor Frankenstein was perfect. All that remained was to secure his passage to my homeland and to prepare a laboratory equal to his talent and ability.

I HAD retired to my bed that night with a volume of Aristotle, thinking to procure the wisdom of the ancients as a likely balm for sleep, and in this I was successful. Scarcely had I taken up the volume when my eyes felt heavy. I laid aside the book and plunged into the waters of Lethe. My sleep is necessarily deep, as is usual for those of my kind, who often find ourselves wearied by the requirements of our hereditary duties. I had known my father to sleep uninterrupted for some twenty hours until, fearful he had somehow died without their noticing, his servants made a terrible din to wake him.

It is therefore not surprising that I slept on through the noisy breaking of my windowpane and the subsequent invasion of my rooms. I woke all at once, with the conviction that someone—something—had entered my bedroom. My candle had long since gone out and the room was sufficiently dark as to make clear vision impossible. I merely sensed the interpositioning of some huge, ragged shape between myself and the window. Then his hands were at my throat.

"Do you think you can deceive me, Caleb Donnithorn?" His elegant voice, so cultured at the tea table, was a low rumble in my ears as the huge fingers pressed against my neck. "I know what you are even if my father does not! I have divined your intentions toward him." He shoved me hard against the bed. "You would entice him away to serve you!"

I clawed at him, fighting to draw breath, but my efforts were in vain. He aimed to snuff out my life this night and leave my body in the bed, an empty shell. I summoned every last vestige of my strength and, heaving my body upward, managed to throw him off. With a grunt of surprise, he fell onto his back, and I was able to stand and draw breath. "Get out. Your presence here, this disturbance, has already alerted the proctor. The alarm has been given. Already they are on their way to take you."

"You shall never have him." He climbed to his feet and felt his way to the door. "Never. I will make sure of it. Mark me well, for I mean what I say." He lingered for a moment, his great bulk filling the doorway, and then he was gone.

An hour later, having bathed the abrasions on my throat and set myself more or less to rights, I returned to bed, but had hardly closed my eyes when Norton, whom I knew from lectures, appeared with an urgent message from Victor Frankenstein: I was to attend at once. "He said to come to the farmhouse," Norton advised, "as quickly as you can. His servant said it was dreadful serious."

As before, I made my way to the rented house in which Frankenstein had located his laboratory, but this time I went on horseback, not bothering with a trap or carriage. I had just reached the last bend in the road when I saw the flames, leaping up into the night like living tongues. I dismounted and ran but, the fire being already well under way, there was nothing I could do. Some of the local people had turned out, several of them clutching buckets, and I saw Victor standing to one side, watching as his life's work went up in flames.

"Victor. I only just received your message."

"Caleb… have you seen…? Did you see?" He gestured weakly at the inferno. "He's in there. Darius. I know this. I know he's in there. He's done this to punish me. We had a dreadful falling out, you know. He accused me of abandoning him. He cursed me and called me awful names." His face was a mask of soot, through which paler tracks had been worn by tears. His eyebrows and the ends of his hair were singed.

"What am I going to do?" He clutched my arms and shook them. "Good God, he is everything to me!"

"Calm yourself." I drew him near to me and held him. His slender body was wracked with sobs, and violent tremors ran the length of him. "When the flames die down, I will send men to search for him."

"They will find nothing!" It came out as a strangled sob. "He would never subject himself to the common gaze. He could not. He is not of this world, Caleb! He cannot defend himself." He pressed his fists against his eyes. "Oh God, all of this is my fault. All of it."

"Victor, my dear friend, I will aid you in whatever way I can. It may be that Darius survives this conflagration. We will search for him together, you and I." I managed to persuade him away from the wreck of the burning house, but he would retreat no farther than the road, where he insisted on watching the progress of the fire. He believed—or hoped—the creature still lived and, as its creator and progenitor, could not abandon it.

The fire burned all night, and by dawn there was nothing left of the farmhouse except the foundation stones and a smoking pile of embers. I retired to my own rooms, unable to do anything of use as regarded the fire. When I was certain it had been destroyed, I dispatched a carefully worded letter to Victor Frankenstein, expressing regret over the loss of his laboratory and offering to fit a more suitable location with everything that he might need to carry on his great work. I enclosed a ticket for the tube network and directions to Castle Donnithorn, and before I left, I paid the three men I'd hired to set fire to Victor Frankenstein's laboratory. They had neglected to destroy the monster that Victor, in his fervid and creative madness, had made, but one cannot expect to have everything his own way, and I am a patient man.

Caleb Donnithorn: Inter-European pneuma network. 1850

"IT WOULD appear you have a problem."

I did not need to turn my head. Even if I had recognized his voice, I had no desire to engage in social intercourse with such a man. I moved to exit the compartment, but I was too late: the train had already lurched into movement, its snaking metal body pulled by the expanding vacuum at the other end of the line. If I chose to exit now, I would be rent to pieces. "It would appear," I said, "that you are on the wrong train, sir."

He wore the same long coat and the same brimmed hat as he had in the tavern. After a moment he settled himself into the seat next to me, smiling slightly. "But we are both traveling to the same destination."

"I hardly think so," I replied.

There was something hard, something dark and steely in him, some eminent resolve. Looking at him, I was reminded of the man I had seen in the library all those years ago, and my vision of dark wings. The pale outline of his visage filled the whole of my peripheral vision. I took up the newspaper I'd bought at the train station and made a great show of shaking it open and holding it before me.

"Where is he?"

"Of whom are you speaking?" I asked.

"Victor Frankenstein. He was last seen in conversation with you outside an alehouse. He has not been seen since."

Again... do it again like that... oh my God, my God. His nude body had arched and bent when the frenzy seized him, throbbing his seed over his thighs and belly. He clawed at the bedclothes as a series of powerful secondary shocks rolled through him, wave upon wave.

Yes, I had enjoyed Victor Frankenstein body and soul. His touch upon my flesh had unleashed many years' worth of loneliness and pent-up longing. He had remorselessly stripped me and stood me naked before the cheval glass in his rooms.

You are beautiful, Caleb Donnithorn. Standing behind me, his arms about me, his hard cock pressing against my buttocks, my entire being throbbed to the music of his desire. He leaned in so his silken erection rubbed gently against me, and I listened to myself whimper as my own cock twitched, a trickle of anticipatory fluid leaking from the tip. *Let me pleasure you.* He laid me down upon his bed and took my cock into his mouth, licking and sucking, drawing my desire until it tingled in the soles of my feet and the curve of my spine. I lay still and allowed it, my impending release filling me up, cresting as a swollen river crests. I abandoned all restraint and gave myself over, listened to the sound of my own voice crying out in rapture as he brought me to my peak.

My strange companion regarded me from the other side of the compartment. It had begun to annoy me. "Are you retained by the police?" I asked him. "If so, I insist you tell me the purpose of your journey."

"Surely you can puzzle it out," he said.

I turned a page of the newspaper. "I regret this train has no scheduled stops. You unfortunately will be compelled to accompany me to Transylvania."

"Where is he? He has not been seen by anyone. He has failed to attend his lectures. Everyone who knows him worries that he has fallen upon some... accident."

I could feel the heat of his body through my clothes. We were sitting close together, his thigh touching mine. I wondered what he would do if I turned, without preamble or rationale, and kissed him? Would he strike out at me, curse me? Would he, as so many men did when confronted with their own essential natures, attack me? "Under what authority do you ask me?" I demanded. "Are you following me?"

"What have you done with Victor Frankenstein?"

"I have done nothing with Victor Frankenstein." *Yes, there... oh my darling... oh mein kostbarer Liebling... oh mein geliebtes... so gut, fühlt sich es so gut.* "I have done nothing with Victor Frankenstein that he did not wish me to do."

"And what about Mary Shelley? What have you done with her?"

"You no doubt read of her sad demise in the newspaper." I kept my voice level, and my tone in no way betrayed the irritation I was feeling. "Such a terrible loss."

"What did you do to Victor Frankenstein?" he asked. "I would know."

I laid down my newspaper, turned, and very deliberately pressed him back against the seat. "You are much too inquisitive, sir. I think you must desist questioning me. What did I do to Victor Frankenstein?" I laid my mouth against the side of his neck, my tongue caressing the smooth column of his throat, and I whispered it to him. Clearly he had not expected my assault upon him to be so unabashedly carnal. I whispered and I felt him tense, his entire body held rigid. "I did nothing to Victor Frankenstein that he did not truly want, deep in his most secret heart."

Afterward we had lain together, Frankenstein and I, our bodies bathed with the sweat of our exertions.

Tell me that you love me. Tell me the truth.

Victor, of course I love you… I want you to come away with me. I want you to live with me forever….

Forever, Caleb? Forever is a very long time.

My pursuer caught and held my wrist and turned his face so we were gazing into one another, locked together in some mute and nameless struggle. "Where is Mrs. Shelley?"

"Have you not read the papers, sir?" I slipped easily from his grasp. "Mrs. Shelley is dead." He blinked. "Dead?"

"Yes." I turned up the page so he could see it. "Of a brain tumor. Did you know her?"

He took off his hat and tossed it onto the opposite seat. "You know I did not." His expression was one of profound consternation. He was not unhandsome, but there was something haunted, something desperate in his features. He seemed to be running from some essential and very personal truth. "I did not know her…." He shook his head. "I did not know her at all."

I shrugged. "I cannot think why such questions trouble you, in that case."

"It concerns my business," he said. I wondered what his business was. His hands were smooth and uncallused, the fingernails neatly trimmed, the palm and fingers resolutely clean. There was a tiny spot of ink on the middle finger, just below the tip, and a corresponding callus, most likely created by the pressure of a pen. A scholar, then.

"How did she die, truly?" He wasn't even looking at me now, but at some point on the opposite wall, or perhaps out of the window at the passing scenery. "Did you…. That is to say—"

"No, I didn't kill her—although you should be grateful you ask this question here, instead of in my homeland, where I would be compelled to challenge you for such an assertion." I folded the newspaper away. "Such a fight is usually to the death."

He was silent for a long time, and I wondered if he had slipped into the kind of trance that affects mortals sometimes, a waking dream. "I only ever met the lady once. It is an encounter I have never forgotten." He spoke quietly, as if to himself. The train swayed a little, the seals between the compartments popping gently as the air redistributed itself. "And you, sir—I suspect you are not at all what you seem to be. What are you, exactly?" We were passing over an elevated trestle spanning a river gorge, somewhere in the mountains between Munich and Bucharest.

"What do you mean?" The question made him uncomfortable.

"How much have they told you, these warrior monks? Hm?"

He drew back sharply, as if I'd physically struck him. "How do you know about that?"

I watched his eyes and the attitude of his mouth. Men often betray themselves without knowing what they do. I suspected he was no different. "Where you came from? Have they told you that? How came you to their habitation, sir? Of your own accord, under your own power, walking as free men do with a will of your own? Did those monster-killers tell you what you really are?" In truth, I'd recognized his esoteric nature from the beginning.

The blood drained out his face, leaving behind the deathly pallor of a corpse. He was quite visibly shaken. "Ego te ligo in nomine Jesu, potestate Crucis sancti, potestate pretiosissimi Sanguinis Domini nostri Jesu Christi—"

"Oh, stop." I fought hard not to laugh at him. "You think I'm the Devil? Is that what you're afraid of?" I sat back and crossed one leg over the other. "It's always Satan with you people. If I were truly demonic, and possessed of the powers of air and darkness, do you think I'd be sitting here on this train, like any common peasant?"

"No." He cleared his throat. "I don't suppose so. It isn't something I think about."

"Yes, you do. You suspect, although you have no proof, that your origins are much more complicated."

How could I even begin to frame such a fact? Yes, I recognized him, but it had no bearing on the situation. I could hardly tell the man the essential nature of his being—that he was of an ancient and powerful race; that he could move back and forth through time, not constrained as mortals are; that he and I knew each other now, but the next time we met, and all the other times after that, he would have forgotten me, because such amnesia is necessary if the machinery of this world is to run predictably.

His body was so still, and yet I knew his mind was racing, as was his powerful heart, thudding mercilessly beneath his human-seeming skin and bone.

"Well?"

My question was never answered. The train gave a shuddering heave and, without any further warning, flung itself over the embankment into open space.

December, 1850

Brasov

Diary of Ada Lovelace

THE DOCTORS say it will not be long. I say I have calculated the remainder of my life and, expressed as a series of percentages, it forms a very cold number indeed. When I tell this to my esteemed gentlemen physicians, they profess themselves unamused and appear quite shocked at what I am told is inappropriate humor in a lady. I can do nothing about their shock. Nevertheless, I am a realist and a woman, and I know the signs of the body and, in this, I am correct. I am dying.

Suppose a mortal woman to have endless potential lives, each one stored up in some repository located firmly elsewhere, and suppose this mortal woman might, by dint of her intelligence and her access to reason, find such material in any one of these accessory lives to suitably bind up her own. That is to say, she might seek to supplement her own life force. Alas, there is no such vessel. It is desirable to guard against such exaggerated ideas as they might arise. In considering any new subject, there is frequently a tendency, first, to overrate what we find to be already interesting or remarkable; and, secondly, by a sort of natural reaction, to undervalue the true state of the case when we do discover our notions have surpassed those that were really tenable. Thus I cannot be expected to live. I *cannot* live. I will die.

Outside my window—which is not truly my window, but the window of my borrowed villa, which is itself not even a villa but a lodge, built of native wood, warm and impenetrable to even the coldest northern winds—there is a train line, a narrow thing snaking imperiously through thick spruce forests and narrow mountain passes as if it had every right in God's creation to be there. I have no reason to use Mr. Brunel's fine conveyance, but if I had, there is a little station just down over the next rise, in the village, of which I could avail myself—if I had a reason. I do not. The work continues as it must do, as it has always done, as it will do long after I have drawn my last and am vanished to dust. Yes, there is a little station there and the train might take me anywhere at all in the world, except there is nowhere I wish to go. I have not even the comfort of oblivion, knowing as I do that even a little sedative will inevitably produce those misshapen creatures of the mind we call nightmares, and so I am required to suffer the constraints of conscience. By "conscience" I mean that portion of the intellect which assesses one's position in the world, to the extent that one has either fulfilled one's promise or fallen woefully short. As the sand in the hourglass of my life runs out, I am forced to consider that I, Ada Lovelace, may yet fall short of my own expectations. That is a bitter thought. Too bitter, I fear, to be effectively considered.

I had always thought to make something miraculous of this human life. The drawings I have thus far completed and the calculations I have made will no doubt find their way back to Babbage, as does everything of mine. Would there might be some other, greater project to which my soul and my intelligence could be appended, and thus bring about something remarkable. I fear it is too late now. As my famed progenitor Lord Byron would say, "Sorrow is knowledge, those that know the most must mourn the deepest, the tree of knowledge is not the tree of life." Indeed, that tree of knowledge so often bears a fatal fruit which we must pluck. Have I been born for death alone? Is this to be the summit of my understanding? I am Lord Byron's daughter. Surely there is, at least for me, something more than this?

The little servant girl is here, with my tonic. I fear I am obliged to drink it, even though it does not one jot of good.

December, 1850
Brasov
Diary of Ada Lovelace

THE WINTER snows have begun, and our little hamlet is by now sadly cut off from the surfeit of civilization. I sit by the window, watching particles of white tumbling from the sky and listening to the occasional wind. The air is bitingly cold, and on those occasions when I have ventured out to breathe this ungentle freshness, I have returned with my cheeks and the tip of my nose glowing red. If one did not know otherwise, one would say it is the glow of health.

I slept fitfully and toward morning I felt something loosen, as though a stubborn knot deep within the flesh had become untangled. In my half-sleep I dreamed the whole of my being had begun to dissolve as matter does in the presence of fire. My cries woke the night nurse, who came running. My bed, my nightclothes, all were soaked, the result of a hemorrhage while I slept. At least Magda prevented them from bleeding me. In my present state, such would constitute an excess of good care—or at the very least, the philosophical equivalent of carrying coals to Newcastle.

I have been at work on some Notes supplementary to Babbage's treatise on the calculation engine, which I hope will prove illuminating. There are innumerable good uses to which it might be put, but mostly I would caution against extreme expectations. Nothing salutary can come of wishing a thing to be other than its nature dictates. It is what it is.

December 2, 1850
Brasov
1:15 a.m.
Diary of Ada Lovelace

Magda bade me to keep my bed, but my native curiosity will not be assuaged. A most horrible accident has occurred. A little farther up the line, one of the tubes enclosing the pneumatic railway has come unfastened from the iron bolts that moor it to the rock. The train has fallen some distance and is lying in a cleft between two hills. Already they have dispatched men to go and search for it, but no one is truly certain where it is. Mr. Popesçu, our driver, says they will have great difficulty in finding survivors, as that entire area is quite rugged and full of hidden obstacles.

I am resolved to stay awake until the outcome shall be known.

2:30 a.m.
Diary, Ada Lovelace.
Brasov

A PARTY of local men have reached the train line, but the news is sad indeed: there are but two survivors. Since there is no suitable hostelry in the area, I have directed the men to bring them here. At the very least we can provide accommodations amenable to their recovery until a doctor can be summoned. Magda attempted to remonstrate me. She believes undue exertion will hasten what she calls the deterioration of my "condition." Since I have but a scant handful of days left me, I fail to see how it can matter. I have prepared rooms for them and have directed Magda and the others to see to their needs. I believe this might prove a much more burdensome obstacle than Babbage's fine machine: men are not, after all, analytical engines, but are composed of myriad parts and pieces, the which mere Reason alone cannot suffice to explain.

December 3, 1850
Brasov
10:30 a.m.
Diary of Ada Lovelace

THE FIRST to awaken is, inevitably, the Rumanian. At first he does not speak, and I wonder if perhaps the accident has damaged some vital aspect of the intellectual machine. His eyes are dark, heavy-lidded with fatigue and pain, and his skin is as pale as wax. I send Magda away and tend to him myself, offering at first a little water and then some weak tea and, finally, soup.

"What is this place?" He speaks English most excellently, but with the odd intonation one learns to expect from foreigners.

"You are safe. There was an accident. The train came loose from its moorings and many were killed."

He accepts the news in silence. "Where is Mary? We were to travel together."

"I do not know the lady of which you speak. I am Ada, Countess Lovelace."

He was far too weak to allow more than a mere moment or two of conversation before slipping into sleep, and so I left him. His companion and the only other survivor was a Dutchman who had suffered some small cuts and bruises that obligingly disappeared within a very short space of time. I suppose it possible that some persons, by virtue of their unique physiology, have bodies that heal quickly, and well. He appeared otherwise to be unharmed. He says his name is van Willigen, that he is originally from Maastricht but has been studying at an English university. He thinks he may have been traveling in the company of other students, some of whom were journeying home to the Carpathian region to spend the Christmas holidays with family. When I ask him what happened to his books, he replies, "They were lost when the train fell." His body may be healed but as far as his mind is concerned, he exists in a strangely enfeebled state, much given to tears and sudden outbursts of emotion. I press tea on him and chocolates and some sweet cherries preserved in wine, a Christmas delicacy, but he will not be consoled.

December 5, 1850
Brasov

MY RUMANIAN patient steadfastly avoids the Dutchman, yet when I press him, he refuses—in the most polite manner possible—to answer me. I have asked my doctors to examine him, but he refuses this as well—again, with as much native charm as ever one could wish or expect—and advises me that he has no need of physic. He is as pale as ever he was, and yet his pallor does not seem to arise from an underlying illness. In this I envy him.

"We were told the iron cages holding the train uncoupled from the rock," I said to the Dutchman one evening. We were sitting at table, having long since finished a light repast, which the Dutchman merely picked at, his stomach not yet being strong enough to take solid nourishment. He spent much time in his rooms, reading or resting on his bed, and did not engage in discourse with myself, the Rumanian, or anyone else.

"They make iron cages and these trains...." He had been reading something, a slim volume bound in leather whose title I could not see. "They are clever." He peered at me as if seeing my face for the very first time. "Have you ever witnessed the flooding of the Nile?"

I confessed I had not.

"It is an incredible phenomenon. I think...." He gazed ahead of him and blinked several times in succession, quite rapidly, the movement of his lashes like the wings of a startled butterfly. "Pneumatic trains. Have you ever witnessed the flooding of the Nile?"

It occurred to me that his mind might have suffered damage in the accident, if indeed his body did not....

I find myself weary for a large portion of the day and thus I keep to my rooms, dozing when I feel it necessary, waking sometimes to read or to derive some equations as the mood strikes me. My Rumanian friend looks in on me and now and then engages me in conversations, which are laudable chiefly for their brevity. By this I do not mean to imply our intercourse is labored—God forbid!—but my current lethargy, which daily grows more tedious, has become my nearest interlocutor. He is most interested in my notes on Babbage's difference engine and engages me in discourse on the subject for as long as I am able. His main interest lies in alternative applications for the engine and whether it might be harnessed for medicinal uses, for the curing of diseases or for the more thorough investigation of such afflictions as continually harass mankind.

"You are unwell." He reached for my hand and held it between his own, a gesture that in another would be unacceptably familiar. "Your pulses grow fainter by the day." He sought my gaze. "Might I carry out a cursory examination?"

I gave my consent. "I did not realize you were a medical man."

"My capacities are considerable." He drew down each of my lids in turn, examined my eyes, and blew out his breath. "My lady, you are, I fear, significantly enfeebled." His declaration fell into the silence that lay between us, a chill penumbra.

"Not at all sir. On the contrary, I am dying." I arranged my shawl about my shoulders. "My doctors advise me it is a matter of days."

"Days." His face was suddenly grave. "I am... sorry."

Just beyond the window glass, the world slumbered under a blanket of new snow, and tiny flakes, almost too small to be seen, twirled in the errant breezes. "As am I." The bitterness in my own voice surprised me. I thought myself altogether resigned to my fate. Caleb gazed at me, and it seemed that his observation took in not only myself, the room, and our immediate milieu, but something of infinitely larger scope. I fancied I was dissolved in that gaze and reduced to my component elements, my whole self stripped bare, an assemblage of cold integers, eternal and unchanging.

"So tell me," he said, "about the difference engine."

December 6, 1850
Ada Lovelace
Brasov

SOMETHING IS wrong with my Rumanian friend, Caleb. Yesterday he kept his rooms until well past noon, responding to none of our entreaties. He could not be coaxed into our society by any means whatsoever. This afternoon I saw him making his way up the stairs, and so weak and ungainly did he appear that I sent for my own physicians, but he would have none of it.

"A lingering effect of the accident, my Lady. No doubt it will resolve itself in time."

I would have shrugged off his excuse, except for one curious occurrence: Caleb and I were sitting together, chatting amiably (I thought) when he suddenly and without warning rose to his feet, with such an expression of alarm that I feared some new catastrophe. He reached an arm in front of him, as if desiring contact with some phantasm that only he could see and, without a sound, pitched forward onto his face on the floor.

"*STRIGOI.*" OUR driver, Mr. Popesçu, makes the Sign of the Cross and spits on the floor. The Dutchman only watches these proceedings grimly, unable to keep his gaze from the prone figure of Caleb, lying full length on the sofa. "Get rid of it while you can."

Van Willigen is silent, and so we wait until Caleb regains full consciousness. He is surprised to see us sitting round him like figures at a wake, and he professes incredulity when I advise him of the situation.

"The *strigoi* must feed at least once a fortnight," Popesçu says. "He will want to sate his hunger." He points two fingers at Caleb, a warding gesture I have often seen in the peasant peoples of this region. "*Strigoi*. Devil."

December 7, 1850

Ada Lovelace

Brasov

DURING THE night, there was a significant issue of blood, more violent than any that has gone before. I woke Magda, who summoned the doctors, both of whom discoursed for nearly three-quarters of an hour on how best to treat me. Their deliberations are useless and I send them all away. The loss of blood weakens me, bringing all my emotions to the fore, and I alternately rage and weep, inconsolable. I wonder where my continence has gone, that I cry so easily, that I lose myself in anger.

Toward morning I surface from a dream of dark forests to find Caleb sitting by my bed, holding my hand. His dark eyes burn with an unnatural fire and a compassion I thought never to find in my fellow creatures. "Tell me." His touch is gentle, smoothing back my hair. "I can only do as I am bidden, no more or less than that."

I see plainly the hours of my future, glistening before me like individual gems, so few. I cannot extend my days. I will go out of the world mute and unprotesting. There is no succor anywhere. My life is draining out of me like water from a corrupted cistern, and nothing I do or say, nothing I think, no power in earth or Heaven can save me. This is the hour of my death. I think of Popeşçu, making his warding gesture: *Strigoi, Devil.* Others have sold their souls for less.

With the last of my strength, I give myself to him.

Jacob van Willigen
1850
Brasov

The final confession of Jacob van Willigen, Fellow of the Society of Psychical and Esoteric Research, traveler, scholar, and heretic. Bless me, Almighty God, for I have sinned. It has been ten thousand years since my last confession.

I am not mad—at least, I do not imagine myself insane—but what madman truly knows himself? It may be I am entirely beyond the help of mortal medicine and merely think myself among the province of the sane. For all I know, my entire life until now may have been a florid delusion, the product of a brain fever, a cloud passing across the mind, or a dream. This jarring of the consciousness occurred when the train leapt from its enclosure and fell, dashing itself and its occupants against the mountain and hurtling us into that awful chasm. Since my recovery (I name it thus, even though it seems more a derangement of the senses than a return to them), I have dwelt in a state of profound confusion.

When I consider my previous life—living in England, studying at the university—it has no more solidity than a hallucination.

Like a hallucination, too, is the existence I remember now, a life occurring outside the realm of the usual, and so bizarre in form and substance that even now I cannot reconcile myself to its veracity. When I search my memory for some temporal referent, the only thing I can come up with is that I had somehow, through some agency not my own, been transported to a much earlier era, a time of poverty and plague.

The nearest thing I can remember is coming to myself in an unfamiliar bed—not this bed, here in Lady Lovelace's borrowed rooms, but another, much cruder, made of hempen cloth stretched between poles of rough-hewn wood, unclothed by even the coarsest of blankets, the pillow dank and greasy with God knows which of Perdition's dark elements. The walls around me were naked stone, roughly dressed and brilliantly orange, and for the life of me, I could not determine what sort of stone this was, as I had never seen its like before. A single candle flickered on a little table near my head, and a straight-backed chair had been placed against the wall, underneath a window scarcely large enough to admit even the faintest strains of morning light. The rough robes I wore seemed faintly familiar, as did the plain leather sandals on my feet. My hair had been cut short, and my beard, which until now had never been allowed to grow, was clipped close to my face. I found out these things by the simple method of touch. There was no mirror in the room and the small window was glassless, open to the weather. I waited, hoping some element of my surroundings would stir sufficient memory in me, but nothing in that awful little room seemed at all familiar. It was as if I had been picked up by a whirlwind and deposited in this place, for reasons unknown to me.

Then I heard a sound I thought I recognized: a man's voice, raised in song. He was joined by several others, and I knew at once where I had landed.

I was in a monastery.

"...AND YOU say you remember nothing of how you came here? Of where you were before your arrival?" The monk's name was Theodius, or so he told me; he advised me to address him as Theo. "It is not a Rumanian name," he said, "but then, I am not a Rumanian. You, my friend, are from even farther away if I am not mistaken." He told me they had saved the clothing I had been wearing when some of the monks found me—bloodied, incoherent, and at the point of death—near the monastery's front door. He showed me a homespun tunic of hemp or linen, much stained and spattered with blood but curiously seamless, as though it had been constructed as a single piece, and also the loose trousers such as the peasants wear, and a pair of leather boots. "We were obliged to cut your hair in order to treat the wounds on your head. I have never seen such cuts, very deep, and they bled mightily. I assume you came to us from some great battle, so violent were your injuries. You were a most difficult case, even for us, and we set great store by our physic here." His smile was kindly and his manner invited me to disclose everything I knew, but I feared to do so. I knew that any wounds I might have would close easily, and of their own accord. It had always been so. When I was at university, I stumbled upon a loose paving stone, returning to my lodgings late at night. I struck my forehead as I fell, cutting myself and also scraping the palms of my hands quite badly. I went into my rooms and cleansed my wounds with soap and water. The torn edges of my skin slid together like the edges of two carpets meeting, the injury vanishing as if it had never been. I imagined the flesh of everyone behaved similarly; it wasn't until much later that I realized my case was unique and unprecedented. The bloodied clothing could possibly belong to me, since I bleed as freely as any other man. The story of the scalp wounds I was less inclined to believe, and I wondered what might cause so venerable a Christian to lie to me.

"Indeed you have lain here insensible for several weeks, and there were many times that we feared you might not live. The gates of Heaven stayed open for you, my friend."

Something not quite a memory swam up to the surface of my consciousness. I was suffused with a cold misery. "No. I will never be permitted to enter Paradise."

The silence between us rang with unuttered questions—questions for which I had no answers. I wanted to tell him everything I knew—

indeed, I owed him at least that much in return for their tender care of me—but I remembered absolutely nothing.

"The scars you bear on your back...." Clearly the subject gave him difficulty. "Those we have never seen before."

A sudden flush of heat prickled the skin of my face. "I permit no man to look on them." My fists clenched so hard my forearms ached—*a sword, cutting them down to and fro, a great battle*—and I rose out of my chair, my body throbbing with rage.

An old monk... He is an old monk; he is nothing.

I fell back, weak and sweating. "Forgive me." My tears came in a rush, and I bent my head and cried. "I do not know what I am doing."

The chief blessing of the monastery as far as I could see was the ability it gave me to structure my days and thus to prevent my mind from plunging into the abyss. The constant round of prayer, meditation, study, and work was as healing to me as any tincture or potion, as were the monastery's silent times, when men were encouraged to search their souls. The fact that the building was located on an island in the middle of Lake Snagov meant that any forays onto the mainland—or, God forbid, into one of the larger towns like Bucureşti, where the pleasures of the flesh could be indulged—were unlikely. The abbot kept one boat and that for his discretionary use alone. Occasionally some two or three of the older and more experienced brothers would use it to travel to market, but that was all. We were profoundly isolated in our island fortress, and I was glad. It is said that, given sufficient temptation, even angels will fall.

Our lives in those days—this was long before the invention of the wonderful machines we nowadays take for granted—were agrarian and peaceful. We rose with the sun and went to bed at dusk regardless of the season, rousing ourselves throughout the night to perform the necessary prayers. Our monastery was well supplied with everything we needed by a rich and powerful patron whose generous gifts ensured an unending stream of prayers for his immortal soul.

I was assigned to work the vegetable garden with Brother Elias and Brother Matei. It was thought that exposure to fresh air would speed my healing. Since there were no mirrors in Snagov, I was unable to examine my head wounds except by touch, but Brother Matei advised me that my scalp looked like the proverbial ploughed field. This worried me considerably less than the loss of my memory, which extended back only as far as my arrival in the monastery and no further.

"Perhaps when the voivoide comes he will be able to help you." Matei and I were weeding the potatoes together one afternoon—a sunless day but curiously warm, as if the dove gray sky were emitting an arcane fire. The vegetable gardens were located behind the monastery, in the shade of a great tree whose shape reminded me of the mighty terebinth, from which turpentine is derived and which grows in abundance in the Holy Land.

"The voivoide? Who is he?" Since early that morning we had been busy, bending and walking, pulling out weeds so deeply embedded that at times I could have sworn they were rooted to the very stone itself. My back ached from the unfamiliar work and I was glad of an opportunity to rest.

"The voivoide is the ruler of this region, a very pious man. If you are fortunate, you may be invited to meet him." Matei shrugged. He was tall and fair, with ecstatic blue eyes and the longest eyelashes I had ever seen on a man. His pale skin burned easily under the sun, and his nose and forehead were red and peeling. When the weather was truly hot, as it was today, he frequently stripped to his drawers, a practice frowned upon by the other monks but, it must be said, necessary, for even here the summer sun was hot and our thick woolen robes soon became as heavy as a coat of mail.

I didn't mind when Matei did this; he was a fine figure of a man and I enjoyed looking at him. He in his turn enjoyed being looked at, and if he chanced to turn and see me watching him, he grinned. The monastery discouraged intimate friendship among the men and, although such fraternization was not actively punished, the abbot made it quite clear that any taint of unnatural relations would be subject to reprisals. I believed Matei had already been punished in some fashion or other, for his naked torso was crisscrossed with scars whose pattern suggested whip marks.

The monastery's evening meal was usually a somber affair, with simple food and silence among the diners. The abbot encouraged all of the men to think upon their sins and to repent in their hearts, even as our bodies received the bounty of God's earth. On rare occasions—holy days and days dedicated entirely to prayer—one of the monks would read aloud from the Holy Scriptures while the rest of us ate, and thus our souls were nourished as well as our bodies. A visit from the voivoide, however, required the sort of elaborate preparations I had never in my life seen, and the monastery's humble kitchen was a flurry of activity from dawn until dusk.

"He must be a very important man." I remarked upon it to Matei, as we washed side by side at the basin that evening, our day's work accomplished, our bodies tired and sore. "Have you ever seen such an immortal haste?"

"Curious you should use that word." Matei dunked his head in the water and sluiced his face and neck, blowing and sputtering like an ox driven through a river. "There are some...." He glanced around him, then continued in a lower tone. "There are some who say the voivoide is not a man at all, but a demon."

The hair on the back of my neck prickled. "A demon." I tried to laugh but my face felt frozen. "Surely you don't.... Matei, surely you don't believe...." His expression told me he did indeed believe precisely that. "What evidence is there?"

"Only the evidence of one's own eyes." He scrubbed his face with a rough towel, reddening his pale cheeks. "I have seen him.... I have witnessed the things he has done, and I tell you, it is the truth."

"What manner of man is he? What does he do?" I couldn't imagine what Matei meant by these assertions. "Can he fly? Does he mount the winds and sail away?"

Matei crossed himself. "Jacob, don't blaspheme." He caught hold of my elbow. "Come. Let us go in to the meal. If we are absent, it will be cause for comment." He grinned. "You never know, the voivoide might take a liking to you."

It was interesting, I thought, how he had so completely avoided answering my question. The evasion made me more keen than ever to see the voivoide for myself and, if possible, to meet him.

The monastery's dining room had been transformed into a scene of palatial—albeit Godly—generosity. Great trenchers of food were laid end-to-end down the lengths of the joined tables, and huge baskets of fresh fruit and flowers had been arranged to best advantage. Many of the monks had already taken their places at table, but I saw the abbot in earnest conversation with a man I judged to be about my own age, beautifully dressed in rich robes dyed a deep scarlet. His long black hair was caught back from his face and held with a silver buckle, the remnant streaming over his broad shoulders like a swath of silk. He must have divined my gaze, for he turned and met my eyes, and I saw his were dark, framed by thick, sooty lashes, and he was beautiful beyond the notion of beauty, with the face of an angel. *I am lost,* I thought. *My eternal soul is lost.*

He turned and looked directly at me, as if he'd somehow heard my thought, and one long finger rose and pressed against his lips. *Say nothing.*

Five days later I left the monastery in the early hours of the morning, long before the sun was up.

Matei caught up with me at the front gate, his face wet with tears. "Where are you going? Why must you go?" He gripped my arms, my hands, embraced me. "Take me with you."

"Impossible. Matei, you are a good man. Stay here, where you can continue to do good. I beg you, do not follow me." His lips were salty, and when I kissed him, he clung to me, his long body racked by powerful emotion. I stepped into my small boat, waving to him, and then I turned away. I could not afford a look back. I must be away.

"Jacob!" Matei roared, and with a mighty lunge, he leapt toward the boat—but I had already pushed off from the shore, too far for him to reach me. The brackish waters of Lake Snagov closed over his head and he was drowning.

Horrified, I watched as his hands broke the surface and then his face, mouth open, gasping. I cursed aloud and, stripping off my tunic, dove in. There was a moment of black panic as the cold water rushed into my eyes and ears, but I quickly marshaled myself. *You must do this thing. You cannot leave him here to die.* I swept both arms through the water, searching for what I could not see and grasping nothing. Matei was close enough that I could hear his labored breathing but not close enough to touch. I drew a big breath in and dove beneath the waves, eyes open, my hands extended before me until I grasped a fold of his clothes, but he fought me, panicked, kicking out in all directions, flailing madly.

"Matei, no! It's me. It's Jacob." I caught hold of one shoulder and drew him close to me, clutching his body under the arms and swimming sideways toward the boat. Luckily it had not drifted too far, and I was able—with some difficulty and much unholy cursing—to heave him aboard. I held on to the gunwales, panting, listening to the frenzied hammering of my heart, and then, with a final effort of will, I slung myself over the side and into the boat. "Matei."

He wasn't breathing. His sculpted lips were blue and his eyelids half lowered over vacant eyes. *Please God, no… not him, not this one. Let me at least have one victory. You owe me that much.* I chafed his cold hands and patted his slack face. "Matei… it's me, Jacob."

And the Lord formed man of the dust of the ground, and breathed into his nostrils the breath of life; and man became a living being…. It was the gravest of all sins, I knew, to intrude where the God of all had been, and yet I could not let him die. I laid him on his back in the boat and, leaning low over him, I blew into his mouth and nose and waited, shivering, for some miracle, some transformation. "Matei." I smoothed his wet hair back from his forehead and touched his mouth. How often had I gazed upon him and dreamed of kissing those lips? He was everything good and decent in the world, a truly honest man who asked for nothing and gave much. "I should have saved you."

I clasped him in my arms and held him, and I kissed his mouth, pressing my own lips to his again and again. I sobbed, my back and shoulders heaving, aching with my burden. I leaned down and kissed the death off his lips, tasting the sweet salt of him.

He coughed—very slightly—and his head rolled to the side.

"Matei?" I lifted each of his lids in turn and peered at his blue eyes. "Matei, speak to me."

His body jerked, caught in the throes of a powerful spasm. He clutched at me, his eyes suddenly wide and frightened, and then he rolled onto his side and vomited a mass of dirty water. I stripped off my cloak and wrapped it around him and held him close to me, warming him with my body.

"Don't waste time," he said. "You must row as hard as you can for shore. We have to get away."

"You nearly died—you need warmth, a fire, hot food." I grasped the oars. "We will go back to the monastery."

"No!" He caught my arm and held it. "We will not."

There was a mastery in his tone I had never heard before and, not for the first time, I wondered what sort of life he had led before the cloister. I suspected he had been the leader of men—perhaps a military commander, a warrior of note.

"Matei, you are chilled."

"I am fit enough. Row." He would brook no disagreement. "Row. The sooner we can quit this place, the better it will go for both of us."

WE SET off at once across the country, moving quickly but only at night, for I feared discovery—by who or what, I did not know, but I sensed strongly that something was hunting me, something that very much wanted to find me, something that desired my death. If Matei knew of my fears or suspected something was amiss, he said nothing—indeed, as a traveling companion he was most fit, swift, and silent. As soon as the sky began to lighten, we would seek shelter, hiding ourselves in deserted shepherd's huts and abandoned farmhouses, sleeping uneasily and as long as we dared, our cloaks wrapped around us, our shivering bodies pressed close together for warmth. Matei whispered in his sleep, and many times I woke to find him sitting bolt upright, his back to the wall and an expression of absolute horror burned into his features.

It took us a little under a fortnight before we finally staggered into Matei's village in Bavaria, not far from the famous spa town of Bad Kissingen. The village itself was beautiful, picturesque in the extreme, but not, I fear, without its dangers: the great pestilence had scoured many of the hillside towns, leaving death and disease in its wake. Seeing as how it was early in the morning when we arrived, there was no one about, and I saw no reason for unease.

Matei, however, was unconvinced. "There should at least be a body about." The town was centered on a square of the usual sort, with a common well and merchants' stalls and a drinking trough for animals. "Old Fleugel," he said, "he is always sitting by the well or sometimes on the steps of the church." He indicated a handsome stone building just beyond. "He has nowhere else to go." In the coldest days of winter, this old man, Fleugel, would be given a warm space to sleep in some villager's stable or in the chimney corner of a house. It was his practice, Matei said, to sit by the well or linger near the stalls, pretending to tell fortunes and using his proximity to the villagers to beg for a scrap of bread or a mouthful of wine. He couldn't recall Fleugel ever having done an honest day's work in his entire life.

"Perhaps he has moved to another village." Even as I said it, I knew this was not correct, could not be correct—and then my gaze was drawn to a curious red mark on the door of a nearby house. *Quarantine.* My skin prickled and I was suddenly very cold. "Matei, we must leave immediately." I caught a fold of his tunic and pulled. "Now. We cannot linger. We must leave at once."

He ignored me and started up a steep grade toward a small wooden house set back from the others.

I caught up with him at the door, which had also been daubed with red. "Matei, I beg you, do not go in there. Do not."

Some of the villages, I knew, used a red circle or a star or the shape of an open eye. The mark on this door was an open eye, painted in red, marking the property for destruction. I saw Matei reach out and touch it with his fingertips and put his mouth against the wood and whisper to it: *My God, my God....* The door was unfastened, and I reached around Matei and pushed it open.

The inside of the house smelled like rotting meat, like the carcasses of animals hung up somewhere and left to decompose. It smelled like something had been forgotten, something hidden in a cupboard the way certain succulent cuts of meat are hung up in a larder and left until the flies are swarming in the flesh. We found his parents lying side by side in their bed. They had been dead awhile. The woman—Matei's mother—had her mouth open and flies were flying in and out of it, laying their eggs. They would be in the other bodily orifices as well.

His sister was dead also. Something had eaten her eyes. All three of them had bled heavily from the mouth and ears. All three of them were lying in their beds, fully clothed. Their faces weren't peaceful: this was no careful *memento mori* but a dance macabre. The stench was nothing; far worse was the weight in my chest. *"Et ego te absolvo a peccatis tuis… in nomine Patris, et Filii, et Spiritus Sancti."*

When I next came to my senses, I was on my knees in front of the door, scrubbing at the quarantine mark. I had somehow procured a pail of water and a rag, and the red paint had turned the water a deep, viscous scarlet. My fingertips were bleeding. I had scrubbed so deeply that I had savaged the wood. I had gouged deep holes in the door, and there were scalding tears on my face and the taste of salt in my mouth and I could smell something burning.

Fire, again. Why was it always fire? "They are burning the houses. They will come to burn this one as well." Matei took hold of my hands and raised me to my feet. "Come."

Those who had remained uninfected left their burned and ravaged villages and went elsewhere. They made the arduous journey through the mountains on foot, carrying their belongings in their hands or on their backs or pulling carts full of furniture and clothes. Their elderly and infirm perched atop the tottering piles like the spoils of some long and bloody war. At first they traveled to the great spa towns, hoping to find respite beside the healing waters and seeking spiritual sustenance from the churches. Always they were turned away, often by force, driven out by sword and fire. Finally they founded makeshift settlements in unused fields and by the side of the road. Those who could procure sufficient cloth erected tents, while others fashioned shelters out of whatever was at hand. These crude villages were barely fit for barnyard animals, lacking fresh water or proper privies, the ground a sea of mud and filth when it rained.

Some of the abler young men had gone into the forest and felled trees to build the shaky wooden huts that housed the very sickest, the elderly, the childbearing women, and their infants, but these temporary villages were overcrowded. One had to be careful not to tread on someone. These people wandered all day and all night, coughing continuously. Some were nervous coughs, dry coughs…

some were deeper noises with a wet sound at the end. Those were the ones who almost always died. And children crying, always crying, it never ended.... Little children with running noses and distended bellies, their naked hindquarters caked with filth, roaming like animals, forever crying until they, too, fell ill and were suddenly and permanently silent.

We found ourselves among them, Matei and I, and we wondered how long we had before the deathly buboes appeared in the folds of our skin, underneath our arms, or behind our scrotums.

I wondered why we had bothered to leave the monastery.

I didn't wish to linger, but Matei seemed unable—or unwilling—to leave, nor was he overeager to occupy himself with work. Where once he had gladly labored all day in the monastery gardens, now he slept much of the day away, waking just after dark to roam the margins of the settlement, looking for something he could neither name nor understand. Unable to sleep myself, I followed him, staying well behind so that if he turned he would perceive nothing in the darkness. I was careful to make my footsteps absolutely silent as I followed him throughout the night. Sometimes, weak from hunger (there was no ready source of nourishment for any of us in that place) or fatigue, he fell, and I would stand him on his feet, supporting him with his arm around my shoulders, until he was strong enough to walk alone. He never spoke to me during these curious altercations, nor did he address me by name. I often wondered if he rightly perceived me or (this seemed likely) he had decided I was merely some aberrant phantasm. With every day that passed, he relinquished a little of his reason.

SEVERAL DAYS after our arrival, word began to circulate about a mysterious figure seen at the bedsides of the dying and the most grievously ill. A tall man, many said, richly dressed but astonishingly pale of countenance. He passed among those poor languishing souls and occasionally paused to lean down and speak to them, to touch them. Inevitably, those to whom he spoke were dead by the time he passed along his way. His appearance piqued my curiosity, but by now

Matei was ill, and whatever time I might have passed in examination of this specter was devoted to caring for my friend.

"Jacob, look." We awoke one morning to dark clouds in a lowering sky and the promise of rain. Matei had come back from the forest, his tunic held above his thighs. "It is the sickness."

I touched the swollen places gingerly, afraid to cause him pain. The buboes were not black, as I had been led to expect, but white, pale protrusions of the flesh that resembled small roots. Apart from some little bruising at the site, there seemed no injury that I could readily divine. "Did you fall and strike yourself?" We were forever stumbling about in the dark. "Perhaps an insect bite?"

He pulled his tunic off, and I examined his bare torso, pale and heavily striated with those raised scars that resembled the marks left by a whip. At the base of his neck were two more buboes, smaller than those on his thigh but ominously dark. The tiny hairs on his arms were erect and he shuddered when I touched him. "Cold," he explained. "I might as well be drowning in Lake Snagov. I cannot get warm."

I built a fire out of such wood as I could salvage, defending it against usurpers and those who would steal the precious brands to start their own fires. From the monastery at Snagov, I had taken my Bible and a small prayer book, gorgeously illuminated and much beloved; these, plus the clothes on my back were the only things belonging to me. I spread some dry boughs and made as comfortable a bed for Matei as I could. Over and over he implored me to check myself, to let him search my flesh as he had searched mine, in case I too had been compromised, but I assured him, in as vague a language as I could, that such concerns were not necessary. I am not certain how I knew, but even then I understood I was not as other men, that the illnesses which daily felled them, which robbed them of blood and breath and spirit, had no power over me.

By noon that day he was feverish, his pale cheeks stained with a hectic flush. His hands and feet, he said, pained him horribly, but he assured me he could withstand it. I knew the worst was yet to come. I had seen how those infected with the pestilence died and how, toward the end, they struggled in the grip of painful seizures like men possessed by demons.

Like any other community, ours was beset by gossip, rumor, and superstition. Beliefs arose, seemingly of their own accord and having little or nothing to do with the doctrine of the established church. There were continual prayers and exhortations for mercy to gods and nature spirits and saints of dubious provenance. Three young men in the rough brown robes of the Franciscan order daily flagellated themselves before a wooden cross that had been erected near the massive open pits used to bury the dead, the blood from their streaming backs running down to soak the ground. Others, defiant to the last, decked themselves in their finery and danced to the music of lute and timbrel, or coupled openly, writhing on the filthy ground. An old man, clad only in sackcloth, roamed the encampment night and day, calling out for repentance, and was mostly ignored. Death was swift, sudden, and wholly expected.

By sunset Matei, feverish and ill, had begun to babble, sometimes in our common tongue and at other times in a language I did not understand. He clung to me, weeping, then thrust me away from him. "You are not natural," he said, during one of these episodes. "You are not a natural man. You are something other."

I sat with him, bathed his face and hands, stoked the fire, covered him, and told him the kinds of stories I would want to hear when my own time was come. Now and then I called his name and asked questions of him, but as the night wore on, his answers came more slowly until finally he could make no reply. I leaned over and lifted each of his eyelids and laid my palm flat against his chest. He was breathing—barely—but had slipped into unconsciousness as profound as the grave. I resigned myself to his death, for I had seen many others die like this and I knew what waited for him, what waited for us both.

"You care for him."

I came to myself suddenly, unaware I had slept. A man was standing in front of me, beautifully dressed in rich clothes, his cloak and doublet embroidered with fruit-bearing vines and the tiny, perfect figures of animals and birds. He seemed somehow familiar to me, and yet I knew, even as I beheld him, I had never seen him before. "Do I know you, sir?"

He crouched beside me and reached out a hand toward Matei. "He is near death." He tilted his head and regarded me with great compassion. "He cannot be saved, but I believe you know this."

I shrugged. "Look around you. They are all dying." A dog barked somewhere far off, and the sound of a child's sobbing cut through the darkness. I had seen small children and babies clinging to the body of a dead parent, tiny hands kneading at the putrefying flesh as if to extract nourishment. In their innocence they could not understand how their most fervent cries for help went unanswered.

"Do you want him to suffer?" He held his face close to mine, so close I could smell the faint odor of his skin, the traces of expensive perfumes that clung to his clothes. He gripped my forearms hard. "Or would you prefer a quiet, peaceful death?"

"He is a good man. We have traveled together for a long distance. He has been a friend to me." I felt the sting of tears against my lids. "If such a thing were even possible, I would wish it for a man such as him."

The stranger crouched beside me, heedless of the mud and filth. "I can give him a peaceful death. I am that angel that you seek."

He has taken leave of his wits. The man is insane. "You blaspheme."

"No." His eyes shone with an unnatural brightness, visible even in the dark. "No, I speak the truth. Absolutely the truth." A long shudder ran through him, and he clenched his hands convulsively. "For his peace I would pawn my own soul."

For a brief time, I existed in this moment as well as in some other time and place. I felt as though I were regarding the scene before me through the wrong end of a spyglass. "I will never be permitted to enter Paradise." My throat was dry, and my voice sounded strange to my own ears. I walked a small distance away and sat down on a large stone with my back to him. I could hear him moving around, could hear the slushy sound of his boots traversing the sticky mud, but I had not the courage to turn and look at him. I clasped my hands together to try to quell the shaking that seemed to reach into the very marrow of my bones.

He murmured a string of words I could not make out and then there was a silence more profound than anything I had ever heard.

"It is finished."

Caleb Donnithorn. Castle Donnithorn
April 17, 1850

WHEN I first explained my theory to Ada—that a machine could be constructed to capture the essential human essence at the moment of death—she dismissed it as entirely too fanciful to exist in truth. Victor has already begun his preliminary research into the qualities of the human soul, and this, coupled with an investigation of my physiology, will form the backbone of the mission. Working with such minds as these, the dual problem of my hereditary gift and the replacement of the soul should be solved in very short order. As soon as she had arrived, I made haste to introduce Ada to Victor, who had agreed to procure such materials as she might need. I explained no expense was too great and she must be both honest and explicit in her desires. "It is my wish that the work be completed as swiftly as possible, but also as completely as possible," I explained. "I am aware that such is outside your usual realm of expertise, but I have every confidence that your great intellect will no doubt bend itself accordingly."

Ada's brows arched. Already my gifts were at work in her, refining the shade and texture of her skin, adding a gloss to her hair, her eyes, a subtle shimmer of something not quite mortal. "You make it sound like a threat, Caleb."

"Never that." I had hoped she would be more compliant than Mrs. Shelley, but clearly I had underestimated what was obviously a strong will. "Merely a desire to see the completion of what will doubtless be a great work."

Ada requested a space of her own in which to work and, seeing as how the castle is much too large for my own needs, I happily acquiesced. Procuring the materials and equipment she required took some little time, even given the scope of my influence, but ultimately we were able to equip one of the castle's empty towers to her purpose, and she settled in to begin.

Victor's laboratory we chose to situate below ground, given that the cellars were the largest uninterrupted space available and because his portion of the work required electrical lines and other similar conduits to be strung, something not possible on the higher levels. I offered him the use of my Roma servants, but he declined, saying the equipment needed a delicate touch.

He was not entirely recovered from the fire and its aftermath—he had arrived at my castle still reeking of smoke—and would not take any nourishment or drink. "Darius is out there, Caleb, I know it."

"Of course," I said, careful to sound as if I believed it. "For certain. I know he will be found and you will be reunited."

"The work we are doing, you and I, is God's work, I know."

"Of course," I repeated. God's work? Let God do His own work. Let Him dirty his own hands. I would have nothing to do with it. "Very important work, Victor."

And so it began.

Diary—Jacob van Willigen
Castle Donnithorn

THE SEQUELAE to recent events are no more and no less than I would have expected, given circumstances and the reason for my journey. Since I had not taken the trouble to inform Brother Inish of the mission's status, it was inevitable a missive should arrive, and it did. Shortly after dawn this morning, one of Caleb's Roma servants looked in at my door and wordlessly handed me an envelope. It had arrived by the village pneuma network, he said, which surprised me. Inish could have sent the letter directly to me, unless this method provided him assurance of its receipt. Inish has never, to my knowledge, issued orders that were not properly witnessed. It is a tenet of our Society that an operative never acts alone: every action, every initiative, no matter how insignificant, must be vetted by at least one other member. If no member is available, any reasonable adult will do.

The communiqué was brief and very much to the point. *You are directed and enjoined to locate and destroy the abominable machine of one* Caleb Donnithorn *immediately. Any delay will constitute disobedience and will be dealt with accordingly.*

I'd pulled a chair in front of my window and sat for a while, watching the sun rise over the Carpathians, the slow spill of carmine light. Nothing stirred, but now and then from the valley below there came the tentative cry of a bird—a low, fluting noise that might have come from the mountains themselves. I thought back to my days in London, when I had done the bidding of Inish and the Society and considered myself well served. I remembered cool autumn evenings in the motherhouse, supping with the other members while discoursing on a myriad of subjects, our palates wet with wine or the Society's excellent cider, pressed from the best apples in our orchards. *At last*, I thought, sitting among them, *here is where I belong. This place is my home.* The great library was ever at my disposal, and I had passed many a pleasant winter afternoon sitting under its glorious ceiling with its scenes of demons and saints and angels, and likewise the chapel, a vaulted space of golden light, smelling of prayer and incense.

I thought also of the furtive looks and the muffled whispers that followed me wherever I went, or the air of suspicion with which some Society members regarded me. I thought of awakening in Snagov monastery in the midst of the medieval plague some four hundred years before, wearing monk's robes and tending the garden with Matei, and Brother Inish's strange reserve when I questioned him about my dreams, and the scars on my back that no one could explain. Surely I must have a history, as all men had a history, but why did I recall so little of it? Why did my memories leap from one century to the next— an improbable supposition, given my years—with no true coherence? What manner of creature was I?

"Jacob." His soft voice recalled me to myself. I had not heard Caleb come in. He stood just inside my door, still in his nightclothes, his dark hair shining like a raven's wing. "What is it?"

I shook my head. "I was sitting here, watching the sun rise."

He came to where I sat and laid his hands on my shoulders. His touch was gentle, his flesh warm, and yet I knew without a doubt that, despite his mortal origins, he was no longer truly human. "There are a great many questions in your mind, Jacob." He came to sit on the bed, where he could see me. "You are very troubled."

"Yes." Tears sprang to my eyes, and I scrubbed them away.

"My servant tells me you have had a communication from London." He saw the letter and picked it up. "With your permission…?" I nodded that he should read it. "You are to destroy my machine. This is as I expected. Your Brother Inish seems rather impatient that this should be accomplished soon. If I offer you resistance, you are instructed to dispatch me." He bent his head to gaze into my lowered face. "This afflicts you greatly. Why?"

"I feel I have just set foot upon a path which will, in time, guide me to all truth. I would not stray from it, and yet I must."

He nodded. "Would you like me to help you?"

"Help me?"

He drew a slow, meditative breath. "Jacob, whether you think it possible or not, I am able to restore those portions of your life that you have lost—rather, those portions that I believe were taken from you by Brother Inish and the Society. It is not unknown, this practice of removing memory. There are many alchemists now and in ages past who would create an elixir which, when consumed, would effectively erase a man's entire knowledge of himself."

His words frightened me. "I have never heard of such things."

"Nevertheless." He got up from the bed and went to stand at the casement. A narrow shaft of sunlight pierced the valley fog and lit up the forest, and here and there wavering fingers of smoke rose from certain of the houses. "Insofar as your Society has been researching me, I have also been researching it. Your Brother Inish and his confederates have grievously misled you, Jacob. Had they told you the truth, you would have long since cast off their ideology. Knowing what you do, a creature of your provenance, as old as the universe itself—"

"Stop." The words were like a clamor of bells. "No more."

"No, you must listen. It is vital that you understand the truth." In one quick, fluid movement, he pulled his nightshirt over his head and dropped it in a pile on the floor. Thus he stood before me, gloriously nude, a man wholly imagined in perfection, his skin as pale as ivory, his muscles standing out in sharp relief. He turned his back and showed again to me the two immaculate scars—livid, purple, great weals running from his shoulder blades to the curve of his waist. "The last thing they took from me before they bid me Fall, Jacob. My immortal wings."

"I don't believe you." My eyes felt hot and my pulse thudded in my throat. "It isn't possible. You are Caius Dumitrescue, in English, Caleb Donnithorn, son of Caleb the Younger, a Rumanian nobleman who immigrated to America."

"Yes." He nodded. "Yes, Jacob, I am all of those things, and more." He tilted his head to one side, regarding me. "Shall I tell you the rest? Would you like to hear my tale in its entirety?"

I may have nodded, but I don't actually remember. My whole being was caught up in him; my gaze full of his imperishable glory. He retrieved his nightshirt from where it was lying and slipped it over his head. Then he came and stood near me, his sight trained on the open casement.

"The obvious tale I will not tell, because you already know it— every soul in Christendom knows it. There was a war in Heaven, and Lucifer, the Great Dragon, did battle with God and his angels and was thrown down, and for a time, I and others like me occupied the medial regions of the air, neither living nor dead, neither divine nor... otherwise. Then the essence of myself, the remaining spark of divinity, fell from the heavens like a burning star and struck a mortal woman on the shoulder. This scorching brand burrowed into her flesh, causing her great agony, and after a time it took root—I took root—in her mortal womb. Some say she was the Princess Cneajna of Moldavia. Others say she was an anonymous noblewoman, but she was either the wife or the mistress of Caleb the Younger or Dark Caleb, a Rumanian warlord. Thus I was born: *filius tenabrae, filius dei*—which is to say, the son of the devil, the son of God.

"The story of my mortal life is as I have told you. I was born in what is now Rumania on November 25, 1431. My childhood consisted largely of unrelenting brutality, interspersed with periods of dubious calm. My father was a harsh disciplinarian who used violence to enforce his draconian rules. At his hands I received, however, an excellent education, most especially in the arts of war, at which he was quite proficient. By the time I was five years old, I could ride my horse bareback and in full armor at least five miles at a gallop. I was proficient in the sword, in archery, and in the use of the long lance for warfare and for hunting. By this I do not mean to imply that my father loved me." His mouth twitched, but he recovered himself quickly.

"Rather, he regarded my brother and myself as political pawns—a useful point of view in those times. When I was eleven and my brother seven, we were sent to the Ottoman sultan Mehmed as 'noble hostages' meant to vouchsafe my father's loyalty to his Turkish masters. When I refused Sultan Mehmed's advances, I was imprisoned and forced to witness horrible tortures against the enemies of the Turk and others— whipping, beating, bastinado, the hook, the cross, and of course, the impaling stake. Many of these same tortures were used against me, and there were other liberties my jailers took, much more intimate. I was often raped by them several times during the course of a day, and especially at night, when I was judged to be most vulnerable."

I shuddered in spite of myself. "My God." I had heard his account of this before, but it never failed to unnerve and distress me.

"The effect of witnessing such... atrocities firsthand affected me. For a time I lost my wits. Thus I returned to my ancestral home and took up the cause of freedom. The Turk had been busy, shoring up his defenses, preparing a mighty army which would annex my land. I took up arms against him. I distinguished myself in other ways."

"Yes." I knew the history well. "Tepeș, they called you."

"The Impaler Prince." He squeezed his hands together, then released them. "You cannot know the sheer number of lives I have taken, Jacob. I have tried to reckon them insofar as I remember. I do not seek to excuse myself. These souls I dispatched into eternity—men, children, women."

"It was a brutal time."

"Yes. Yes, it was a brutal time." He turned slightly, the better to see me directly. "I know you, Jacob."

This simple utterance made tears spring to my eyes. "I don't understand."

"I have always known you, Jacob." He cupped my chin in his hand. "You were there at the beginning. Indeed, we two Fell together."

"Then you're a Watcher, as Brother Inish said... one of the Grigori."

He nodded. "And so are you."

"No." I got up. "No, Caleb. It's true, my recollections of myself are confused, and it may be that some supernatural explanation will suffice, but I cannot believe I am as you are."

My denial made him clearly incredulous. "The scars on your back, Jacob."

"Could be from anything." I turned. He was still sitting on my bed, but he looked stricken. "I might have suffered an accident, been thrown from a train, run down by an omnibus or a coach and horses. These could merely be the scars of my birth, Caleb. It doesn't mean that I am as you are."

He tilted his head. "What does it mean, then?"

I ignored the question. "Will you show me your machine?"

"So you can destroy it?"

"I merely wish to see it."

Something in my tone alerted him. "You are leaving, aren't you? Will you destroy it before you go? Or will you leave only to return with your Christian hordes?" He laughed coldly. "Only now I am the infidel and you the defender of the faith. How our places have been changed! Once it was I who wore the red cross on my chest, who rode proudly into battle to save our Christian lands from the scourge of Islam." He got up from the bed and moved toward the door but stopped halfway. "My God! I have never met a man so determined to deny the truth, Jacob van Willigen. What other proofs do you require? Shall I show you your own immortal nature?" He whirled and, reaching toward a pair of swords mounted on the wall, drew one. He brandished it before him like a man intimately acquainted with its use, once more the warrior and Wallachian prince. "Shall I show you, Jacob, what you really are?" He lunged and, before I could step out of his way, drove it through my body just below the breastbone so the steel protruded from my back.

I was skewered, transfixed on the sword's length like an exotic insect on a collector's pin, and yet I felt no pain. I touched the hilt of the sword that projected outward from my chest. The cold metal rode the rhythm of my breaths but did not impede them. My heart still beat. Clearly I was alive. In fact, I felt like laughing, so I did. "How is it possible?"

Caleb reached for the haft and wrenched the blade free of my body. The bloodless wound closed of its own accord with naught but a slight sucking sound. "You are not human. You have never been human. They lied to you, van Willigen. Brother Inish and the others have all lied to you." He threw down the sword and held out his hand. "Come. I will show you the machine."

We went down into the quiet sitting room, where darkness still lay about the corners, to the great fireplace where Caleb lifted down a small box of highly polished wood. He set this box on a table and, lifting the lid, showed me a beautiful—albeit fantastical—apparatus.

How shall I attempt to describe it? It was vaguely pyramid-shaped, its base being wide and gradually sloping up to a point, which was surmounted by a thin tube of brass. The brass tube was surmounted by a clear glass bell, the purpose of which I could not even guess at, but which, by its form and function, suggested an enclosure. A trio of dials on the front of the machine were fitted with needles, rather like a compass or a watch, but neither of these appeared to measure time. Directly to the right of these was a second glass bell, this one being flared open on the far end and connected to the machine by a length of flexible copper tubing.

"Lift it up," Caleb said.

I did as he instructed and drew the glass toward me. Immediately the dials on the front of the machine began to spin and the entire appliance commenced to hum quite melodically, almost musically.

"Breathe into the glass, Jacob, and see."

I breathed. The needle on the first dial spun wildly, then settled at a point approximately due west. I bent to peer at it: **IMMUTABLE**. "Immutable. What does that mean?"

"Your nature is unchanging and eternal." He gestured at the device. "What do the others say?"

The second dial seemed to have difficulty making up its mind. The needle swung at first one way and then the other, pausing at magnetic north and then lunging wildly in the opposite direction. When it stopped, I read: **ANARCHIC**. The third indicator shuddered itself through a series of clicks and settled finally on a small secondary window in which a selection of numerals were displayed. As I watched, each of these numerals—some six in all—flicked over into blankness until the entire arrangement was empty.

"Ah," said Caleb, "your true age is indefinable. The device knows this. It knows, also, that to try to calculate your years would be a mathematical sin comparable to dividing by zero. This indicates that you are not mortal. If a man of normal years were to breathe into this device, his true age would be immediately displayed. For you, the display is blank."

I blinked at him, utterly confounded. "But how does it... it merely measures the breath?"

"It measures the soul, Jacob. The breath is merely the vehicle."

"This has been here all the time? Here, in this very room?"

"Yes." He tilted his head. He was smiling at me. "Should you require a broadsword through your chest again? Or do you believe me?"

"You... use this device to collect souls?"

"I would have, yes."

"You would have. I don't understand."

Caleb took the bell from my hand and laid it gently back on the device. "If the mechanism were to perform as it was intended, yes. I would use it. I have already told you: performing my hereditary duty is extremely unpleasant to me. I would have an analogue, some other means by which I might fasten on to the dying soul and usher it into eternity." He shrugged. "I had hoped to someday capture a soul for myself, some worthy mortal who would not mind spending time without end in this immortal body."

"You're telling me it doesn't work?"

"Precisely, Jacob. We have been searching for some way to make it function, but thus far we have been unsuccessful."

I thought about what Ada had said to me, how Mary Shelley had begged me to set her free. I thought about Victor Frankenstein, laboring in darkness underneath the castle, and for what? To capture a human soul suitable for transposition into an immortal host? "You have a soul of your own, Caleb."

"No." He dropped the lid of the box, and the fantastical machine disappeared from sight. "Fallen, Jacob, without hope of redemption. I shall never be permitted to enter Paradise."

"I don't believe that."

"There is much you do not believe." He smiled grimly. "That does not, however, prevent it from being true. My dear friend, it is still very early in the morning, and the rest of the household will not be awake for hours. Why not regain your chamber and resume your rest?"

I caught his wrist and held his hand against my heart. "It beats in my chest, Caleb, as does yours. We live in these fleshly bodies— immortal, or so it would seem, not human, but bodies nonetheless. As matter passes from one region to another, can it not be transmuted into something else?"

"Theology," he said. "Mere sophistry. Simply a handful of words." He made to pull away, but I held onto him.

"Come with me." I tugged at his wrist.

"Where are we going?"

"We are going to bed."

I shut the door of my chamber behind us and shot the bolt. The golden sunlight of early morning spilled in through the opened casement, touching everything with subtle fire. I lifted the hem of his night robe and stripped it from his body, stripped myself likewise, and folded him into my arms. His kiss was eager, hungry, and desperate, and for a long time, we simply lay together in this manner while the desire between us rose higher and higher.

The hollow of his throat, I discovered, was exquisitely sensitive, as were his nipples and the flat of his belly. I smoothed the long muscles of his thighs before bending and taking his exquisite cock into my mouth. He groaned, his back arching nearly off the bed as I began to suck, and I felt his long fingers insinuate themselves into my hair. Over and over I drew him to the brink of release, never allowing his passion to build to the point that it might discharge itself, but instead forcing him to remain on a knife edge, his entire body sweaty and trembling. With mouth and hands, I teased and pleasured him, leaving no area of his skin unexplored. I licked and sucked wherever my fancy took me, and when I was satisfied that he was indeed passion's slave, I took his erect member again into my mouth and suckled strongly.

He cried out, his strong hands crushing the sheets and coverlet as the spasms took him again and again, spending his desire in jagged bursts until he lay prostrate and still. "Jacob...." He opened eyes whose pupils had contracted to catlike slits and reached for me. "My darling, take your pleasure."

I found a small bottle of oil in the bureau by the bed, and when uncorked, it released a smell of lavender and sage. Parting his languid thighs, I smoothed a little of it onto his skin and also laved my swollen member. Reaching for me, he guided me between his thighs and held me as I moved—at first slowly, then, as my crisis loomed, more quickly, plunging down into the space between us. The world retreated and there was nothing except he and I, the bed and the room, and our passion. A palpable brink loomed before me, and I trembled on the edge of it. I gazed into his eyes as my completion reared its head and took me in its teeth and shook me, and I was in a place of so full of violent, throbbing pleasure that my vision went and was replaced with bliss and darkness.

I drew him into my arms and held him tight against my beating heart.

Caleb Donnithorn: Castle Donnithorn
May 17

HE IS gone. It was Victor who told me. Sometime after the consummation of our mutual desire, he quietly parceled up his things and went back to Bistritz via the diligence, and from there, I assume, to London. He left nothing behind to explain—if indeed he intended to give explanation—apart from the lingering emptiness where he had lately been. The Society sent him here to destroy a machine that, had they but known, was hardly worth the effort.

I was sitting in my study, a small fire kindled against the spring chill of early evening, when Victor Frankenstein approached. He told me van Willigen had gone and said he also wanted my permission to take leave. Where would he go? I asked. Where else in the world afforded him such opportunity for study, for research and discovery? He would go, he said, to search for the creature Darius.

"The creature was destroyed, Victor, when your old laboratory burned." I remembered the conflagration well. "Why seek something that does not exist?"

"Isn't that what you've been doing, all these years?" He came and stood by the fire, warming his hands. "Let us speak plainly to one another, Caleb. I am not the naïve scholar I was when we first knew each other. Nor am I the love-besotted boy who became your willing consort in the winter of 1850. Many years, Caleb, I have spent in your service." He drew a slow, meditative breath, and when he turned his gaze to me, there was steady purpose in it. "I would take my leave of you."

"And if I refuse to let you go?"

"You cannot stay me." He came to where I was sitting and went down on his knees before me. "But I am hoping that with love you will let me go."

I stroked his cheek and forced myself to smile. "You go in search of phantasms, Victor. What you seek cannot be found."

"But it is my right to seek," he said. He caught hold of my hand and kissed the palm. "I will go whether you allow it or no, but I would rather depart with your blessing."

It began to rain. Huge drops spattered against the windowpanes and rattled down the flue. "Victor, have I ever told you about my wife, Elizabeta?"

He blinked. "I don't believe so."

"On a day rather like today, many years ago, she leapt to her death from the battlements of this very castle because she said she could no longer live with a man such as myself. Our child had died three days before of an incurable illness that sapped his strength and drew him inexorably toward the grave. I could not, as his father, continue to witness the slow and painful degradation of a child I loved more than my own life, and so I did the only thing I could do, which was to alleviate his suffering."

Frankenstein's eyes were moist, yet he said nothing.

"Late one night, while my wife was sleeping, I went into our son's room and I picked up his little fevered body and I held him close to me and I sang to him all the old songs that I had learned as a child. I spoke soothing words to him and I—I took away his suffering." This memory, centuries old, still has the power to strike at the very heart of me. "Some years later my second wife, a young Frenchwoman named Justine, divined one night what I really am and threw herself from the battlements. I grieve her still."

"And you wonder if you have a soul." Frankenstein rose from his knees. "Caleb, I take my leave of you. I have dismantled the laboratory. Sergei and Andrzej helped me." He handed me the key. "Thank you for everything you have done."

I watched him walk away, leaving me as so many others have left me. I thought about running after him, forcing him to return, but I would retain some semblance of dignity. I listen to the sound of the rain, and slowly, inexorably, the impetus of sleep comes stealing over me, a sleep the likes of which I have not indulged in for many centuries. Doubtless there are a great many arcane texts and alchemical pamphlets describing the diurnal cycle of my kind, but I have never slept in a coffin, and although I despise garlic on general principle, I have no overweening fear of it.

I climb the stairs to the rooms that were van Willigen's and I strip myself naked and climb into his bed. The rain sounds exceptionally loud through the open casement and I suppose I ought to close the window, but I no longer care about such things. I will sleep until I no longer need the calming solace of my dreams.

Diary—Jacob van Willigen
September 21
London

FOR THE first three weeks of September, it has been ceaselessly raining: a cold, unseasonable rain that strikes like bullets on the skin. Since my return, Brother Inish has made it his business—and the business of the other Society members—to keep a close eye on me in case my recent sojourn in the wilds of Transylvania has conspired to turn my mind. Rather than permitting me to prosecute my own outstanding cases (a haunting in Bath, reports of a suspected lycanthrope in Coventry), Brother Inish has set me to working in the library, cataloguing some recent additions to our collection and supplementing our card catalogue. It is work usually done by novices, work designed to humble or even to humiliate, but I am careful not to show this. In truth, I am grateful for such quotidian distraction, as it leaves my mind free to range where it will.

For some time now I have thought ceaselessly of Caleb, and even in my dreams, I am embroiled in what seems like a never-ending search for him, scouring London alleys and crossing Rumanian mountains. When my day's duties are ended and I am free to amuse myself, I walk, and in walking, I perceive him everywhere. The streets of Marylebone, where our great motherhouse was long ago established, now seem to be the darkest of grim prisons, and every glance from a stranger is like a dagger to my heart. He has become frightfully real to me. I see him—I hear him—everywhere. It has become my habit to walk until I am exhausted, and only then am I able to sleep. I range the width and breadth of Westminster and beyond, to Lambeth and Camberwell, Rotherhithe and Deptford. My journeys stimulate my memories, so that in my walking state I am privy to all the little moments that constituted my time with Caleb.

Although it has been many months since I returned from Transylvania, and although I have arguably done nothing which would raise the Society's ire, I have been banished from the confidence of my fellows as surely as if I had murdered one of them. I am no longer privy to the essential consultations which preface each assignment, nor am I welcome in Brother Inish's private study. My quarters, too, have changed. While I was away, my belongings were moved out of the room I shared with another member of the Society, and I have been relegated to a small room behind the chapel, located in a disused corridor. It is barely large enough for my narrow bed, a chair, and my books. This, too, does not trouble me. It is best that I remain separate from them in preparation for the more final schism I will soon initiate.

I have been much occupied of late with a thorough search of the Society's records. As my duties in the library require my attendance to archival matters, I am ideally positioned to conduct a most thorough search on a subject dear to my heart: myself. I have discovered a great many things in the Society's archives that alternately intrigue and discomfit me. These things I have corroborated, courtesy of the City archives and diverse other sources of which I, as a gentleman scholar, may easily avail.

Brother Inish was sitting at his desk this forenoon when I knocked at the door and asked whether I might enter. Inish, it must be said, has aged in the months since my return, or else he has always appeared thus and only my great regard for him has prevented me from seeing what is so much in evidence.

"What is it, van Willigen?" He indicated a stack of documents on the desk before him. I recognized Mandeville's handwriting on them. The case involved a demonic apparition in the Cotswolds and was originally assigned to me.

"It would appear I have been anticipated." I nodded at the papers he was reading. "Or does Mandeville handle all of my cases now?"

Inish assumed a blank expression. "I'm afraid I don't understand. If you are referring to the reduction of your workload since your return from the Continent, I thought you understood that I acted in your own best interest. You were quite unwell upon your return, van Willigen."

This was nonsense, and both he and I knew it. "Unwell? I think you are mistaken, Brother Inish. On the contrary, I have seldom felt so well in my life." I toyed with the idea of telling him how I had been impaled on a three-foot Rumanian broadsword, suffering no ill effects, but I decided he probably would not believe me. He might even summon the others and have me exorcised or turn me over to a lunatic asylum. I reached into my pocket and pulled out a set of papers— evidence of a sort that I had copied from our official records. "I find that I should like you to answer some questions."

"Questions." A note of irritation crept into his voice. "You can doubtless see that I am much occupied at the moment."

"That is unfortunate." I laid my evidence on his desk, papers containing vital pieces of information about my own personal history, painstakingly culled from the Society's records. "Brother Inish, you have lied to me." I held up a hand as his face suffused with dark blood. "No, do not make your excuses to me, if you please. The proof is, as you will see, irrefutable. I found it written down in your own hand, Brother Inish."

The proofs I presented were thus: a letter from one Brother Alban in the year 310, requesting permission from an early precursor to the Society to administer Holy Communion to a group of lycanthropes living on the edges of Londinium and reporting, also, the presence of a "wild man" who came out of the forest at night to forage for food, but who, according to Alban and his fellow monks, was not himself a lycanthrope. One of Alban's fellows got close enough to this feral creature to make a thorough report of what he saw and described "something very like a man, walking upright, with great scars on his back as though cut with a scythe." When Alban approached this creature to offer him the solace of Holy Communion, the man ran into the forest and was never seen again.

In 1226, a young boy drawing water at a well in the Berkshires was approached by a man dressed in the clothing of a mendicant friar, who asked him for a drink. When the boy asked the man's name, he said "Jacob," and turning, went away. Near the end of the year 1406, this same Jacob was heard discoursing on the nature of the Holy Trinity in a market square in Bergen. In 1657, a parish priest in a small village near Dublin heard his confession. Jacob—as he called himself—occupied many years in this fashion, traveling the length and breadth of Europe until finally, in the year 1850, worn away by the hunger and fatigue of his endless sojourn, he fell down in a dead faint on the steps of a particular building in London, whereupon he was taken in by the brothers of the Society of Psychical and Esoteric Research and trained in their methods.

A thorough physical examination by one of the Society's trusted doctors revealed a pair of livid scars extending from the shoulder blades to the small of the man's back. This, coupled with certain other "proofs" (I cited the term as it was used in the original document), marked the wanderer as a possible Grigori or Watcher, one of the few Fallen remaining on earth.

Brother Inish was pale as wax. "You should not have had access to such documents. These documents are the property of the Society. It was not your business—"

I stopped him by the simple expedient of wrapping my hand around his throat. "I remember there was a dark room, and a single candle, and a mirror." He was turning blue, so I released my hold on him. "I remember gazing into the mirror and hearing someone speak certain words. You gave me something to drink. I remember." I removed my hand from his throat. "You told me I had been born in Maastricht, that my father, although not a rich man, was wealthy enough to send me to university, that I had studied theology and law—"

"You did!" Inish averred. "That much is true. We sent you to the finest university—"

I continued speaking as if he'd not spoken at all. "—that I entered the Society of my own free will. You told me the details of a life that I, to my knowledge, have never lived."

Inish massaged his throat with one hand, his breath coming in harsh gasps. "Jacob, I assure you, I can explain."

"He was right." The realization felt like a thread of cold steel running through the center of my being. "Caleb was absolutely right… and you sent me to kill him. You knew the machine didn't work—it was never the machine. It was him. You sent me to Rumania and you hoped that I would kill him, that we would kill each other." My heart was thundering in my chest and it was suddenly hard to breathe. "We are the only two left."

"The Grigori—the Watchers—were bound in the deep places of the Earth until the final judgment." Inish got up and went to a wooden cabinet that stood against the wall. I had often noticed this cabinet but had, for some reason, never wondered what it contained. Inish took a key from a chain at his waist and unlocked it, and I saw it was full of books—very old books by their appearance, and very precious, seeing as how they were locked away. He extracted a long, narrow volume that had the guise of an accounts ledger. It was bound in pale, yellowish leather with its title stamped in gold upon the spine: **THE BOOK OF NAMES**. Inish brought it to the desk and opened it, turning the volume so I could see. "This is a list—entirely complete—of those entities with which the Society has done battle. Since the earliest days of our organization, such records have been kept." He turned to a page near the middle of the book and pointed. A faint inscription was still visible, made in a spidery hand: **GRIGORI**. Under this there ran a list of names, all of which had been crossed out save for two. I did not need to bend close to the page to ascertain the names. I already knew them. **JACOB VAN WILLIGEN, VLAD DRAGULIA/CALEB DONNITHORN**.

"My God." My flesh was pricked with a pervasive chill. "You have been killing us… all of you. You have been killing us. Will you kill me, now?" Anger, sudden and violent, surged through me. "Have you sent your minions to Wallachia? Is that your holy mandate, monk?"

He reached into his desk drawer and pulled out a small metal crucifix, and holding it in front of him, he began to intone the Rite. "I command you, unclean spirit, whoever you are, along with all your minions now attacking this servant of God, by the mysteries of the incarnation, passion, resurrection, and ascension of our Lord Jesus Christ, by the descent of the Holy Spirit, by the coming of our Lord—"

I slapped the instrument out of his hand. "Please, I beg you, do not shame yourself or me in this manner. Where are your holy flunkies now?"

Inish regarded me, his head on one side. "This battle is out of your hands, van Willigen." The room seemed to contract around me and grow a little darker. "There is nothing you can do. They are on their way to his castle. They will destroy him utterly."

November 2: All Souls' Day
Bistritz
Diary—Jacob van Willigen

THE COLD is all pervasive, deadening, a chill fist closing round me with a viselike strength. I am waiting now, as I have waited before, at the inn where the diligence will take me to the Birgau Pass, and from there one of Caleb's Szegeny servants will convey me to the castle. I do not know what to expect when I reach the top of the mountain. He has no idea I am coming. Every missive I have sent him has gone unanswered, and I am terribly, horribly afraid the news brought to me this fortnight by the most unlikely of messengers is true.

My last days at the Society motherhouse have been excessively uncomfortable for me, and I have passed my time in study and in searching the desires of my own heart. In the end Brother Inish did not tell me anything I did not already suspect, the same facts confirmed by Caleb and indeed by the Society's own records. I decided immediately to go to Transylvania, to find Caleb, and to save him from the awful fate decreed for him by the Society, or barring that, to stand and fight by his side until the day of my own destruction, if such was necessary. I threw into a bag the few belongings I had managed to acquire during my years at the motherhouse: my clothes, a pair of sturdy boots for walking, and a volume or two of theology and poetry. The rest I left behind.

There have been delays, too, in the preparations for my travel, and I suspect Brother Inish's influence has been at work. My attempts to secure passage over land and water have been excessively trying. Those who sold me my tickets did so only reluctantly, and acquiring the necessary travel documents demanded an inhuman effort. The unnecessary delays wasted valuable time, during which I was obliged to wait in London while Inish's emissaries were already at Caleb's very doorstep. Anything that could be done to delay or prevent my going to Rumania was done: the airship passage I had booked was mysteriously unbooked; steamship agents to whom I had confided the details of my journey were suddenly amnesiac; a packed valise containing my clothes and travel documents vanished from my room. My sudden lack of allies—for there was now no one in the Society to whom I could turn for help or guidance—coincided with the cancellation of my privileges and the withdrawal of any favor I might have previously enjoyed. I was permitted to keep my room at the motherhouse only because Inish wanted to keep an eye on me, something he could not do if I were to quit the establishment and seek lodging elsewhere. Were he any other man, he might err in thinking he or his minions could kill me...but only one Grigori can kill another. We are not prey to mortal death, only the fatal touch of another.

The night before I was due to leave for Rumania saw me greatly troubled in my soul. I had just retired to bed when the sound of scratching from the windowpane alerted me that something was amiss.

I got out of bed and, lighting the candle on my nightstand, I carried it to the casement. "Who is it?" I demanded. "Tell me at once who is there."

"Open the window, van Willigen. I have a message for you."

"A message from whom?" I raised the sash, wondering if some of the Society brethren had decided to conspire against me, and saw no ordinary man, but a creature out of legend—a shambling mass of flesh at least nine feet tall that seemed rooted to the ground like the mightiest of oaks. "Good God!" I cried. "What do you want?"

"Do not fear, good van Willigen. I am Darius, son of Victor Frankenstein, and I have come from my father with a message for you." The voice was masculine, full and rich in tone and beautifully modulated. I could see nothing of the face except the mouth, with its richly red lips and fine white teeth. "I pray I do not startle you. I understand my physiognomy is rather unconventional."

The nature of Frankenstein's work was again borne in on me. "I did not realize Doctor Frankenstein's research had been... successful. Will you not come in and warm yourself?"

"Thank you. I will not. My presence would doubtless be discovered, and I fear I would be the cause of much alarm and panic."

I dressed quickly and went out to him, carrying the candle with me. He was dressed in the robes of a Franciscan, a hood pulled over his head. On his feet he wore a pair of stout boots, much larger than would be necessary for any ordinary man, and he carried a staff in one enormous hand. His uneven features gazed out at me with no emotion save patience and perhaps a gentle piety and the light of keen intelligence shone from his eyes. His countenance, it is true, was most unfortunate and appeared to have been culled from the various parts and pieces of other men, but there was gentleness and grace in his manner. "What message?" I asked.

"You must go to Transylvania at once. The enemies of Caleb Donnithorn are massing round the castle. My father has removed himself to the home of his family, but he impressed me that the message was most urgent. There is very little time."

"How do I know you speak truly?"

"You do not." He reached into the depths of his robes and brought out a small leather pouch. "Hold out your hand." He tipped the contents into my waiting palm, and I saw it was a ring, of very fine and intricate design in enamel and gold: a dragon rampant with a cross behind it. "He said you would know what it meant."

"Yes." The Order Draconis. "I will come immediately. Will you wait?"

"I cannot. My task was to deliver the message. I have done so." He turned to go, but my hand on his arm stayed him. "Yes?" He seemed astonished that another being had touched him. I imagined his was an austere life.

"Please, let me give you something for your trouble." I fumbled for my purse, but he would not hear of it.

"I have no need of anything. I yearn only to serve." He inclined his massive head. "My father spoke well of you, van Willigen. I only hope his faith in you is not misplaced." His going was as quiet as his coming had been, his enormous figure swallowed up by the night. It was the last time I ever saw him.

The proprietress of the inn has just given me the news that the diligence is approaching. I am on my way to Castle Donnithorn. I pray my visit will be useful or, failing that, a culmination of my fate. All that I was I have left behind. I am merely Jacob van Willigen, warrior angel and damned soul.

November 2

Castle Donnithorn

The true account of Caleb Donnithorn, known also as Vlad Dracula

WHAT REMAINS of my castle is but a smoking ruin, a set of broken walls enclosing air. The attack came, as I knew it would, from the village. They are no longer content, it seems, to have one such as I among their number. I was sleeping when the attack occurred, and at first I imagined I was merely dreaming. By the time I gained the staircase, the entire great hall was in flames, a hellish conflagration that devoured every destructible thing in its path. The chairs and tables, the gorgeous carpets underfoot, the massive tapestries that had belonged to my great grandfather—all were in their turn destroyed, and worse, the *geis* which had bound William and Mary and Ada to my side had been irreparably broken. As the castle is ravaged, so too are the wards and enchantments I placed upon it. I am as alone as I have ever been.

They have destroyed precious works of art, some thousands of years old. In the stairwell at the back of the castle, Justine's portrait hangs undisturbed. I consider taking it with me, but it isn't possible. The portrait is large, a life-sized likeness of her, commissioned early in our marriage. She gazes serenely out from a dark background, her hands folded in her lap, her dark eyes calm and unconcerned. She was so beautiful—not merely a physical beauty but a beauty of the spirit, an illuminating fire that drew others to her and made them want to linger at her side. "I wish that you might speak to me, my dear." I touch her hands with my hand. I stroke the painted folds of her wedding dress as high as I can reach. Her static form entices me as few things ever have. She loved me—and I was the instrument of her destruction. I press my eyes closed, and when I open them again, the noises of devastation are closer. They are coming up the stairs. They have discovered this hidden staircase, originally built to ensure a quick evacuation in the event of an invasion, complete with embrasures and arrow slits.

I open my eyes and she is smiling at me. The surface of the portrait glows from within, pulsing to an unheard cadence. The outline of Justine's form grows luminous, swelling to fill the frame. She rises from her chair and stands for a moment, confined by the painting's physical barrier. Then she steps forward, out of the picture, and descends toward me slowly and gently, picking her way down an invisible staircase. As she comes nearer, she takes on form and substance, until she appears entirely solid.

"Justine. My love." I open my arms and she comes into them, warm and real. "We are ended, my darling." I draw back to look at her. She is beautiful, entirely untouched by the ravages of time. "I fear I cannot hold them back."

She smoothes my brow with her small, cool hand. "Is there nothing to be done?" And, when I shake my head, "Then we are indeed ended." She tilts her head to the side and smiles. "Eternity isn't all that bad, Caleb. You might even like it."

I wind a curl of her dark brown hair around my index finger. "I have no patience for harps and golden thrones," I say. "Besides, I shall never be allowed to enter Paradise. You know this." I change the subject. "I see you are still wearing your wedding dress."

"You are displeased?" She pats my cheek. "Or would you rather see me in widow's weeds?"

"Do you remember our wedding?" I wish to recall some comforting piece of history, some seldom-told fable to take with me to my destruction. "You came all the way from Martinique. A French Creole—society would never let me forget it. Everyone said I had chosen unwisely." The memory warms me. "But you were so beautiful, so willing and responsive. You were eager for me, just as I was for you."

"Caleb, you cannot stay here." She presses her fingers against my lips. "You must go. I'll hold them off as long as I can." Her pretty brow creases with worry. "I can be terrifying when I wish it."

"Justine, I—"

Her fingers rise again to press my lips. "Go to him."

I catch her wrist and kiss her hand, her fingers. "I fear he doesn't want me."

"You're wrong, Caleb." She stands on tiptoe and kisses me. "Go to him. I will hold them off."

FOR SOME hours now, I have been obliged to hide myself, for there are invaders in my castle, a barbarian horde of priests and monks, the remnant of that esteemed Society of which my dear van Willigen was lately a member. They have come to accomplish what he could not. I hear them calling to me, shouting out the many names by which I am known: *Lucifer, Apollyon, Abaddon, Belial, Satan, Donnithorn, Dracula.* They seem surprised when I answer to none of these.

I made my way below, to where Elizabeta's corpse, encased in glass, sleeps away the centuries. The fires which drive the great network of pipes and conduit have long since gone out, and my Szegeny servants are fled. The glass of Elizabeta's coffin, deprived of its chill air, has begun to cloud. The body, I know, is decomposing. Like all mortal things, my Elizabeta is subject to the tyranny of Time.

"Donnithorn!" Something thumps hard against the floor above my head, and a trickle of sand sifts down. "You have nowhere to go! You must come out."

"What would you have done, my darling?" But she does not answer me. In life she had no great love for me. She merely tolerated me and counted herself blessed that she was married to a fine young Wallachian noble, rather than consigned to a life of toil and drudgery, slaving in the fields or in childbed. She was no Justine, full of fire and spirit. Justine, who loved me with her whole heart until she happened to stray one day where she never had before, into the castle's ancient depths. She found me bending over a dying man whose family had brought him to the castle, begging me to offer him release. She at once understood what I was doing and cried out—I can't remember what it was she said—and ran, horrified.

She ran and did not stop running, until she leapt over an open casement, her body falling, soundless, to the mighty Argeş. Two wives, both fed to the river. I believe I have paid my penance to whatever gods there are.

Perhaps van Willigen's erstwhile companions imagine they are capable of destroying me, when in truth I could lay all of them to ruin and their precious Society as well. "Perhaps a restoration of history." I lay my hands flat on the glass that lies directly over Elizabeta's face. "A forest of stakes as far as the eye can see… would they understand, then? Would they fear me?"

"Belial, son of darkness." A voice comes from behind me and I turn. A young monk, pale and frightened, with an absurd crop of blond hair and bright blue eyes set flat in a stupid face. "I command you to come forth." The smell of smoke permeates the air. The fire is spreading, as fires do.

"My son, go back the way you came."

"Belial, come forth." He yanks a crucifix out of his tunic and holds it before him in a trembling hand. "I command you in the name of Christ."

Outside, the crowd grows louder, and those who came merely to witness my destruction have begun to lend their hands and backs to the larger task. They will be busy trying to break the door down. They will heap combustible materials in my rooms and set other fires. They will douse the floors and walls with oil. They will leave not even so much as two stones laid one upon the other.

"Go now." I take hold of his shoulder and turn him about. "While you still can. These villagers will kill you. It's all they want to do. In the name of this God you profess, I beg you, save yourself."

I leave him by the simple expedient of stepping sideways out of time, emerging on the northwest battlement of my castle. The entire village seems to be massing underneath my gaze, pressing with farm implements, with staves and axes and even their very flesh against the gates. Men have thrown crude ladders against the walls and are climbing into windows. I turn a corner and duck into a passageway, and there is another of van Willigen's peers, this one wielding holy water and a wooden stake. He sees me, comes rushing at me, and I turn adroitly, grasp his wrist, and wrench his arm away, breaking the bone. Two more approach me from Elizabeta's chambers, wearing strands of garlic around their necks and chanting from a prayer book. They run at me, their eyes wild with a holy madness, and I throw them down. Do they think I can be so easily defeated? Do they imagine I am weak?

A great shout rises from outside. The villagers have broken through the gates and are rushing as one body into the castle. I find an egress through one of the narrow passageways I had constructed centuries before and emerge to find myself on a slender lip of ground high above the Argeş. The wind is bitter and it begins to snow hard little flakes that strike the skin like a flurry of fine sand. Where will I go from here? Shall I seek refuge in some other place, attempt to establish myself there? Everything mortal eventually succumbs to fire or the death of the flesh, and the smell of burning timbers is strong now in my nostrils. All I have loved was here. All I have loved is gone. There is nowhere left for me to go.

Diary—Jacob van Willigen
November 5
Donnithorn Castle

I DISMOUNTED some distance from the burning castle and went the rest of the way on foot. The snow had begun to thicken by now, making travel difficult. Within three-quarters of an hour, I had gained the outermost battlements, over which a pall of greasy smoke hung, staining the sky. The trees for some distance around the castle were burned and blackened, and even the stones bore evidence of recent violence. The courtyard was empty, but the churned-up mud and broken flagstones told me only recently a great company had been there, wreaking havoc and destruction. The huge gates, so beautifully carved with Caleb's personal emblem of dragons rampant, hung loose and broken on their posts. The castle's great wooden door had been battered in, and as I crossed into the foyer, I saw the great hall was littered with blackened roof beams and broken glass. No one was about.

"Caleb?" My boots crunched on fallen embers as I made my way up the stairs, and someone had daubed the word *ucigas*—'murderer'—on the wall in scarlet paint or blood. "Caleb, are you here?"

In the same corridor where my own chambers had been, there were heaps of broken furniture, the burned detritus of everything Caleb had owned, smashed crockery and shattered window glass, and—most vile of all—someone had defecated on the floor. I found one of the little clockwork cleaners turning in an endless circle, round and round, chattering to itself. I picked it up, found the switch, and turned it off. There was nothing here that would benefit from cleaning. There was nothing here that would not forever stink of blood and pain and ordure. "Caleb?"

The scene outside on the battlements was little better, but here, at least, there was clean air. The outer walls had been breached, as if by catapult or cannon, but I knew the Society's methods, knew the damage had been inflicted by what amounted to magic. They would have worked as a concentrated force to unsettle and unseat him, stopping short of absolute destruction only because they couldn't find him. He could, I knew, evade them for as long as necessary, and even with their vast array of arcane knowledge, there was no way the Society was capable of destroying him. He was simply beyond their power. In the castle's ancient cellars, I found the smashed coffin in which Caleb's wife, Elizabeta, had lain these long centuries, the finely etched glass lying like splinters of ice, the broad brass conduit twisted and broken. Her corpse was nowhere to be seen, and I hoped Caleb or some conscientious servant had seen the remains respectfully buried in consecrated ground.

I gained the inner staircase and followed it up to Caleb's personal chambers. The door had been smashed inward and now swung lazily on its hinges, and there was a pronounced smell of burning in the room. "Caleb?"

The bed where we had coupled so ecstatically had been blasted to splinters, the fine bedcovers and hangings lying in shreds on the floor. On the balcony just beyond, I caught a glimpse of a slender figure, hatless and coatless, his black hair blowing in the wind. The air was freezing cold and the snow had thickened, and the wind howled and moaned in the open casements like a dying animal.

"It is finished, Jacob."

"Caleb, please come inside." I held out my hand to him. "Let's go away from here."

"Where?" His expression was bleak and haunted; his eyes the eyes of a man who has lost all hope. "Forgive me. I have nothing to offer you. I fear my hospitality is most wanting." His voice was flat and uninflected. He sounded as if he were reciting the words from rote. "Where did you want us to go?"

"Away." I caught hold of his arm and drew him to me. "Please, let us leave this place." He smelled of smoke and his fine clothes hung in tatters. There was blood on his face. "They will return, next time in greater force. There will be more of them. You must come with me."

"Jacob, you came back." He patted my arms and shoulders. "You have returned to me. When you went away, I feared you had gone forever." He gazed into my eyes and nodded. "Did you make them tell you the truth?"

The proof is, as you will see, irrefutable. I found it written down in your own hand. "I did." I left Inish with the memory of my voice, speaking those words, tearing down the artifice of centuries that he and the others had erected around themselves.

"That is good." He gestured to the ruined castle with its burned timbers and broken glass. "I thought that you would send others in your place. I was not surprised when they arrived."

"In my *place*?"

"There were three who came at first. They said they were your emissaries, sent to finish the task because you lay near death." He nodded again, as if in agreement with something I could not hear. "I am glad you are well and unharmed. I am very glad. *Omul nu stie la ora nici pe zi.* They did battle with the dragon, and the dragon was thrown down. You see? I still remember." He started toward the balcony again but stopped as if remembering an errand. "Have you seen my wife? Elizabeta would want to greet you herself, I know. Justine wanted very much to take brandy with you in the library." His entire body was trembling violently, as a man in a paroxysm of fear. "Jacob." The snow dropped a curtain white around us. "Jacob?"

I shrugged out of my heavy topcoat and threw it over his shoulders. "It's time for us to leave, Caleb. We can't stay here anymore."

"Of course." He gazed at me, then reached out and touched my face. "Mehmed hasn't harmed you?" He bent his head and murmured, "Do you know what the Turks do to such deserters as they find? *Ţepeş!*" He began to weep. "They made me watch it. They made me *Ţepeş.*"

I did not pause to carry anything away with me, for the castle was already in ruins. I hurried Caleb out into the courtyard and down the narrow road that led to Sighisoara, the village of his mortal birth. There would be aid and sustenance for us, but not yet, and I had still to get him out of Rumania and safely onto the Continent. I helped him mount my horse and then I climbed on behind him.

"Where are we going, Jacob?"

"We are going home, Vladislaus."

"Home." His head lolled back against my shoulder and I felt his body relax. "We are going home."

I flicked the reins and we moved off—silently, in the gathering darkness, leaving the burned and broken wreckage far behind us.

LETTER: JACOB van Willigen to Brother Coilm Inish, Society for Psychical and Esoteric Research, London W1

Cable code #459-12-A/Eastern European Aethernet via Ragusa hub

My dear Brother Inish:

This letter will serve as formal notice of my resignation from the Society, effective immediately. I have decided, by the light of my own conscience, to remain with Caleb for the foreseeable future.

Please advise my former fellows that they may divide my personal effects between them as they see fit. My only directive is that Lipinski receive his choice of my books, as he has always been extremely kind to me. Despite the rift that has so lately developed between us, I am indebted to you for all you have done. Your manifold kindness to me shall never be forgotten. I remain your servant,

Jacob van Willigen

J.S. COOK was born and raised on the island of Newfoundland. She holds a BA and an MA in English Language and Literature and a B.Ed in postsecondary education. She makes her home in St. John's, Newfoundland, with her husband Paul and their spoiled rotten dogter, Lola. Sheppie passed over the Rainbow Bridge in August, 2013. He is ever remembered, and ever loved.

J.S. Cook also writes as JoAnne Soper-Cook.

Twitter: https://twitter.com/jsopercook
Website: joannesopercook.net

Also from J.S. COOK

COME
TO
DUST

J.S. COOK

http://www.dreamspinnerpress.com

Also from J.S. COOK

A Little Night Murder

J.S. Cook

Also from J.S. COOK

VALLEY
OF
THE DEAD

J.S. COOK

http://www.dreamspinnerpress.com

Writing as JOANNE SOPER-COOK

JOANNE SOPER-COOK

The Eye of Heaven

http://www.dreamspinnerpress.com

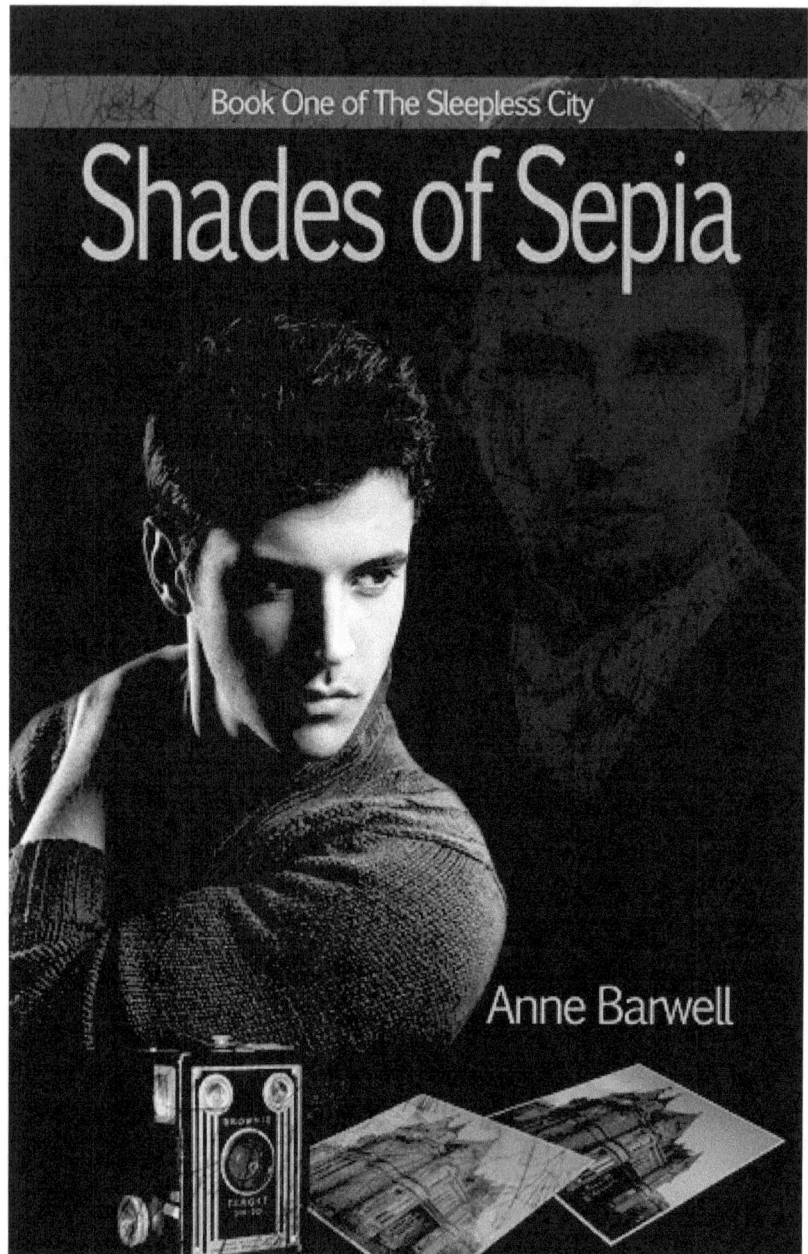

Book One of The Sleepless City

Shades of Sepia

Anne Barwell

JANA
DENARDO

If Two of Them Are Dead

www.ingramcontent.com/pod-product-compliance
Lightning Source LLC
Chambersburg PA
CBHW060102260626
47160CB00005B/1771